Praise for Mary Anna Evans

The Faye Longchamp Mysteries

CATACOMBS

The Twelfth Faye Longchamp Mystery

2020—Oklahoma Book Award Winner

"Fast-paced, well-plotted… Those who like richly textured, character-driven mysteries will be rewarded."

—Publishers Weekly

"Overall, a solid entry—based in part on an actual Oklahoma bombing—in a popular series."

—Booklist

UNDERCURRENTS

The Eleventh Faye Longchamp Mystery

2019—Oklahoma Book Award Finalist

"The Longchamp mysteries combine history and mystery in a gritty way that makes them feel different from most amateur-sleuth fare—dark-edged rather than cozy. Faye, too, is not your traditional   sily anchor a gritty thril   n that genre a run for the

—Booklist

"Evans expertly juggles a host of likely suspects, all the while breathing life into the city of Memphis, from its tourist-filled center to its marginal neighborhoods and the spectacular wilderness of the state park."

—*Publishers Weekly*

BURIALS

The Tenth Faye Longchamp Mystery

2018—Willa Literary Award Finalist, Contemporary Fiction
2018—Will Rogers Medallion Award Bronze Medalist, Western Fiction
2018—Oklahoma Book Award Finalist, Fiction
2017—*Strand* Magazine Top 12 Mystery Novels
2017—*True West* Magazine Best Western Mysteries

"This is a highly successful murder mystery by an author who has mastered the magic and craft of popular genre fiction. Her work embodies the truism that character is destiny."

—*Naples Florida Weekly*

"Evans's signature archaeological lore adds even more interest to this tale of love, hate, and greed."

—*Kirkus Reviews*

"Evans sensitively explores the issue of how to balance respecting cultural heritage and gaining knowledge of the past through scientific research."

—*Publishers Weekly*

ISOLATION

The Ninth Faye Longchamp Mystery

2016—Oklahoma Book Awards Finalist

"Evans skillfully uses excerpts from the fictional oral history of Cally Stanton, recorded by the Federal Writers' Project in 1935, to dramatize the past."

—*Publishers Weekly*

"A worthwhile addition to Faye's long-running series that weaves history, mystery, and psychology into a satisfying tale of greed and passion."

—*Kirkus Reviews*

"Well-drawn characters and setting, and historical and archaeological detail, add to the absorbing story."

—*Booklist*

RITUALS

The Eighth Faye Longchamp Mystery

"A suspenseful crime story with just a hint of something otherworldly."

—*Booklist*

"A superior puzzle plot lifts Evans's eighth Faye Longchamp Mystery…Evans pulls all the pieces nicely together in the end."

—*Publishers Weekly*

"The emphasis on the spirit world makes this a bit of a departure from Evans's usual historical and archaeological themes, but it's certainly a well-plotted and enjoyable mystery."

—Kirkus Reviews

PLUNDER

The Seventh Faye Longchamp Mystery

2012—Florida Book Award Bronze Medal Winner for General Fiction
2012—Florida Book Award Bronze Medal Winner for Popular Fiction

"In her delightfully erudite seventh, Faye continues to weave archaeological tidbits and interesting people into soundly plotted mysteries."

—Kirkus Reviews

"Working in Louisiana, archaeologist Faye Longchamp doesn't expect a double murder and pirate plunder, but by now she's used to the unexpected."

—Library Journal

"The explosion of the Deepwater Horizon rig in the Gulf of Mexico provides the backdrop for Evans's engaging, character-driven seventh mystery featuring archaeologist Faye Longchamp."

—Publishers Weekly

"Details of archaeology, pirate lore, and voodoo complement the strong, sympathetic characters, especially Amande, and the appealing portrait of Faye's family life."

—*Booklist*

STRANGERS

The Sixth Faye Longchamp Mystery

"Mary Anna Evans's sixth Faye Longchamp novel continues her string of elegant mysteries that features one of contemporary fiction's most appealing heroines. The author also continues to seek out and to describe settings and locations that would whet the excavating appetite of any practicing or armchair archaeologist. Mary Anna Evans then commences to weave an almost mystical tapestry of mystery throughout her novel."

—Bill Gresens, Mississippi Valley Archaeology Center

"Evans explores themes of protection, love, and loss in her absorbing sixth Faye Longchamp Mystery... Compelling extracts from a sixteenth-century Spanish priest's manuscript diary that Faye begins translating lend historical ballast."

—*Publishers Weekly*

"Evans's excellent series continues to combine solid mysteries and satisfying historical detail."

—*Kirkus Reviews*

"This contemporary mystery is drenched with Florida history and with gothic elements that should appeal to a broad range of readers."

—Booklist

FLOODGATES

The Fifth Faye Longchamp Mystery

2011—Mississippi Author Award Winner

"Mary Anna Evans gets New Orleans: the tainted light, the murk and the shadows, and the sweet and sad echoes, and the bloody dramas that reveal a city's eternal longing for what's been lost and its never-ending hopes for redemption."

—David Fulmer, author of Shamus Award–
winner Chasing the Devil's Tail

"Evans has written a fascinating tale linking the history of New Orleans's levee system to the present and weaving into the story aspects of the city's widely diverse cultures."

—Booklist, Starred Review

"Evans's fifth is an exciting brew of mystery and romance with a touch of New Orleans charm."

—Kirkus Reviews

"Evans's fifth series mystery…reveals her skill in handling the details of a crime story enhanced by historical facts and scientific discussions on the physical properties of water. Along with further insights into Faye's personal life, the reader ends up with a thoroughly good mystery."

—Library Journal

FINDINGS

The Fourth Faye Longchamp Mystery

"Evans always incorporates detailed research that adds depth and authenticity to her mysteries, and she beautifully conjures up the Micco County, Florida, setting. This is a series that deserves more attention than it garners."

—Library Journal, Starred Review

"Faye's capable fourth is a charming mixture of history, mystery, and romance."

—Kirkus Reviews

"In Evans's fine fourth archaeological mystery…the story settles into a comfortable pace that allows the reader to savor the characters."

—Publishers Weekly

EFFIGIES

The Third Faye Longchamp Mystery

2007—Florida Book Award Bronze Medal Winner for Popular Fiction

RELICS

The Second Faye Longchamp Mystery

"An intriguing, multi-layered tale. Not only was I completely stumped by the mystery, I was enchanted by the characters Evans created with such respect."

—Claire Matturro, author of *Wildcat Wine*

"The remote setting engenders an eerie sense of isolation and otherness that gives the story an extra dimension. Recommend this steadily improving series to female-sleuth fans or those who enjoy archaeology-based thrillers like Beverly Connor's Lindsay Chamberlain novels."

—*Booklist*

"Evans delivers a convincing read with life-size, unique characters, not the least of whom is Faye's Indian sidekick, Joe. The archaeological adventures are somewhat reminiscent of Tony Hillerman's Jim Chee mysteries. While the story is complex, *Relics* will engage the imagination of readers attracted to unearthing the secrets of lost cultures."

—*School Library Journal*

"A fascinating look at contemporary archaeology but also a twisted story of greed and its effects."

—*Dallas Morning News*

ARTIFACTS

The First Faye Longchamp Mystery

Also by Mary Anna Evans

The Faye Longchamp Mysteries

Artifacts

Relics

Effigies

Findings

Floodgates

Strangers

Plunder

Rituals

Isolation

Burials

Undercurrents

Catacombs

Other Books

Wounded Earth

Your Novel, Day by Day: A Fiction Writer's Companion

Jewel Box

*Mathematical Literacy in the Middle and Secondary Grades:
A Modern Approach to Sparking Student Interest*

WRECKED

WRECKED

A FAYE LONGCHAMP MYSTERY

MARY ANNA EVANS

Poisoned Pen
PRESS

Sourcebooks, Poisoned Pen Press, and the colophon
are registered trademarks of Sourcebooks.

Published by Poisoned Pen Press, an imprint of Sourcebooks
P.O. Box 4410, Naperville, Illinois 60567-4410
(630) 961-3900
sourcebooks.com

Library of Congress Cataloging-in-Publication Data

Names: Evans, Mary Anna, author.
Title: Wrecked / Mary Anna Evans.
Description: Naperville : Poisoned Pen Press, an imprint of Sourcebooks,
   2020. | Series: A Faye Longchamp archaeological mystery
Identifiers: LCCN 2020014718 (trade paperback)
Subjects: GSAFD: Mystery fiction.
Classification: LCC PS3605.V369 W74 2020 (print) | DDC 813/.6--dc22
LC record available at https://lccn.loc.gov/2020014718

Printed and bound in the United States of America.
POD

For my sister Suzanne

Prologue

The drone flew like a bird, cutting through sea breezes as if it could feel the joy of a living creature. Sometimes it flew high, though not so high as to lose sight of the Florida Panhandle's battered coastline. Sometimes the drone dove like an eagle and its camera got a close look at colorful fish swimming in water as clear as air.

The fish fluttered through the wrecks of newly sunken boats. Perhaps they remembered the hurricane as they swam below seacraft still able to float. Perhaps they didn't. The drone didn't care. It just snapped their picture and moved on.

The drone's camera captured everything in sight—clean water, broken trees, littered sand, swimming fish, flying birds, and shattered houses—because that is what cameras are made to do. They record everything they see. There is no hiding from them.

When the drone was flying low, its camera caught the faces of exhausted people spreading blue tarpaulins over splintered roofs. It saw the sun-bleached hair of people on pleasure boats, rubbernecking at destruction. It saw the bobbing heads of swimmers brave enough to share the water with floating wreckage.

The camera captured light reflected from the silvery backs of sharks and barracudas who swam wherever they pleased.

When the drone was flying high, it captured the contours of the coastline and the fractured light of sun on floodwater and broken glass. It saw the enormity of what the hurricane had done.

What is more, the camera's images were stamped with a date and time and, over time, the images recorded the movements of each boat. A careful observer could look at the drone's images and guess where all the boats and swimmers had been and where they might be going next.

If the drone made multiple flights that day, and it did, all of its pictures together gave a sense of the passage of time. The drone knew when the highway running along the Gulf of Mexico had seen heavy traffic that day. It noticed that the same boat had sat here in the morning and there in the afternoon, moving someplace else in the evening before cruising home. With a drone and a bit of ingenuity, an enterprising person could find fishing spots that had been family secrets for generations.

Almost everything captured by the camera was inconsequential, a series of instantaneous incidents that would be forgotten by morning, but not everything. The drone saw a place that had been the home of people long dead, generations of them. Barely visible, the stone outcropping marking its location had been exposed by the scouring waters of a hurricane after years and years under the seabed.

But that wasn't all. Someone was taking things that belonged to someone else, hoping to get rich. Someone was stealing something irreplaceable.

The drone saw it all.

Chapter One

Chain saws roared. Voices chanted "One. Two. Three!" as clusters of people lifted chunks of trees too heavy for one person to lift alone. Neighbors cried "Thank you so much!" as one driveway after another was cleared.

Short and skinny Faye Longchamp-Mantooth was struggling to do her part in carrying the big logs. She had friends who were sleeping in tents where their houses used to be, and she knew how much they would suffer under the broiling July sun. She had begged them to come stay with her, but there were looters prowling Micco County, and they were terrified. They'd rather live outdoors with the mosquitoes than lose the very few possessions that the hurricane had left behind. She struggled to think of ways to help them—fill their ice chests, swap out their propane tanks, bring them food and water—but these things weren't enough. Nothing was enough, not really.

Faye recognized the peculiar clarity of the sunlight that shines in the aftermath of a hurricane, because she had seen it before. It was as if swirling winds had drawn the moisture right out of the air, leaving nothing but oxygen, nitrogen, and traces of the usual stray gases. She felt as if she could see forever through the clear air, or at least to the point where the Earth curved and hid itself. And everywhere she looked, she saw something that the hurricane had crushed or shredded or twisted beyond recognition.

Faye and her husband, Joe Wolf Mantooth, had been lucky. The hurricane had dealt their home on Joyeuse Island a glancing blow on its way to pummeling Micco County. Eventually, they would need to sweep the roof and replace some missing shutters, but those chores could wait. Whole towns were without electricity and water. Cell phone service was spotty, even for people who had electricity to charge their phones.

The sheriff's department was stretched thin, because the disaster had rubbed the veneer of civilization right off of some people. Faye had heard about a knife fight over bottled water, right in the middle of a suburban grocery store. With her own eyes, she'd seen three men brandishing handguns as they robbed a convenience store, led by three men brandishing handguns. She thought that Sheriff Rainey had done an excellent job of restoring order. He'd arrested some key players and put his entire staff on overtime. His deputies were constantly visible, prowling rural roads and patrolling Micco County's tiny towns. Faye felt safer, but she didn't feel safe.

Hospitals and nursing homes were running on generators, staffed by doctors and nurses who were running on no sleep. Shelters were full and they, too, were running on generators. Micco County wasn't a wealthy place, so a lot of people had already been living on the edge before they got flattened by nature. Faye and Joe were losing money every day that they did no archaeological work for their clients, but they'd find a way to make their bank accounts last until the crisis passed. People needed their help.

Faye and Joe had strong arms and backs, and they had functional cars that they could use to get supplies to people. Their nineteen-year-old daughter, Amande, had found her own way to help as she drove loads of donated food and water to people too old or sick to get to the distribution points.

Faye had argued against Amande's plan to make these delivery runs. She'd said, "Your father and I are helping people get back on their feet. If you stay at home to take care of Michael so we can do that, you'll be helping, too."

Faye hadn't said *I feel safer when the two of you are at home. I'd wrap you both in bubble wrap if I could*, but it was the truth.

Amande had out-argued her, which was the downside of having assertive and intelligent children. "I'll take Michael to hang out at Sheriff Mike and Magda's every morning. He'll be as safe as he is at home. Maybe safer, since Sheriff Mike will stop packing heat on the day they put him in the ground."

Faye knew that this was true. She also knew how strict Mike was about safety when it came to kids and guns. She trusted him to keep everyone around him safe.

Amande was still making her case. "I'll be in a car that you and Dad make sure is perfectly safe, just like I am on any normal day. I'll only be traveling on roads that have been cleared. Deputies are keeping the roads hot with all their patrolling. Michael and I will be out of your hair, so you and Dad can focus on what you need to do. I really want to do this, Mom."

And so, with her imagination conjuring danger at every turn, Faye had watched her daughter drive away every morning for a solid week. More, actually. She'd mostly lost track of how much time had passed since the storm, but somehow she knew that today was Monday. She mostly knew this because it felt like a Monday.

For days now, Faye had watched little Michael sitting behind Amande in his car seat, and Joe had watched Faye watch them. Every morning, he'd said what she was thinking, and it sounded so ridiculous when he said it out loud that it made her laugh every single time.

"There go all our eggs in one basket."

And each time, their laughter calmed her. It made her able to wave good-bye to her children and get to work helping her friends.

The hurricane had taken a human toll—two people had been killed when their car slammed into a fallen tree and two people were still missing—but it could have been much worse. Still, months—years, probably—would pass before life in Micco County was anything like normal again.

Faye and Joe were helping their substitute mother, Emma Everett, and her neighbors clear the downed trees blocking access to their homes. By lunchtime, they'd made visible progress, but Faye's muscles—biceps, triceps, quads, hamstrings, glutes, all of them—were trembling. It was time to sit down, drink a lukewarm bottle of water, and eat a peanut-butter-and-honey sandwich, because peanut butter doesn't have to be refrigerated and neither does honey.

Joe's muscles didn't seem to need rest. He was loping down the street, his long, straight black ponytail swinging like a pendulum. Faye's own black hair, short but just as straight, was stuck to her brown cheeks with sweat. She was a little jealous of Joe's energy after the morning's hard work. She figured that it helped a lot to be made of six-and-a-half rawboned feet of muscle. Five-foot-tall Faye wouldn't know. And also, he was nine years her junior. Those years might have something to do with the fact that she wanted a nap and Joe looked almost perky.

Joe was on a mission, and it was a mission that Faye would never have imagined for him. Who would have thought of Joe as the passionate pilot of his very own drone? He was beside himself over this chance to make his fanciful hobby useful.

Faye had assumed that Magda and Mike were wasting their money when they'd bought Joe a flying, picture-taking robot for Christmas. She'd figured that it would get about as much use as the food processor she'd been foolish enough to buy him. He'd given her a sweet thank you, then tucked it deep into a cabinet so he could go back to making cole slaw with a sharp knife and patience.

Faye fervently loved her solar panels and the air conditioning they made possible. Joe? Not so much.

He tried to live as close to the traditional ways of his Muscogee Creek ancestors as he could. If it had been practical for people living on their remote island to get along without boats that had motors, Joe would have chucked everything they owned that didn't exist before the Industrial Revolution. Yet he had bonded to his twenty-first-century flying gadget so completely that he'd given it a name.

And maybe that name, Osprey—Ossie for short—explained Joe's fascination with his new hobby. Faye thought that Joe loved Ossie because he himself moved easily on earth and sea, but he would never be able to take to the air.

Ossie could fly. The little drone gave Joe a new way to see the natural world that he loved so much. It was probably no coincidence that their son's middle name, chosen by Joe, was Hawk.

Today, Ossie would be hard at work doing something useful. She—and, yes, Joe had gifted his inanimate flying sidekick with a gender—would be taking aerial photos that would come in handy when their friends needed to do battle with their insurance companies. Since people who live in hurricane zones rarely have much trust in the companies that collect their insurance premiums, everybody wanted Ossie to get pictures of their shredded roofs and totaled cars.

They called out "Hey, Ossie! Take my picture!" whenever she zoomed by.

A crowd gathered around Joe, cheering as he sent Ossie skyward. She was white, like a living osprey's breast and head, but she had four white rotors instead of two glossy brown wings. Her four slender legs were as white as her namesake bird's legs, without the black talons.

As she rose above their heads, the camera attached to her underside looked back at them. Joe expertly manipulated the levers on Ossie's controller to guide her as she paused over each house to get images of the hurricane damage. Then, just to make them all smile, he sent Ossie roaring away at top speed to get video of the Florida Panhandle's coastline, still gloriously beautiful under unending piles of debris.

Ossie sped down the coast to the west as far as they could see before Joe steered her out over the Gulf of Mexico and flew her back their way. As she swooped over their heads, the cheers grew louder. Joe was focused on the drone's controls and on the drone's-eye view scene on his phone's display, but not so focused that he didn't crack a smile.

Faye leaned over his shoulder to watch the images on his phone, which was attached to the drone's controller so that he could see to steer. It seemed like Ossie's onboard camera could see forever. Beaches the color of confectioner's sugar stretched out ahead as she flew far above them. They were strewn with chocolate-colored seaweed and the wood from obliterated boat docks.

To the drone's left, beyond the damaged beach houses, the phone's screen showed tall trees, some snapped in half with their topmost branches dragging the ground. Even broken, the pines and cypress trees appealed to the eye, but it was the luminescent water to Ossie's right that held Faye's attention.

She had lived on an island for a long time, but she hadn't gotten used to the beauty of the Gulf of Mexico yet. She hoped she never did.

In the shallows, where long docks and piers had collapsed under punishing waves, the water went from emerald green to spring green, shading quickly to a pure turquoise so clear that she could see objects on the white sand beneath it. An area of murkier water marked the mouth of a broad, deep creek. It also marked the location of the marina that Faye's family depended on to switch from their boats to their cars, and vice versa, making their island life possible. She enjoyed seeing it from the sky, admiring the stark geometry of the rectangular buildings and straight docks against the softness of nature.

In an instant, Ossie flew beyond the creek and all murkiness left the blue, blue water. Out beyond the barrier islands, the water's color deepened to a strong aquamarine. If she focused her eyes in that direction, she could imagine that the hurricane had never happened at all.

Just as Joe swung Ossie around one last time, she flew over their home, Joyeuse Island, separated from the green-black coastal swamps by a narrow channel. When the crisis was past, Faye would ask Joe to fly the drone over their island to see whether the hurricane had uncovered more of the old buildings her family had built back in the 1800s. She'd been exploring the archaeological traces left by her ancestors since she was a child, and those happy years digging for historical treasure had made her into the archaeologist she'd grown up to be.

For now, she was happy to stand among her friends and watch the drone return to Joe. Hardly bigger than an unabridged dictionary and not nearly so heavy, Ossie settled herself at Faye's husband's feet like a faithful pet.

The crowd applauded, and Joe said quietly, "Good girl, Ossie."

———

Far away, much too far for Ossie to fly, a woman was running. With a single bag in one hand and a child's hand in the other, she wondered whether it was even possible to disappear these days. Even her credit card would give her away. And everybody knew there were cameras everywhere.

Chapter Two

"Hey! He's got a newspaper," somebody called out, and Faye looked up from her sandwich. A crowd was forming around a man who'd just come back from a food-and-water run.

Another man's voice emanated from the cluster of people, calling out, "Joe, you're a star."

A woman spoke up to argue with him. "Not Joe. Ossie's the star."

Faye rushed over to see what they were talking about. There, dominating the front page and above the fold, was one of Ossie's photos in full, glorious color. She didn't know when Joe had found time to send it to the newspaper, but he must have done it from home or from his phone during a trip to town, because they certainly had no cell service where they were working at that moment. One of Joe's fishing buddies, Nate Peterson, was credited with writing the story, which explained how the newspaper even knew Joe's photos existed.

Below the fold was an article memorializing the dead and the missing. Their photos haunted Faye. Her eyes were drawn to the school photo of an eighth-grade girl. They lingered on the cropped, blurry snapshot of a mother who'd been killed during the time of life when she was always the one taking the pictures. Mother and daughter had died together when a massive live oak toppled in front of the speeding car that was supposed to be taking them to an emergency shelter and safety.

Another photo showed a smiling woman holding her five-year-old son. Both of them had been missing since the storm. It was printed beside a brief article asking for help in locating them. Faye knew that this request was optimistic. They'd gone missing at the height of the storm, when the hurricane had peeled the roof off their double-wide and toppled what was left of it. In all likelihood, floodwaters had washed their bodies into a swamp where they'd be found when the water finally receded.

Faye couldn't look at their faces any longer. She flipped the still-folded paper over and rested her eyes on Joe's peaceful photo.

"Is our street in the picture?" Emma asked. "People need to know how bad it is here."

Joe shook his head. "Nate wanted a big-picture shot, so I sent him one that I took east of here from pretty high up. He also said they'd been running pictures of torn-up houses all week and he wanted something that showed what the storm did to nature. So I got him a shot that shows the torn-up beaches down toward our house and all the downed trees in the swamp. Look. That sandy point that used to stick out into the water west of Joyeuse Island is just gone. And see those snags piled up in the shallows? People around here are boaters and they're going to have to navigate around that stuff. Those things will get people's attention."

"Well, I hope their attention strays a little farther inland," Emma said tartly. "My house will be fine with a few tarps, but everybody wasn't so lucky."

Faye raised an eyebrow at her.

"Oh, okay. Sooner or later, I'll need some carpenters and

roofers, and maybe a plumber and a couple of electricians, but they'll get the place livable again. The houses on both sides of mine? They're gone. And all the people in the trailer park across the highway lost everything, too."

Emma Everett was past seventy now. Her deep brown skin was starting to wrinkle and her cap of tight short curls was more gray than black, but she still funded college scholarships for poor Micco County teenagers, and she still spent her Saturdays tutoring them for their college admissions tests. Her late husband, Douglass, had remembered what it was like to be poor. He would have been proud to see how Emma was using her time and their money.

"Your pictures are beautiful, son, and this one reminds people that it's not going to be so much fun to fish or go to the beach for a while, but that's not enough," Emma said. "You need to tell that Peterson man to come out here himself and interview my neighbors." She swept out an arm that encompassed a bunch of people who hadn't bathed in days. "They're hurting."

Joe said, "Yes, ma'am. I'll tell him."

Mollified, Emma gave him a big hug and said, "I'm proud of you." She pulled Faye in close, so that the three of them could look at Joe's photo together.

Newspaper images are low-resolution by nature. The photo's blurred haziness made the damaged coastline look better than it did in real life, like an aging Hollywood actress who had trusted her face to a photographer who knew how to use lighting and filters.

The picture was oriented with north facing up, so the coastline ran along the top edge and water dominated the rest of the photo. Faye's eyes went straight to her home, Joyeuse Island, hugging the coast in the top right corner and extending off the right side of the photo. The tin roof of their house shone silver through trees that had survived the big fire. A lot of other trees were on the ground. From this altitude, her island looked like a giant had dropped a box of matches on it.

The water just below Joyeuse Island was dotted with a handful of small pleasure boats and a…well, she couldn't say, but it made her archaeologist's heart sing for joy. It made her desperate to see the image at full resolution. Her brown eyes found Joe's green ones, and she tapped her forefinger hard on the photo.

"What's that dark blotch in the water southwest of our house?"

Joe's shrug said he didn't know what the blotch was, either, but he was grinning. He could see how excited she was.

Faye hadn't seen it in any of Ossie's photos taken before the storm. It was slightly smaller than the boats floating nearby. That meant it was probably too small to be that holy grail of underwater archaeology, a shipwreck.

Faye supposed it could be a shipwreck that was still mostly hidden under the sand, but she doubted it. She snorkeled in that area all the time, and she'd never seen anything like a debris trail on the seabed that screamed "Shipwreck!"

She had, however, found two chipped stone points lying on the sand, as if they were pointing toward something truly ancient. Maybe the hurricane had uncovered a dugout canoe to go with them, hundreds or thousands of years old. Maybe it had exposed a midden made of the piled-up shells of oysters eaten by long-ago people. Or maybe that dark blotch was just an old tractor tire.

Joe asked, "Is that The Cold Spot?"

Faye nodded. "I'm pretty sure."

Their family spent a good chunk of every August swimming at The Cold Spot, an area where the water felt chillier than the surrounding Gulf. Faye had always thought that The Cold Spot must mark a submarine spring dumping cold groundwater into the Gulf.

Maybe Joe's photo was evidence that The Cold Spot looked totally different now. Maybe the hurricane had scoured centuries of sand and debris out of a spring vent, revealing it to Ossie's all-seeing camera. Faye sure hoped so.

At times in ancient history, Faye's island would have been on dry land, and so would The Cold Spot. A spring there would have been a water source for thirsty animals…and thirsty people. She knew that archaeologists had found Paleolithic tools at Wakulla Springs. They'd even found mastodon bones there. The Cold Spot might have looked a lot like Wakulla Springs, back in the day.

What could be cooler than mastodon bones and Paleolithic tools? Well, a 13,000-year-old hearth where people had once sat around a fire would be cooler, to Faye's way of thinking. And maybe it was waiting for her, right off the coast of her very own island.

"Joe," she said, trying to be nonchalant while she nearly poked a hole in the newspaper with her forefinger, "want to go wading out to The Cold Spot, once we get our friends comfortable?"

He grinned. "Might be a few weeks before we're home much in the daylight. And we'll have to go when the tide is right, but our chance will come. We'll get out there and see what the storm uncovered."

Chapter Three

Faye was behind the wheel of Joe's car, a white Chevy Cavalier that was ancient but utterly reliable. Getting supplies to the cleanup workers was Priority One, but she had a second mission that was more selfish. She wanted more information on the mysterious dark blotch on the floor of the Gulf of Mexico, and she was pretty sure she knew where to get it.

People with cash or functioning credit cards had pooled their resources for this trip to civilization. Faye had used those dollars to fill the Cavalier's trunk and back seat full of bottled water, energy bars, baby formula, diapers, and wet wipes. Since Faye was good at making cash go a long way, she had stretched the budget enough to fill the passenger seat with practical luxuries. Handing out things like apples, oranges, peanuts, deodorant, and dry shampoo was going to feel like playing Santa Claus.

It was sheer luck that there were open stores in Crawfordville, close enough for her to make a round trip in a single afternoon with time to spare. If that weren't true, people would be a lot hungrier and a lot thirstier. Those in the storm's path had been lucky in some ways, if one is willing to call being walloped by a Category 3 hurricane lucky.

First of all, at least the storm hadn't been a Category 5. It had pulverized the lightly populated Micco County coastline, but it had spared the beach resorts to the west and the popular fishing areas to the east.

Second, there had been luck in the storm's small size. Like the Category 5 Hurricane Camille, one of the most powerful of all time, its eyewall had been a fierce but small circle of wind and rain. Hurricane force winds had extended barely sixty miles from the eye, so the counties to either side of the storm's center were windblown but functional. This meant that the Wakulla County towns of Panacea, Crawfordville, and Sopchoppy were open for business. When Faye and Joe had first ventured out after the storm, they'd been shocked to find that the marina where they kept their boats was barely touched.

It was as if God had pointed at Micco County and said, "Here's a good place to try out my new wind tunnel." Faye didn't want to think about what would have happened if the thing had been the size of fellow Cat 3 Hurricane Katrina.

Unfortunately, mere Cat 3 storms don't get a lot of media attention, unless they're Katrina, so the news cycle had moved on. Government-sponsored help was falling into place, but it was inadequate. Insurance money hadn't started flowing. In short, people were largely on their own.

The small size of the devastated area meant that its residents were within reach of the trappings of civilization. Faye and Joe had access to gasoline at the marina, so they fetched the fuel that kept people's cars and chain saws running, and they did a lot of driving themselves. Today, it was Faye's turn to make the afternoon supply run.

As she drove away from the grocery store, she detoured to her friend Captain Eubank's house. If anybody could help her identify the dark blotch off the coast of Joyeuse Island, he could.

She turned her car into his driveway, parking near the free-standing garage behind his house. The captain leaned out his side door before she'd even put the car in park. He was a slim, gray-haired man with gray eyes that surveyed the world with a sharp intelligence. The captain was past retirement age, but he still carried himself with a military bearing.

"Come in, come in. It's always so good to see you, Faye."

He lived in a white wood-frame house built shortly after World War II. It was surrounded by a neat green yard, front and back, and a white picket fence. The house looked freshly painted, but then it always looked freshly painted. If the hurricane had dropped a single twig on its grassy lawn, it was gone now.

The captain seated her at a table smack in the middle of a 1950s fantasy kitchen. "Have a seat in here while I fix us some tea."

His sink was shiny white porcelain, his refrigerator was shiny white enameled steel, and his counters were shiny red laminate. Faye didn't know you could still buy kitchen wax. Maybe Captain Eubank had a lifetime supply stashed in his garage.

The captain was a big tea drinker, so the teakettle on his stove was permanently hot. He made a pot of tea and poured Faye a cup, then he dropped in a sugar cube and a splash of milk, because people who operated at his level of efficiency never forgot how their friends liked their tea.

Picking up his own cup, a celadon-green antique that suited the captain's love of the past, he said, "Now that we've got our tea, do you want to sit in the library? It's more fun in there, because that's where the books are."

Faye never passed up a chance to soak in the ambiance of the captain's fabulous library. "Absolutely."

Captain Eubank's body might live in Crawfordville now, but

his heart had never left Micco County. It was where he had lived the first sixty years of his life. His passion for Micco County history knew no bounds, and his book collection showed it. His personal library held documents so rare that they brought historians to him.

He lived for those historians' visits, which gave him opportunities to ply them with tea and pick their brains. His door was just as open to people researching their family trees, Civil War re-enactors trying to get their uniforms just right, and school kids working on history projects.

Faye wasn't sure what branch of the military the captain had served in, or when. She'd never wanted to ask him, maybe because she wasn't convinced that he'd actually served. She'd always harbored a private suspicion that "Captain" was his first name, until she'd read the inscription on the plaque that had pride of place on his library wall. It read:

In Recognition of Long and Faithful Service to the Citizens of Micco County, Florida, Captain Edward Eubank is Hereby Awarded the Title of Honorary County Historian.

For a time, she'd thought that this inscription had finally answered her question. Then she'd decided that the inscription didn't actually clear things up. Yeah, the captain had another name and it was Edward, but Captain could still be his first name. The mystery remained, and Faye decided that she liked it that way.

The plaque adorned a room that most people who weren't Captain Eubank would have called the living room. He had filled it full of books. Then he'd filled the dining room full of old maps. And he had crammed two of the house's three bedrooms full of old newspapers and ephemera. If the captain didn't stop collecting stuff, he would need to move out of his bedroom and sleep on the couch.

His books were labeled and shelved just as they would be in a public library. The captain had told Faye on more than one occasion, with some vehemence and more than a little passion, that he favored the Library of Congress system over the Dewey Decimal system. He'd never specified his reasons but she did not doubt that he had them.

Since the captain had lived most of his seventy-ish years without computers, he still maintained a physical card catalog made possible when the Micco County Public Library went digital and gave him their card cabinets. They had also given him their old stamp-and-ink book checkout equipment. These things had brought his system into the 1970s. The metallic smell of library ink pervaded his home, and it took Faye back to her childhood bookmobile visits. She always left Captain Eubank's house with a daffy smile that made her look like she'd been sniffing glue.

Faye and the captain sat down at a reading table in the center of the living room library, and he said, "To what do I owe the pleasure of your company?"

"Well, I mainly wanted to be sure you made it through the storm okay. From the looks of things, you certainly did. Your yard looks like we never even had a hurricane, so I'm guessing that you spearheaded efforts to make every other yard on the street look just as good."

The captain grinned, but he didn't say no. "We're all fine. It wasn't near as bad here in Crawfordville as it was over in Micco County."

"What about your sister? She lives in Micco County. Do I remember that Jeanine has been ill?"

"I don't know that Jeanine's ill, really. Maybe old age is just creeping up on her, but she doesn't get around like she used to. Her legs don't want to go, and her breathing's not too good. I've been beside myself worrying about her. You know how far she lives from town. Her phone wasn't working—still isn't—and I can't get a call through. Haven't been able to get through by car, either. And, believe me, I've tried. Every day since the storm, I've tried. Can't even get halfway there. Still too many darned trees in the road."

"I bet you have."

"Every morning, I'm in my car, trying to find a way to get to Jeanine. Every afternoon, I'm working with my neighbors to get this town cleaned up. I'm so happy you caught me here when you stopped by."

Now Faye was really concerned. "It was that bad where she was, and you still haven't seen her? Or heard from her?"

"No, no, no, don't worry. She's okay. One of her neighbors was able to chain-saw his way out far enough to get a cell signal. He called to say that her house is in terrible shape but she's fine, just scared and lonely. He thinks the road to her place will be open tomorrow. She may even have cell service by then. I'm heading out bright and early to lay eyes on her, maybe even bring her here. If she's willing to leave her house, that is."

"Well, I'm glad she's okay, and I'm glad you're going to able to see her."

"I was actually more worried about your family, living out there on that island, but I saw Joe at the store. He said you missed the worst of the storm."

She began, "Thanks, but speaking of my family, Joe took a picture that you really need to—" but he was too excited to wait for her to finish.

"I saw it!" he said. He reached into a pile of papers on his desk and pulled out a newspaper, smacking it down on the table with Joe's aerial photo facing up. He jabbed a finger at the dark spot off the coast of Joyeuse Island.

"That picture is why I'm here. Well, besides making sure

you're okay," she said. "I thought you'd be interested in that spot. Actually, I thought you might know what it is."

"I don't know what it is, but I have a theory."

His face had an ask-me-please glow, so she did. "What's your theory?"

"Somewhere near here, a ship went down during the Civil War."

Chapter Four

Joe loved to send Ossie into the sky, so nobody had to twist his arm to get him to send the drone up. Just let a little kid say, "Hey, Mr. Joe, I haven't got to see Ossie fly yet," and he'd be fetching her from the back seat of his car. He felt a little guilty playing with his toy instead of chain-sawing more dead trees, so whenever he made a kid smile by flying Ossie, he justified himself by taking aerial shots of storm-damaged roofs while she was up there.

Really, though, he couldn't feel too bad about spending his time with Ossie. People's spirits rose when she rose. When Ossie flew, they smiled, and Joe saw. To keep people smiling, he took the time put her through her paces, every time. He sent her straight up. He brought her back down in a steep dive. He sent her far out over the water and brought her home. He spun her in the air over their heads and everybody cheered.

When they were happy, Joe was happy.

———

Not far away from where Joe's happy audience watched him send Ossie out over the water, someone was aboard an anchored boat, working at a task that was nowhere near so generous as help-ing neighbors dig themselves out after a disaster. Ossie was a quiet machine, so there was almost no sound as she approached the boat. The waves drowned out any sound she made, but her shadow slid across the boat as she passed overhead.

A face looked up as if to say "What's that up there? Is this okay?"

Ossie took a wide turn out over the water, and then passed above the boat again, lower this time. Its passenger was quick-witted enough to lean far out over the gunwale, putting a human body between the drone's lens and the boat's registration num-ber. Crouching there, hat brim flipped low to hide a guilty face, the interloper pondered whether the drone posed a real threat and, if so, what to do about it.

Chapter Five

Faye didn't think she'd ever seen the captain this excited.

"You think Joe's picture shows a sunken ship, Captain? Confederate or Union?"

"Neither, not really. Blockade runners did their own thing."

Now Faye was intrigued. Blockade runners had risked their lives during the Civil War, doing extremely dubious things for money. They ran cash crops from the Confederacy past the federal blockade and brought cash and trade goods back in. And guns. When there's a war on, the value of a gun skyrockets. Blockade runners were smugglers by any definition— criminals, actually—but Margaret Mitchell had draped a cloak of roguish respectability over them in 1936 when she created *Gone with the Wind*'s notorious blockade runner, Rhett Butler.

Sometimes blockade runners lost their cargo. Sometimes they lost their ships. Sometimes they lost their freedom. And sometimes they lost their lives. But the successful ones got rich, some of them beyond their wildest dreams. There was an air of romance around their memory, and Captain Eubank was a sucker for historical romance.

"I think it's the *Philomela*," he said. "I've been hoping for years that somebody would find her, and they have certainly been looking. You wouldn't believe how many people come in here, asking me where I think she is. Treasure hunters. Historians. Conspiracy theorists." He smiled. "Even archaeologists like you."

He slapped his hand on the clipboard holding the stack of the sign-in sheets that kept track of the foot traffic coming through his library. These careful records proved that his work was valuable, and they had paid off several times in the form of grants to support his collection.

The captain shook his head. "The people who come to me looking for the *Philomela*? They're all starry-eyed dreamers. They all think she was loaded with gold. But why would she be?"

And there it was, the romantic belief that all sunken ships carried hoards of gold. But then, maybe the *Philomela* did. Blockade runners were all about buying and selling, and both of those things involved money. The value of waterlogged paper money, especially Confederate money, was sketchy at best, but this wasn't a problem with gold. So yeah, maybe some of the money onboard the *Philomela* when she sank was in gold. And maybe you might call that treasure, but this was beside the point for the captain. He didn't care about the treasure. He cared about the ship.

She hated to disappoint her friend, but it couldn't be helped. "I don't think it's the *Philomela*. First of all, it's a very small anomaly for a ship that size—"

Ever hopeful, he said, "But maybe most of it's still under the sand. Maybe the storm only uncovered a little of it."

"That's possible, I guess, but I've done a lot of swimming in that very spot. Snorkeling, too. So has everyone in my family. I just can't believe that none of us has ever seen anything related to a shipwreck. No timbers, no anchor, no cargo, no nails.

Nothing. I guess Mother Nature could have buried it that well, but she's not usually such a perfectionist."

He didn't look convinced, but he didn't argue. He just changed his tactics, like the military man he probably was. "Well, then, what do *you* think it is?"

"I think it's a submarine spring, a place where fresh groundwater from down below seeps into the saltwater above. When the flow from a spring like that is strong enough, you can see the surface of the seawater over it mound up and churn. People call that a 'boil.'"

"I fish enough that I've seen lots of boils in creeks, but I didn't know you could see a spring boil offshore. You think your spring was stopped up and the hurricane opened it again?"

"Could be."

His lips were pursed and he drummed his fingers on the table. She could see that he wasn't convinced, but the captain was a logical man. If he couldn't marshal a strong argument to refute hers, he wasn't going to waste her time.

"Hmmm." He drummed a while longer. "You seem pretty excited for somebody who thinks she might have found a wet hole in the ground underneath a really big wet hole in the ground."

The captain knew her well. Faye pulled her phone out of her pocket, pulled up a photo, and handed the phone over. "Take a look at these."

On the screen was a photo of two chunks of nondescript beige stone. Faye knew that Captain Eubank would recognize them for what they were, hand-chipped projectile points. But he might not realize how old they were, so she told him.

"I think they're pre-Clovis. Fourteen, fifteen thousand years old. I found them years ago, when I was a kid. They were right near the spring, if it is a spring. I wasn't even looking for anything. I was just snorkeling around but there they were, lying on the sea bottom like they were pointing at…something."

She remembered the feel of wet stone on her palm as she pulled them out of the water and lifted them up to the hot sun.

"Well, you're not nuts to think they might be that old," he said, holding the phone on his palm to study the photo, exactly as she had held the points themselves. "There's been some papers published about pre-Clovis sites in the Aucilla River. Seems to me like finding something under a river is different from finding something under the Gulf, though."

"That's just it. It's not different at all. The sea level was a lot lower then because the Earth was colder and lots of its water was tied up in the ice caps. If that spot's a spring, it wouldn't have been underwater then. It would've been on land and it would've made a handy watering hole for thirsty animals."

"Humans are animals," he said, holding the phone closer to his face and squinting.

Faye reached over and used two fingers to expand the photo so that the tech-phobic captain could get a better look at the points' meticulously shaped edges.

"You do have a point about springs," he said, "being as how they've found artifacts kinda like these at Wakulla Springs."

"There are subterranean springs in the Aucilla River, too." Trying not to let her excitement show, she said, "There really could be a Paleolithic occupation site right off the coast of Joyeuse Island, practically in my back yard. How cool would that be?"

"Pretty cool." He opened a drawer in the desk behind him and pulled out a stack of photos, big and glossy eight-by-tens. "Do you see anything in these pictures that might help you find your precious occupation site? Or my precious blockade-running ship?"

"We both have our own personal Great White Whales that we'll do anything to find," she said, reaching for the stack of photos.

"Don't I know it? I think everybody's got one. I get the biggest part of my foot traffic from people looking for their Moby Dick. People come here looking for shipwrecks. Mysterious ancestors. Rare maps that will help them write the book that earns them tenure. Legendary fishing holes. Family histories. Hidden beaches. Even archaeological sites."

Faye grinned, because this was how they had met.

"And all that foot traffic gets me the grant money that keeps this place afloat. Everybody wins."

The captain handed her the photos and she spread them out on the table. They had to be some of Joe's photos, because they looked so much like the one that had appeared in the newspaper. They might even have been taken within a few minutes of that one. Faye's heart beat quicker. The newspaper photo had been fuzzy, as newspaper photos always are. These originals were sharp and clear. Joe and Ossie did good work.

"Joe gave me these that day I saw him in the store," he said, picking one up and studying it. "He knows I don't do computers, so he was kind enough to bring me print copies. The resolution is astonishing. I'd get myself a drone like his, but then I'd have to buy a computer and a cell phone. And I'd have to learn to use them. I'm an old man. I don't have that kind of time left."

"You won't be old until you stop being excited about shipwrecks and library books, Captain. Tell Joe what photos you want, and he'll take them for you."

Faye scrutinized the images. She loved aerial photographs as much as Captain Eubank did, so she and her friend had a geeky good time studying Joe's pictures and comparing them to old maps.

"You sure can see how the storm changed the coastline," she said. "And look. It almost cut this little sandbar out by Seagreen Island in two."

She handed him a photo so he could see for himself, then she said, "It didn't take the pleasure boaters long to get out there. Look at them all."

"Don't know why. The fishing's terrible right now—not that this is keeping me from going out every day and hoping I catch a few. Takes two weeks for things to get better after a big storm, minimum."

This was a fisherman's response. Sometimes people boated just because they enjoyed the water and the sunshine, and there had certainly been plenty of both since the storm cleared. Most of the boaters in the photo had responded to that day's bright sun by raising their bimini tops, awning-like pieces of canvas mounted on metal frames that could be raised to shade the boat's passengers. While it was possible to boat in Florida and allow oneself to broil in the unshaded sunshine, biminis made everything more fun.

Biminis were usually chosen to match the boat, so they came in shades that were common boat finishes and trim colors. Though only a handful of boats were visible in any of Joe's photos, the spots of color drew the eye. Blotches of blue, red, black, burgundy, and white, set against the Gulf water, made the boats look like a handful of marbles tossed onto a blue slate tabletop.

Seeing all the boats on the water made Faye hope that nobody else had noticed the dark spot. She did not need sightseers and treasure hunters hanging around so close to her house.

Faye sighed. "I don't see that dark spot in any of these shots. It's out of range of every photo but the one in the newspaper. I'll have to get Joe to make me a copy of my own."

"Here, take one of these with you," the captain said, holding out a photo that was only subtly different from the one on the paper's front page. It covered the area just east of the missing photo, so most of Joyeuse Island was visible.

Faye knew that Joe could make her a print of any one of the photos in the stack whenever she asked, but the captain's offer was a symbolic gesture. By holding out the photo, he was saying *Fellow researchers share what they find.* She took it.

"Some of these are almost duplicates," he said. "I don't need them all for my library."

The captain was right. The only real difference between this photo and the one in the paper was the slightly shifted field of view and the slightly changed pattern of boats. One of them, located near the bottom left of the frame, hadn't been in the newspaper photo. She knew this for sure, because its light-yellow bimini stood out. She would have remembered it.

"You planning to go out there and see what's waiting under the water?" he said. "I know you are."

"I absolutely am, once I get a spare minute. If you're right, the *Philomela*'s been waiting for a century and a half for somebody to find her. And if I'm right, that Paleolithic occupation site could have been waiting for me for fifteen thousand years. Neither of them is going anywhere."

She hugged the captain goodbye and headed out, taking a carload of baby wipes and bottled water to people who would be very glad to see them.

Chapter Six

The job at hand could be done in the daytime, when the water was warmer and brighter, but the danger of discovery was high. Nighttime was safer. This job was tailor-made for night diving. For a diver with the right skills, experience, and equipment, doing this work at night didn't require much more than handheld lights and patience. And time, which was unfortunately in short supply.

Because time was short and the potential rewards were long indeed, the occasional daytime dive like this one was worth the risk. It had been a productive morning and it would be a productive night. In the meantime, though, there were things to be done.

Attention to detail was critical, but this was a fact of diving life. When swimming so far underwater, a single error could kill. Duplication of equipment helped guard against a deadly mistake.

This meant carrying two lights at all times. Even in the daytime, the water at this depth was too dark for safety.

Two specially built contraptions hoisted the contraband thirty feet or more to the surface. And if either of them failed, the redundancy kept that dive from being a complete failure.

Two knives strapped to an arm and a leg guarded against sharks, but also against the constant risk of entanglement when diving in tight, unfamiliar spaces.

These precautions had paid off. They were still paying off. Night after night, and occasionally in the daytime, a fortune was emerging from the dark water.

There was danger afoot, but it didn't lurk in the water. It existed in the form of a man who asked too damn many questions. He hadn't proven receptive to suggestions that he might want to keep his mouth shut.

Finishing the work quickly, before the blabbermouth could endanger the operation, wasn't possible. The process couldn't be rushed, not safely, but cutting things short was equivalent to pouring money down the drain, piles and piles of it. Or setting it on fire.

It was time to visit the blabbermouth, and it was time to silence him.

Chapter Seven

Captain Edward Eubank was in an opalescent heaven. It was like no place he had ever seen.

He had been boating on the Gulf of Mexico hundreds of times during his long life. He had swum in the Gulf and fished in the Gulf. He had sat on the deck at the marina, beer in hand, and simply enjoyed looking at a million colors of blue and green. But he had never donned scuba gear and slipped into the warm water, drifting down so far that he saw nothing but blue in all directions.

He'd done a lot of snorkeling, so he moved comfortably with the swim fins on his feet. The regulator in his mouth wasn't so very different from his snorkel's plastic mouthpiece. It brought air to his lungs, and they sent it to all the rest of his body. The tank on his back made swimming awkward at first, but he stopped noticing its weight after about thirty seconds of watching sunlight filter through the lovely water.

He knew the fish around him on sight. He had caught so many speckled trout in his life that he recognized them like old friends. Tawny redfish moved among them. So did black drum, with their dark scales and pugilistic faces. When he held out a hand, schools of tiny fish hovered around his fingertips, covering them in tiny kisses and then scattering in a million directions.

As he swam slowly downward, he left the opalescent blue and dropped into a blanket of translucent gray. The water grew chilly and continued to cool as he went deeper.

Visibility quickly dwindled to ten feet or so as he descended still farther. He could see his own outstretched hand but not much more. If the *Philomela* really lay below him, and he believed that she did, then she was on the sand at the bottom of the murk, and underneath the sand, too. He dipped his head down and, with a few flicks of his fins, began his descent in earnest.

The water around him cooled with depth and the gray water grew darker. His eyes darted here and there, peering through the dive mask adhered to his face. Somewhere below him was a wrecked ship that had been loaded with cargo when it went down. There would surely be guns aboard and very old ammunition. There would be rusted iron hoops of rotted barrels that had held the ship's supplies of flour and salt pork. Probably, there would be rotten silk and spoiled books.

Maybe there would be gold and silver, too, but not in fabulous quantities. The *Philomela* was no treasure ship. She was a smuggler's ship. The captain didn't mind the lack of treasure. He loved history, so he was more interested in things like rotted barrels and spoiled books. Money had never held any meaning for him beyond the value of the books it would buy.

The sea bottom had not yet come into focus when he felt peace suffuse him to his fingertips. It felt like magic.

It made no sense to him for the chilly water to suddenly grow comfortable and welcoming, but it did. And he felt buoyant, as if a deep breath would float him all the way to the surface, which was a long way away by now.

He had been afraid without realizing it, afraid of the dark and afraid of the deep, but he realized that he simply wasn't now. The captain looked around for his companion and saw nothing but soft gray. Even his aloneness failed to frighten him.

One part of his mind refused to be distracted from self-preservation, and it rang an alarm. That part of his mind knew that he wasn't supposed to feel no fear, not down here where it would be so easy to die. And he wasn't supposed to be alone. His companion had agreed to help him, because fellow research-ers helped each other. He would need help to get down to the *Philomela*, since he'd never even put on a scuba tank before, and his friend had promised.

His eyes drooped. His body screamed for sleep, and this is what finally told him that something was wrong. Despite the fact that his pressure gauge said that he had plenty of air to breathe, his body was starving for oxygen.

Lifting his face to search for the sun, he wondered how far he would have to rise to find air.

How deep was he? Twenty feet? No, more than that. The surface was much too far away.

Even with fins, he didn't have the power in his legs to kick himself to the surface before this pervasive fatigue trapped him underwater. He knew he couldn't do it while wearing such a heavy weight belt. He still had the presence of mind to fum-ble with the belt, but it was long past the time when removing it would have helped him. The buckle opened, allowing the webbed belt to slide between the steel teeth that held it closed, but it didn't slide enough to free him from the belt. That was when he panicked and that was when he was lost. That was when he knew he would never see the *Philomela*. He would never see anything, not ever again.

No longer sure which way was up in the dim, deep murk,

he kicked hard. He rose out of the murk and into the soft blue water, but he was fatally disoriented. His fins propelled him more sideways than up.

The end was quick.

Within the hour, the weight belt would slide off his body as the rocking of the Gulf's deep currents and eddies worked the last inch of webbing free of the teeth that held it. In such warm water, buoyant decomposition gases would form rapidly in his body. The lift provided by those gases and his buoyancy compensator would do their work. The captain would rise. The currents and the wind and the tide would bring him back to land, one more time, but he would no longer care.

Captain Edward Eubank had almost no time left, but he spent it dreaming of shipwrecks and blockade runners and beautiful things lost to time.

Chapter Eight

Faye's sore muscles woke her early. She'd slept hard, like a woman who had been moving trees for days. Now that she was awake, her muscles were complaining about all that work, and her kids were complaining about having to get up so early during the summertime. Nevertheless, she needed to get to shore and punish her muscles some more, because people needed her. And also, the sooner the cleanup work got done, the sooner she could get out to The Cold Spot and see what was there.

Michael was glaring at his scrambled eggs. He'd wanted the sugary breakfast cereal that he ate at Emma's house, and he'd been willing to make his mother suffer in order to get it. He'd lost the battle, but this didn't mean that he would necessarily agree to eating the eggs. He actually liked eggs, but he hated losing arguments with his mother.

Amande's surly expression was inextricable from her status as a nineteen-year-old still living at home with her parents, and Faye was mightily tired of it. Her daughter had tried to flounce out the door without eating breakfast, but Joe had blocked the door bodily, holding out a plate of bacon and eggs. She was sitting at the kitchen table with the rest of the family, but she wasn't speaking to them.

For reasons Faye didn't comprehend, Joe was less bothered than she was by all the unpleasantness around them. He lived in a world where love truly did conquer all, so he was actually smiling at his scowling children as he gathered up their dirty dishes. Faye did not live in that world, and she blamed the people who made sugary breakfast cereals for most of the problems with this one.

Despite the squabbling, all four of them were in the boat on schedule. As Faye used her foot to shove the boat away from the dock, she looked longingly in the direction of The Cold Spot. Sooner or later, she'd get home before dark and wouldn't be utterly exhausted. The tide would be low enough to walk out into the water where she wanted to go. Or, at most, she'd be able to use a snorkel to get there, and thank heaven for that. Fathoms of water above her head freaked her out, so she had no plans to learn to scuba dive.

As the marina came into view, Faye watched Amande perk up. This made Faye surlier than her surly children, because she knew the reason her daughter was starting to glow. That reason was Manny.

Joe elbowed her and grinned as Amande started her about-to-see-Manny routine. As the boat slowed down to enter the marina's no-wake zone, she removed the orange scrunchy that had kept her long hair from whipping in the wind. Once released, honey-brown curls framed her golden-brown face, hanging down her back below her shoulder blades. Next, she pulled a tube of lip balm from her pocket and made her full lips shine.

Joe cut the motor and let the boat drift into their slip. The sudden silence made it easier for Amande to hear her dad as he made lame jokes at her expense.

"Hey, my lips are dry," Joe said. "Can I borrow some of that stuff? What do you call it? Lip gloss? It smells like mangoes."

She gave him her best withering glare. It said, *You embarrass me.*

Joe lived to embarrass Amande. "I wanna borrow some of that conditioner you use, too. Your hair always looks great and that stuff makes you smell like a watermelon."

Faye was biting her lip to keep from blurting out, "Does Manny like fruit salad or something?" There was only room for one comedian in the family, and Joe easily outshone her.

Amande was way too busy tying up the boat to take the bait. She'd been running around in boats since she was in elementary school, so the job was done quickly and well. Without making eye contact with her parents, she leaned down into the boat and grabbed her little brother. After she'd deftly removed his life jacket and tossed it in the direction of Joe's head, the two of them disappeared into the marina's grill. The sight of Michael's back with its stubby black ponytail and chunky, little brown legs normally made Faye smile, but she was too busy stewing over her rebellious daughter.

"We're going to have to do something about this," Faye muttered as they followed Amande and Michael.

"About what? Manny? She's known Manny longer than she's known us. He'd never do anything to hurt her."

While both those things might be true, they didn't change the fact that Joe was a starry-eyed dreamer. They also didn't change the fact that Manny had befriended Amande when she was an awkward and lonely little girl in Louisiana and he was a handsome twenty-something. Faye and Joe had adopted her when she was sixteen and moved her to Florida, so she hadn't seen Manny in three years. Time had turned her into a whole new person physically during those years, but she was still heartbreakingly young. Anyone could see that she was no longer awkward, but she was probably still lonely.

But now here Manny was, the brand-new owner of the only marina within a practical distance of their home. He was impossible to avoid. If they wanted access to civilization, then they had to go through Manny. He was back in Amande's day-to-day world, and Faye knew in her bones that it was no coincidence that Manny had chosen Micco County as the place to start his whole new life.

Manny met Faye's eye when she passed through the door, and she knew at a glance that the two of them understood each other. She didn't like him, but she would tolerate him for Amande's sake, and the feeling was mutual.

He manned his own grill at breakfast time. Savvy restauranteurs know that their customers are friendly over pancakes and that they bond to the person who flips them. Manny knew that cooking breakfast for his customers would keep them coming back for life.

"Been hitting the books, Missy?" he said, holding out a full cup with a hand that was darker than the espresso in it. She sat on a bar stool and took it from him as if he were handing her champagne.

Asking Amande about her studies was Manny's way of kissing up to Faye. He knew it. She knew it. Amande knew it. It wasn't working.

Faye had been secretly thrilled when Amande chose to take a gap year after high school. It would have hurt her too much to send their new daughter away so soon after she joined their family. They needed time to bond. But now Amande had put college off for another year, mollifying her mother by taking a few online courses, and Faye was not okay with it. She saw Manny as an obstacle standing between her brilliant, studious daughter and her future.

Amande was looking at Manny when she said, "I'm ahead of schedule in all three classes. Getting an A in every one of them, too," but she was really talking to Faye.

Faye was self-aware enough to admit that Manny was a handsome man with his rakish grin. His perfectly coiffed black hair set off hazel-brown eyes that were fascinating because they were never the same color twice. Manny carried himself like a man who spent a lot of time on the water, with the fluid grace of a dolphin. Or a shark. He was unquestionably a hard worker, and the marina's booming business showed it. And he adored her daughter. None of those sterling qualities outweighed the fact that he was well past thirty.

Faye had grave doubts about a man Manny's age who was interested in a woman who was only barely of legal age. Granted, Faye herself was nine years older than Joe, but they had gotten involved when he was thirty or thereabouts. She didn't consider the two situations to be remotely comparable.

Plus, Joe's age made the Manny-and-Amande situation creep Faye out even more. While Faye was old enough to be Amande's mother if she'd started having children in her early twenties, Joe was in high school when their daughter was born. Yeah, he was technically old enough to be her father, but just barely. It gave Faye the willies to see Amande flirting with a man Joe's age.

Manny plunked a plate of pecan pancakes in front of Faye's daughter, saying, "This is your favorite dish since you were a little kid. I keep real maple syrup around just for you."

Faye didn't think. She just blurted out, "Amande, you had breakfast half an hour ago."

She wasn't trying to hurt her daughter's feelings. She certainly wasn't trying to say, "Do you know how many calories are in those pancakes?" If she were honest with herself, she was saying, "I don't want you to spend another minute chitchatting with this sexy man who is all wrong for you."

But Faye knew that Amande didn't hear either of these things. She heard, "I'm your mother, and I think you're fat."

Amande was almost a foot taller than Faye, so she naturally weighed a lot more than her mother, and her build was far more muscular and curvaceous than scrawny Faye's. Faye knew that this bothered Amande, but she honestly thought her daughter was goddess-beautiful.

Despite the difference in size, and despite the contrast between Amande's long brown curls and Faye's straight and close-cropped black hair, Faye clung to a belief that her daughter looked like her, at least a little. They both had strong jawlines, up-tilted eyes, and mid-brown skin. If she were honest, she'd admit that they also both exuded the same try-and-stop-me approach to life.

Deep down, Faye harbored the adoptive mother's fear that Amande would someday turn to her and say that she'd never loved her, not like she would have loved her biological mother... her real mother. She held tight to any physical resemblance she could find.

None of these things changed the fact that she'd just said what amounted to "Are you really going to eat again?" to a teen-aged girl.

"Why would you say that?" Amande demanded. "Why would you ever say that? And why would you say it in front of somebody?"

There were tears in her eyes, and Faye had put them there.

"Sweetheart, I didn't mean—"

"You don't respect Manny. You don't respect my college just because it's teaching me online. For some reason I don't freakin' understand, you want to ship me off someplace far away to study, even though I practically just got here. I'd go, but then I'd miss Dad and Michael. And, yeah, I'd miss Manny, too. What's wrong with that?"

She shoved the plate away from her so hard that it crashed on the floor at Manny's feet. The pitcher of maple syrup went with it, sloshing stickiness over his stylish deck shoes.

"I think maybe I'll go someplace far away after all."

And then Amande had slid Michael off her lap and handed him to Joe, so she could run full-tilt out the door. Maybe she was running for the old-but-safe used car they'd bought her. Or maybe she was running for the battered oyster skiff she used for exploring or fishing or escaping her annoying parents. Faye didn't care which avenue of escape was calling Amande. Either option meant that her daughter was running away from her.

The problem with having a daughter who is nearly six feet tall is that she can outrun you with those long legs. Long, tall Joe's legs stretched farther than Faye's, of course, and so did Manny's, but Manny was trapped behind the bar, and Joe was holding Michael. And also, surefooted Joe was so rattled that he tripped over his own bar stool. They were all still gathering their wits when the door slammed behind Amande and took her out of their sight.

Faye's legs were short but speedy, and she was determined, so she beat the men through the door by a split-second. Amande was nowhere to be seen.

Faye knew that Joe spent sleepless nights worrying over Amande wrapping her car around a tree, so it was only natural that he would head right to the parking lot at a time like this.

Manny had watched her tooling around in boats since she was a preteen, so he knew how far from civilization she was capable of going in that skiff. He headed left toward the dock.

Faye was between Manny and the dock. She had once been

a teenaged girl with a boat, so she too knew how far away the water could take Amande. What was more, she had an island-dwelling parent's nightmares about drowning. And also, she would be damned if Manny was the one who found her daughter. She turned left, too, trying and succeeding in keeping her head start.

Faye still couldn't see Amande, but she could hear her daughter's feet striking the dock. She and Manny had clearly chosen the right place to look. A long line of boats in their slips obscured Faye's sight line, but they wouldn't for long. She ran hard.

In a moment, Amande would be in view. There was no question about it, because the dock was only so long. At its end, there was no place to hide.

Before Amande came into sight, she gave herself away. Faye knew where her daughter was because she could hear her scream.

Chapter Nine

Where was she? Where was Amande?

The sound of her daughter's scream hit Faye hard. She was shaky, weak, nauseated. Knowing that these things were caused by adrenaline did not help at all, because she needed to find her daughter with all of her being. She flung herself in the direction of Amande's heart-stopping scream.

Faye stubbed her toe on a loose board and almost went down, but determination kept her on her feet. Behind her, Manny dragged the rubber sole of one of his deck shoes on the same board. She heard him go down, but he was cool, smooth Manny, so he probably did it gracefully.

The scream morphed to a long continuous wail that tore Faye's heart out. It only stopped when Amande took a breath. The next sound out of her mouth was a single word.

"Mom."

There was another ragged breath before the next wail. *"Mom!"*

When Faye reached Amande, she found her standing in the spot where Manny let her keep her boat for free, but she wasn't looking at the battered skiff. She was staring down into the water near where it floated, rising and falling with the moving water. Something long and narrow floated on the same waves. It was covered in black and maroon rubber, with an air tank painted a dull, matte maroon strapped onto it.

At one end of the long narrow thing was a pair of flippers the same dark red color as the air tank. At the other end was a head covered with wet, stringy gray hair. Two long, thin arms dangled in the water, and so did two legs with stringy musculature that was beginning to atrophy from age.

The man hung in the water, motionless, and Faye knew two things instantly. This was her friend Captain Edward Eubank, and he was dead.

Faye knew to her core that, somehow, he had been killed by his own curiosity.

———

The marina wasn't fancy. Manny had worked hard to spruce it up, but it would never be without damp and mold. This was the way of watery places.

Regardless of the mold, the marina served its purpose. It provided a way station for people moving from land to sea and back, and it was a place for them to drink, eat, and enjoy each other. It was a place of community. Faye had spent happy hours at the marina, but she thought it was a shabby place to die.

Manny's Marina sprawled along the shore of a creek, near the place where it emptied into the Gulf. Long docks lined with boat slips extended into the water, and a wide ramp served people who trailered their boats. Several buildings sprawled across the marina's grounds. They held the things boaters needed—a bar and grill, a convenience store, a dive shop, storage sheds, and a barn for dry boat storage.

Manny lived in an efficiency apartment above the bar and grill. Faye was grateful to him for opening it to her family. The sheriff wanted to talk to them, but how awful it would have been to wait for him with Manny's other breakfast guests, knowing that the captain's body was being retrieved not far away.

Amande sat slumped on Manny's couch beside Faye, her head on her mother's shoulder. They were both weeping. The feel of her daughter's shuddering chest against Faye's was both comforting and heartbreaking.

Joe sat in an easy chair beside them, also weeping. At first, he'd done this while bouncing a confused Michael on his lap, but Manny had silently taken the little boy, leaving Joe, Amande, and Faye to grieve without upsetting a preschooler.

"The captain was such a nice man," Amande said between sobs. "I was just at his house last week, working on a project for my history class."

"Nothing made him happier than seeing somebody make good use of his library," Faye murmured. "And for him to see a young person like you poring over his maps and books? He must have been in heaven."

Faye almost said, "I guess he's in the actual heaven now," but now she was crying too hard to talk, and this was bad. Talking kept the truth at bay. Silence gave her space to think the horrible thought that she'd been pushing back ever since she looked into the water and saw Captain Eubank's lifeless body.

He had probably died within sight of Joyeuse Island, her home, and she hadn't been there to help him.

Where else would he be? His romantic obsession with history was essential to everything that he was, and he believed he'd found his own holy grail, the historic wreck of a very old ship.

Why else would he be suited up in scuba gear? He had probably gone out to Joyeuse Island as soon as Faye left his house. He would have known that her family was all ashore doing hurricane cleanup, leaving him free to explore alone.

No one would have seen him drop an anchor at The Cold Spot and hoist himself overboard. Nobody would have known that he was swimming beneath the water's surface, looking for an old, old shipwreck.

She should have offered to help him look for it. All she'd had to do was say, "I can't go today, but let's make a date to go exploring next week. Okay?"

If she'd done that one simple, kind thing, Captain Eubank would still be alive.

———

Dr. Longchamp-Mantooth kept saying, "This is my fault. It's all my fault."

Sheriff Ken Rainey knew it wasn't, of course. He couldn't say how many times he'd sat with a bereaved family and heard one person after another repeat, "It's my fault," like a prayer of absolution. It was only human nature for a person to claim responsibility for a loved one's death. The only other comfortable option was to blame the dead person or to blame someone else or to blame God. It was too terrifying to admit that nobody had much control over anything. Certainly not death.

This family had a logical, controlled approach to life, particularly the mother. It oozed from all her pores. She didn't tolerate uncertainty well.

"I should've known that he'd go looking for that shipwreck." She stopped herself. "Not that I think it's a shipwreck, Sheriff. I already told you that I think it's a submarine spring, and I told him so. It's just that I should've gone with him and made sure he was safe while he checked it out."

The sheriff sat up straighter in his chair. "'Spring' is just another way to say 'underwater cave.' Lots of divers swim into caves and never swim out alive. Maybe he swam into the spring vent and got lost."

He could tell that Faye didn't like that idea.

"If a cave that size were right up next to my island, it would have been obvious before the storm. Even a hurricane wouldn't be enough to clean out something that big," she said.

"Then why do you think there's a spring near your island, if you've never seen anything obvious like a vent?"

"The water's always cold there, probably because groundwater was seeping out of a little crack that was clogged up with something like a wad of sand. I'm thinking the hurricane cleaned that crack right out, but I really doubt that it uncovered a cave big enough to get lost in. You're describing something more like Wakulla Springs. The water doesn't seep out of a cave like that. It comes roaring out like a firehose."

Sheriff Rainey thought "firehose" was a bit of an exaggeration, but agreed Faye had made a reasonable point. "If you're right that the spring vent is just a narrow little crack," he said, "maybe he got a foot caught in it and couldn't get it out."

The sheriff noticed that she didn't really respond to that idea. She just said, "I never thought he'd go out there, certainly not by himself."

"People who have lived alone all their lives are pretty independent, as a rule," the sheriff said. "I can absolutely see the captain diving by himself. It's not smart, but nobody's smart all the time. And who's to say that he was anywhere near your island when he died? There could certainly be other, bigger springs and caves under the Gulf."

This woman wanted to think Captain Eubank had died off the coast of Joyeuse Island because it made her feel better to blame herself, but that didn't mean that it was so.

She also wanted to think that he'd had some kind of accident.

It was just as likely, though, that he'd suffered a heart attack or his equipment had failed or he'd made a fatal error far underwater, in a world that tolerated no error. There would be an autopsy and the captain's equipment would be checked out, but it was overwhelmingly likely that the cause of Captain Eubank's death was something very simple and very sad.

———

Faye couldn't stop looking out Manny's window. From her second-story vantage point, she could see all the way to the waterfronts, both creek and Gulf. She would have been able to see the captain's motionless form, if someone from the sheriff's department hadn't set up barricades that blocked her view. For this she was profoundly grateful. The image of his body floating facedown would always be with her. She did not need to add more images to her nightmares.

Even the simple retrieval of the body was unthinkable. Was he still floating in the water, or was he already shrouded in a body bag and waiting for transport? How many people would it take to lift him out of the water and onto the dock? Would they do it with a sling and a winch, or with their bare hands? Would they lift him onto a gurney and roll him to a waiting hearse? A sheriff's department van? And then what would happen when the medical examiner took charge of his body?

She did not want to know.

Faye had seen someone official-looking pass below her window carrying a camera and a notepad. Later, she had passed again, heading back toward her vehicle, and then returned with a video camera. While Faye was focused on her, she'd lost track of what the sheriff was saying. His voice had shifted into a warm and calming, but unintelligible, audio blur.

As he spoke, she thought of a question and blurted it out, knowing that she was interrupting him. It bothered her that she was so upset that she couldn't even force herself to be polite.

"It looks to me like you're treating this like a crime scene. Do you think somebody—"

She couldn't say "murder," especially not in front of Amande, so she tried again. "Do you think somebody did this to him?"

"I don't. There's no evidence of foul play. None whatsoever. But drowning investigations are tricky, so I've assigned Lieutenant Baker of our Criminal Investigations Division to make sure we tie up all the loose ends. And please know that when I say 'Criminal Investigations Division,' I'm speaking of Lieutenant Baker and one evidence technician. That's as close as Micco County gets to the kind of CSI work you see on TV."

Faye nodded. She knew this. Her friend Mike McKenzie had done the sheriff's job for years, and she knew exactly how much funding he didn't have.

The sheriff was still talking. "We owe it to the captain to be sure we learn as much as we can about what happened to him. It's very easy to jump straight to 'Accidental Death' when you're dealing with a drowning, especially when someone drowns alone. There's a school of thought that says we miss some murders when we do that. Lieutenant Baker's expertise in forensic investigations can keep us from making that mistake."

Faye didn't want the sheriff to make that mistake, either.

"Now, you can't do much of an investigation when you don't have a crime scene," the sheriff pointed out. "We've got nothing but a body, really. Nevertheless, Lieutenant Baker will tell us if she finds anything unexpected. If she does, I promise that we'll stretch our budget to give the captain what he deserves."

Joe said, "We've lived here a long time. We understand about 'small' and we totally understand about 'no money.'"

Sheriff Rainey almost laughed, but his stone-faced act held. "Then you know what our budget is like. It's even tighter at the moment, since the hurricane. Everybody's working overtime, night and day. We've still got people missing. I can't spare anybody else to work this case. Actually, I can't really spare Baker, but we're going to try to do it all. We always do try. I wouldn't ordinarily be here now myself, but the captain was my friend."

He turned his head to clear his throat, and Faye thought he might also be wiping his eyes.

"Lieutenant Baker's going to do a walk-through of his house. We'll talk to some people—like you folks—to see if we hear anything suspicious. Will we find any evidence of a crime? Probably not, because I do honestly think that this was an accident, but we're going to tie up the loose ends. The captain deserves that much."

Chapter Ten

Sheriff Rainey excused himself when Lieutenant Baker stuck her head in the room and said, "Can I speak with you, sir?"

Faye stayed put, perched on Manny's sofa and peering out the window of his apartment. From this vantage point, she could see the captain's car. It was far away, under a tree on the far side of the parking lot, but the sedan's weathered red paint was unmistakable.

She rose and crossed the room to another window where she could get a better view of the marina's creekfront facilities— slips, docks, and ramp. The captain's boat slip was empty.

It was possible that she'd been the last person to speak to him. He might well have hopped in his car right after she left, driven to the marina, gotten in his boat, and made the questionable decision to dive alone, all without meaningful contact with another person.

She slipped her phone out of her pocket and dialed Manny. Part of her wanted to apologize for the scene at the bar that had sent Amande running and the other part of her wanted information.

She opened with, "I'm sorry about what happened. I'll pay for the plate and the syrup pitcher."

She thought he was about to laugh, and she thought maybe he was hysterical. He, too, had just discovered his dead friend's body. Then she heard his voice crack and he fell silent.

Faye didn't know what to say, so she just started talking. She wanted information, and talking to Manny was the price of that information. "Is it weird that the captain's car is here and his boat isn't?"

She could hear the steel-on-steel sound of Manny's whisk whipping up somebody's eggs or pancakes.

"It wasn't weird that he drove here and parked his car." His voice was still trying to crack, but it held. "And it wasn't weird that he took his boat out. He does those things every afternoon. The weird thing is that he didn't stop to talk to me on his way through. And, of course, the other weird thing is that he didn't come back. His car was out there when I got up this morning, parked all by itself."

She wasn't convinced that these things were all that weird. "There's a lot of little islands out there, places where you can just drag your boat up on the beach and throw up a tent. Maybe the captain did that last night."

Manny's whisk kept whisking. "If he did, it was the first time. The captain was a man of habit. You know that. He liked to sleep at home."

She did know that. "Are you saying that he was dead by bedtime?"

The whisk went silent. After a moment, Manny said, "Yeah. His body would have needed time to get here. Unless he died practically within sight of the marina, it would have taken hours for him to float here on the currents and the tide."

This tracked with Faye's understanding of the timeline. She knew that the captain had planned to see his sister bright and early that morning. Faye had been sitting in his library early the previous afternoon. If he were going to take a foolish solo dive, the only reasonable time to do it was shortly after she left.

Faye looked at the eaves of the buildings around her, checking for cameras. "Do you have surveillance video?"

"Are you kidding? It's all I can do to make payroll these days. I'm saving up for cameras, but I ain't got any now." He paused, and Faye heard the refrigerator open and close. "If I only had those cameras, we could get one last look at him. I'd give anything to be able to say goodbye."

———

Once the door was shut behind him, the sheriff stood on the landing atop the outdoor stairs leading to Manny's apartment and jumped straight to the point. "Did you find any witnesses, Lieutenant Baker?"

"Nobody admitted seeing the victim recently. Not today. Not yesterday, except for Dr. Longchamp-Mantooth. I'd say he drove here, got in his boat, and made the fatal mistake of diving without a buddy. End of story."

She looked down at her close-clipped fingernails, and the sheriff noticed her unconscious need to break eye contact. She didn't leave it broken for long.

Meeting his eyes again, she said, "Can I tell you what I really think?"

"Sure thing, but thanks for asking. It makes me feel important."

"You know, and I know, that this is a waste of time. The man made a mistake or had a heart attack. Maybe it would make sense to spend my time and the county's money on a full-out investigation of his death if we were having a slow month. But we're not. Every minute that I'm chasing this wild goose is a minute when a missing woman and child lie dead in the swamp. There is no chance that they're still alive more than a week after the hurricane washed them out of their own house, but it eats at me to think of them out there alone. It's like nobody cares."

He tried to interrupt the flow of words, murmuring, "I hear you, Baker," but she wasn't finished.

"How can I face that child's grandmother if I walk away from her case to launch an investigation that simply has no point, just because this dead man was apparently lovable enough to have a million friends? Where are that child's friends?"

And now the sheriff really appreciated Baker's razor-edged mind. She could tiptoe right up to saying he was wasting money on the captain's death because the man had been his friend, without passing into the unforgivable subordination of suggesting that he was making poor decisions out of grief.

Well done, Baker, but I'm still in charge.

"It's my job to stretch my little budget far enough to do the impossible," he said in what he hoped was a calm tone of voice. "And that includes finding out what happened to the captain. You've been talking to witnesses for a while now. Is it true that nobody saw him get in the boat? A talented interviewer such as yourself must have found out something."

She shook her head. Her hair didn't move because it was cropped into a blond buzz cut. "Nothing helpful. Most of them just said, 'I didn't see anything,' and waited for me to tell them they could go. The marina owner was the only one who was willing to get involved."

"Manny? I know Manny. More days than not, he cooks my breakfast. What did he have to say?"

She checked her notes. Her long, rawboned fingers clasped her tablet computer with a surprising gentleness. "Manny's best guess is that the captain took his boat out yesterday afternoon, while the marina was really busy, and then he didn't come back. He thinks he would have noticed a boat motor starting at a weird time, like late last night or early this morning. He's sure the captain left yesterday afternoon without talking to him, and that's weird."

She looked Sheriff Rainey straight in the eye. "Or so Manny says."

Chapter Eleven

Lieutenant Baker had gone back to her work, but the sheriff still stood on the landing outside Manny's apartment, gathering his thoughts before speaking to the grieving Longchamp-Mantooth family. A popular misconception about officers of the law is that they are stoic and without feeling. The sheriff knew that anyone who believed this believed a lie.

The sheriff had lived in Micco County all his life. One of the great benefits of a job like his was that he was personally acquainted with a decent fraction of the people he served. This meant, of course, that when he dealt with death on the job, it was a reasonable bet that he knew the dead person. The sheriff had known Captain Eubank to be argumentative, opinionated, and completely likable. He would miss him.

It seemed like a cruel twist of fate for a man to up and drown after spending every afternoon on the water for literally decades. How could such a thing happen?

Sheriff Rainey sometimes thought that this marina was cursed. A woman named Wilma had owned it before Manny, but she'd let the place go. When you let a waterfront property go, it goes to rust and rot. And then the customers find someplace that isn't rusty and rotten to do business. Exit Wilma.

But Wilma's failure wasn't the worst thing to happen here. The two previous owners, Liz and Wally, had both died violently. He'd be inclined to say that this third death proved that the marina was cursed, if the captain had died at the marina, too.

Where did he die? Who knew? But just for the sake of jurisdiction, he was going to say that the captain died within Florida's seaward boundaries. Nine nautical miles was a long way, so he was on pretty solid ground claiming the case as his own.

Sheriff Rainey's best guess was that the captain had indeed died within those boundaries. He'd probably floated in from someplace well offshore, toward the barrier islands or beyond, or else somebody would have found his boat. It made no sense to think that he'd died right here at the marina, like Liz and Wally. It seemed to him that Faye, Joe, and Amande might want to know this.

Now that he had something constructive to say to the people on the other side of the door, he was able overcome inertia and push himself through it.

He was talking before he sat. "I don't want you people to think that this is like what happened to Liz or to Wally. They got murdered. I honestly don't think that's what happened to the captain."

Faye, Joe, and Amande looked at him as if they were hoping that he would say something, anything, to make the situation less horrible.

He wasn't sure he could do that, but he was going to try. "There's some important differences to remember."

He held up a hand and started counting those differences on his fingers. "First of all, Liz and Wally died right here, and I've got some reasons to think that Captain Eubank didn't. And,

second," he said as he held up a second finger, "they had enemies. Liz was an innocent victim, but Wally earned his enemies
the old-fashioned way. Can any of you think of any reason at all
for somebody to want the captain dead?"

They all shook their heads.

"He had enough money to get by, but I don't think he had
the kind of money that people get killed over." This brought him
up to his third finger, but he knew his point here was weak. He
moved on to his next point quickly, before the exceedingly logical Dr. Longchamp-Mantooth could arch a skeptical brow and
remind him that people sometimes got killed for their pocket
change.

"Fourth, suicide is a possibility that we can't ignore. I can't
imagine him doing that, although we will certainly interview
people who knew him better than I did. I'll start with you folks.
Have you ever known him to be suicidal or depressed?"

Amande's curls bounced and her parents' straight hair swung
as all three shook their heads.

Moving on to his fifth finger, which most people would call
a thumb, he drove home his point, which was *This was a terrible
accident, and you nice people shouldn't feel guilty.* "Fifth, I don't
think this happened because he was doing something illegal and
got tangled up with the wrong people, like Wally did. The captain just didn't care that much about money and material things,
not as long as he had enough to buy books and bait. What else
would he have committed a crime for? Can any of you imagine
him stealing anything or…I dunno…selling drugs?"

Everybody laughed at the idea, and that lightened the
moment.

"You don't think he maybe got crosswise with somebody
who *was* running drugs?" Joe asked. "Maybe he saw them doing
something illegal and they were afraid he'd turn them in."

"Could be, but to tell you the truth, the worst crime we've got happening lately is onshore. Every two-bit criminal around is thinking, 'Hey! Nobody's minding the store and it's half blown down.'"

When they all laughed again, he followed up with, "Please know that I'm spending my whole year's overtime budget on keeping my people out and about. Keeping 'em *visible*. The criminals will be crawling back under their rocks any minute now."

Faye said, "That's good," in a weak voice.

"Look. It's not out of the question that he got crosswise with some of the same two-bit crooks that are making my life miserable, but I'll say this much. If somebody killed him, they sure were careful not to leave a mark on him."

The sheriff could feel their eyes on his face, so he went ahead and laid out exactly what he thought had happened. "Based on the condition of the captain's body, I think he probably washed in from somewhere farther out. The marina was just unlucky enough to be the place where it happened. For one thing, there were no drag marks on his hands and feet, like there would have been if he'd spent much time floating in shallow water. That's what makes me think that this young lady found him almost as soon as he got here."

It was hard to watch their faces as they thought about the things that happened to a human body floating in shallow water with a rough sand bottom, filled with sea creatures looking for a place to feed.

"I promise you people that we'll investigate as closely as we would any unexplained death—we're doing that now, actually— but I truly believe that this was just a tragic accident and that it happened somewhere offshore."

"You do?" Amande said. "I keep picturing him drowning…

dying...right here in a place where people love him. And none of us were here to save him."

The quaver in the teenaged girl's voice cut Sheriff Rainey's heart. He spoke directly to Amande. "It makes no sense for him to be diving right here. All those boats coming in and out of the marina keep the water too stirred up for a diver to see anything. If the captain left on his boat alone, like he always did, then he was away from shore. There's no reason on this Earth to think that anybody was nearby who could have helped him."

He heard Faye try not to sob. Oh, hell. He'd reminded her of her belief that the drowning had happened at Joyeuse Island and that it was her fault. This was not what he had been trying to say. He kept talking, trying not to keep blundering into statements that would make these good people cry.

The girl nodded slowly, so she wasn't hysterical. She was capable of following a logical train of thought. Her mother wasn't out-and-out weeping. Her father was holding it together. These things were good.

"Like I said," he emphasized, "there was no sign of a struggle. No injuries at all. You saw it for yourself. His wetsuit stopped at his knees and he wasn't wearing gloves, so there was a lot of skin exposed. You would have seen it if he'd been banged up like he'd been attacked—by a person or by a shark or whatever. Even if he just got tangled up in something and ran out of air, you'd still expect to see scrapes or bruises on somebody who had fought for his life."

He could see Faye working to get hold of herself, so that she could put on the calm, logical face that she wore like some people wore makeup. It was important to her that she didn't fall apart in front of her daughter.

"But you said you're going to do an autopsy," Faye said.

"Certainly. If somebody did kill that man, then I will be

damned if they get away with it. And you should know that I've made sure that the person doing the autopsy has been trained to do them on people who died diving. That's a specialty. Here in Florida, we see more diving deaths than anybody wants to see, so we have people who know how to handle those cases right. Honestly, though, my guess is that the captain just made a mistake. Maybe he pushed his luck too hard or maybe his equipment failed. Once that happens, people tend to panic, and then things don't go well."

"Could it have been something like a stroke or a heart attack?" asked the daughter. "Something that could've kept him under the water until all his air was gone?"

He'd heard that Amande was raised by a grandmother who had died right before she came to live with Faye and Joe. He guessed that a kid who had lived her life with someone that old would be a lot more aware of cardiovascular disease than most teenagers.

"The autopsy should answer that question. Don't you worry, Amande."

And now he was treading on the line of dishonesty, a line that he made it a point to never cross. He knew something that these people didn't, which was that autopsies on drowning victims were tricky. Those who didn't spend their time looking at dead people's internal organs would be justified in thinking that confirming a drowning death would be a slam-dunk. There was in fact a classic lung presentation—"boggy, voluminous, and crepitant" were the insider's terms for it—but time and decomposition could complicate things.

Still, the captain hadn't been in the water too terribly long. Sheriff Rainey had every hope that he wasn't lying to this young woman.

"I can't believe he's gone." Joe had been silent most of the morning. It was as if he'd been saving up his grief for this moment. "Everybody liked the captain. Everybody. He was always smiling, always kind. It must have been an accident. Or, like you say, he got sick while he was in the water and couldn't save himself from drowning. There just isn't any reason for somebody to kill him."

"Baker and her technician will be going to his house soon. If he left a suicide note, we may know today. They'll look for signs of a break-in and things like that, even though the captain's house was long on books and short on the kinds of things thieves usually steal."

They all nodded half-heartedly, then Joe spoke up again.

"I guess I'm confused about why his body...well...why was it floating? He was wearing that heavy air tank, and I guess he was wearing a weight belt. When he drowned, it seems like his body woulda just sunk to the bottom and stayed there."

This was a question that the sheriff was prepared to answer. Training in how to investigate diving deaths came with the territory for the sheriff of a coastal Florida county. He skipped right over a major part of the answer, which was that bodies tended to sink at first, but that decomposition gases would eventually float them back to the surface. Amande did not need to hear this.

Instead, he focused on a factor that was less upsetting, the captain's diving equipment. "None of you scuba dive, right?"

They all shook their heads, and Faye said, "We snorkel all the time, but none of us has taken the time to get certified for scuba."

"Me neither," he said, "but I do have training in investigating scuba deaths. First of all, I can tell you that a lot of diving fatalities stem from incorrect weighting. Sometimes, a diver's carrying too much weight, which is something you'd expect to cause problems, but too little weight can be deadly, too."

"Will you be able to tell if he was carrying the right amount of weight?" Amande asked.

Bless her heart, she was trying to be as analytical as her mother, and she was doing a damn fine job.

"In this case, we can't even try to judge. He wasn't wearing his weight belt when you found him."

He saw the same look on all of their faces, and it said, *That can't be right.*

He hurried to reassure them. "He probably ditched his weights when he got in trouble. This didn't save him, but it was a logical move. And he was wearing a buoyancy compensator that he set when he was wearing the weight belt, so that would affect where his body hung in the water. Those things go a long way to explain why he was floating near the surface when you found him."

There was no way he was going to talk to these people about the buoyancy of a body's decomposition gases, so he stopped talking. He may already have given them too much information. The horror on their faces was obvious. He kept talking, trying to distract them.

"Nobody is sure how much diving experience he had. The overwhelming possibility is that he just made a rookie's mistake. Or something happened with his health and he wasn't physically able to save himself."

Not that the sheriff was as convinced as everybody else was that Captain Eubank was a diving rookie. More likely, over the course of a long lifetime spent in proximity to the Gulf, he'd done more diving than anybody thought, but that didn't mean he hadn't made a mistake. The captain was getting older. Maybe his reflexes and judgment weren't what they used to be.

"So what happens now?" Joe asked.

"I'll get a report soon from the walk-through of his house."

"And the autopsy. You may still get information from that."

"Yes, and we've contracted with somebody to check out his gear." They were still looking at him expectantly, so he kept talking longer than he probably should have. "Here's what I think. I think he got excited because he thought he'd found a treasure ship. He got in his boat, put on some diving gear that he hadn't used in years, jumped in the water, and got in some trouble that he couldn't get himself out of. It's the simplest explanation, and it fits all the facts that we know."

Faye sniffled, and the sheriff knew what she was thinking. She was pretty sure she knew where the captain had died, and she was pretty sure that she herself was responsible. She was going to torture herself this way unless he managed to clap a pair of cuffs on someone she could point to as the person who had killed her friend.

———

As the sheriff walked down Manny's stairs, his mind kept straying to the submarine spring Faye kept talking about, the one nobody had ever seen. Well, maybe Captain Eubank had found it, or one like it. The sheriff had heard fishermen talk about tremendous craters—caves, really—in the seabed where fresh water flooded out of the earth. They'd never shown him one, though, because fish were said to adore those craters. People who loved to fish didn't share their favorite spots with just anybody.

If the captain had found a cave out in the wide-open Gulf, anything could have happened to him. Divers loved to explore caves, and cave diving was an exceedingly dangerous hobby. More than that, Faye herself had said that archaeologists often found things like arrowheads and stone knives in spring vents. Mammoth and mastodon bones, even.

It was so easy to imagine Captain Eubank following one fascinating find after another, like Hansel and Gretel's breadcrumbs, until he was deep in a submerged cave with no idea of how to get out.

The more the sheriff thought about it, the more he favored that theory.

Chapter Twelve

Faye said, "Let's go talk to Manny," and Joe thought maybe he should check her pulse. Most of the time, Faye acted like Manny was her mortal enemy. Joe thought that this was dumb, but even a smart person like Faye was entitled to act dumb sometimes.

"Why?" Joe asked. "So we can get Michael back?"

"I need to ask him whether the captain was a diver."

They trooped downstairs from Manny's apartment and went into the bar and grill. He was standing in his usual spot, handing off his spatula to the day cook. Michael was perched on a bar stool in front of him, chowing down on bacon-studded pancakes with his face covered in maple syrup. Her son's brown-green eyes were half-shut and dreamy, as if he were rethinking his affection for sugary breakfast cereal because he'd found something way better.

"So, Manny," Joe heard his wife say, in the friendly tone of someone with a regular habit of making pleasant conversation with her daughter's friend-whom-she-did-not-like. "The captain came in here a lot, right?"

"Sure thing."

"Have you ever heard the captain say anything about going scuba diving?"

"Nope. I've only been in town a few months, but I know the local divers well. I sell them equipment. I fill their scuba tanks. Stuff like that." He paused, as if reconsidering. "Well, Cody fills their tanks sometimes. He runs the dive shop for me when I need to be doing something else, like flipping pancakes or keeping happy hour happy. The rest of the time I take care of the shop while he works for himself, running a boat repair business out of space I rent him in the barn. I'll ask him if the captain's done any business with him in the dive shop, but I doubt it. I arrange my schedule so I can be in the store during high-traffic times, and I never once saw Captain Eubank buy anything diving-related."

"You sell bait and groceries out of the same store, right?" Joe asked, because it was sometimes dangerous to let Faye do all the talking.

"Yep. Out of the same register. The only way this business can stay afloat is if the owner does as much of the work as humanly possible."

"That's how Liz and Wally did it," Joe said. "God rest their souls."

"Wilma? Not so much," Faye said. "And it showed."

"That's how I got this place so cheap. And it's why I'm close to working myself to death, cleaning up her mess. So, yeah, I know the divers. I sell 'em ham sandwiches to eat while they're out on the water. Sell 'em beers when they get back. While I'm doing all that, we shoot the breeze and I pretend like I'm as laid back as they are. Like I said, I know 'em and the captain wasn't one of 'em."

He paused and smiled. "I liked that man. Good Lord, he could talk. I think he saved it up all day, living by himself. Mostly, he talked about fishing. I sold him live bait, snacks, stuff like that. He loved his beef jerky and his root beer."

And now Joe could see that Manny knew what he was talking

about, because the captain really had liked a cold root beer almost as much as he had liked a cup of hot tea. With his own eyes, he'd seen the captain slurp down three root beers at a sitting. He'd always said that the sweetness was just right when you were eating something salty, like beef jerky.

He could see that Faye was remembering the captain and his root beers, too. The memories were making her eyes tear up again.

"I never saw any scuba gear on his boat," Manny continued, "and he never once mentioned diving. If he liked to dive, I think he would have said so. Like I said, the man could talk."

"Was he a good enough boat pilot to get out to Joyeuse Island?" Faye asked. "Or someplace farther out, maybe?"

"Oh, yeah. Many's the time I watched him handle that little boat of his, and he was real comfortable on the water. He didn't look all that comfortable in his diving gear, though."

This comment must have struck Faye wrong, because Joe heard a sharpness in her voice as she asked, "Why would you say that, if you never saw him in it while he was alive? Can a dead body look uncomfortable?"

Manny stammered a bit, but he finally managed to get his thoughts out. "It's hard to say why, but something about his body in that wetsuit looked wrong. I guess it just didn't look to me like gear a man his age would wear."

Faye was watching Manny's lips, like she hoped they'd miraculously reveal his motives. He always wore a too-cool-for-you expression, which meant that Joe's wife never quite believed Manny was telling the truth. Joe thought the too-cool attitude was an act, so he took what Manny said more seriously than Faye did.

"So that's why you think his dead body looked uncomfortable," she said. "Not because it didn't fit right?"

"Yeah, though you can't be sure of that, because a dead body ain't the same as a live one. But…hmm, how to say this? His wetsuit wasn't new but it wasn't real old. It was the latest style maybe five or seven years ago. Captain Eubank didn't strike me as a man who'd be wearing something with a fancy swoop of 2013 maroon across his chest and around the back. A plain black wetsuit would have been more his style."

Joe actually agreed with Manny on this. The captain had died dressed like someone who spent money on looking good underwater. It would have been more like the captain to wear gear that was really out-of-date, like maybe he'd bought it in the 1970s when Jacques Cousteau was still diving. And, yeah, Joe would have pictured him in something black and utterly plain.

Joe decided to insert himself into the conversation. It was one way to keep Faye on her toes. "So you're saying that he didn't buy the gear he was wearing from you? And you didn't fill his tank?"

Manny shook his head. "Nope. I was selling gear in Louisiana in 2013, when that gear was new. And nope. Like I said, he never got a tank filled here unless Cody did it."

"Is there any other place nearby where he might have gotten his tank filled or bought some gear?" Faye asked.

"Yeah, at Thad's place. Thad's Surf and Dive Shop. It's in Crawfordville. You know him?"

"I know of him," Faye said.

"Me, too," Joe said. "His store's right down the street from the captain's house. Maybe the captain did business there and that's why you didn't know he was a diver."

"Maybe so. Maybe he did buy every last thing from Thad," Manny said. "But I sell a lot of last-minute equipment to divers who get to their boats and find out they don't have everything they need. I imagine that most all of Thad's customers have bought diving gear from me at some time. Never the captain, though. Not once. It just seems weird to me."

"I guess it's possible that he never once forgot anything. He was extremely organized. Still, nobody's perfect," Faye said. "I have to make deliveries to shut-ins this afternoon, so I'll need to pick up food and water in Crawfordville. I could stop by that other dive shop. Do you think Thad would talk to me about the captain?"

"No, Mom," Amande said. "Making those deliveries is my job. You don't need to drive all the way into Crawfordville."

"You're way too upset to be driving today, sweetheart. I'll do it. I want to do it."

Amande turned away, obviously angry at her mother for trying to spare her a hard job on a hard day. Joe knew it wasn't fair of her to feel that way, but she did.

"I'll call Thad and tell him you're coming. We're competitors, but we're not cutthroat about it. I throw him some business sometimes, and he gives me a cut of his profit on the deal. He throws me a little business sometimes, and I give him a cut of what I make. It works out."

Joe presumed, but was not sure, that Manny's business relationship with Thad was legal. As long as he kept his distance from Joe's daughter, he did not care. Much.

———

Faye thought of the captain as she paid Manny's cashier for overpriced supplies she could have bought elsewhere. She'd rubbed her last drop of sunscreen onto Michael's face when they left the house that morning. There was no way she was putting her family on the water on a bright summer day without protection, so this poor planning was going to cost her big-time. Manny's sunscreen offered forgetful boaters their last chance to avoid third-degree sunburn, so he charged top dollar for a little tiny tube of it.

His convenience store was small, with a concrete floor and concrete block walls. Two walls were devoted to coolers full of unhealthy vacation food like sodas, beer, cold cuts, and ice cream. Four rows of metal shelving dominated the center of the room, two of them loaded with candy, bread, and chips and two of them loaded with convenience-sized toiletries like the sunscreen in Faye's hand. The dive shop consisted of racks of dive gear and a tank-filling station with pressurized cylinders of oxygen, nitrogen, and helium. This merchandise was technically in another room, but the two spaces were separated by an open archway so that one person could keep an eye on everything while they ran the entire operation.

It was hard to believe that the captain had been a secret scuba diver who never ever forgot anything critical. Surely he had spent money in this dive shop if he liked to scuba dive, but Manny said no.

Faye studied the tanned blond man silently taking her money. This must be Cody, Manny's tenant and part-time employee. She'd already tried and failed to make idle conversation with him.

Cody's eyes darted around the room, then returned to her face, disappointed.

She suppressed a smile. "No, Amande's not with me."

Oblivious Joe, standing behind her, gave a grunt of surprise. He kept forgetting that their daughter was constantly on the radar of men on the prowl.

Now Cody loosened up and smiled a little, giving her a glimpse of white teeth framed by his deeply tanned face. "I *thought* you were her mother. Nice to meet you." He pulled a dollar out of his pocket, put it in the cash drawer, and slid a couple of miniature chocolate bars across the counter to sit beside the tube of sunscreen. "She likes these. Tell her they're from Cody."

Michael said, "Ooh, Sissy's getting some candy!"

Cody retrieved one of the chocolate bars and held it out for the little boy. Michael said, "Mom?" and Faye said, "You're a good boy for asking. You can have it."

As Michael grabbed the candy bar and commenced peeling off the wrapper, Faye watched Cody revert to his all-business stone-faced act. She watched his hands as they bagged up her purchase and took her money. They were calloused, with nails clipped so closely that he was able to scrub away almost all of the engine oil that a mechanic's work left behind.

She was tempted to say "Hey! Sold anything to a dead man lately?" but she decided she'd let the sheriff have that special joy.

As if she'd conjured him up, the sheriff walked into the store. He didn't come right over to talk to them. Faye figured that he'd already said all he had to say to her family. She didn't have anything left to say to him, either, but Joe was too straightforward for uncomfortable silence.

He strode over to the sheriff, shook his hand, and said, "I've been thinking about something. Is it weird that the captain's boat is missing?"

"Not so much. The Gulf's a big place. It'll be a real trick to find it, if it's made its way to shore and grounded itself in one of those coastal wetlands, but we will."

"Would it help to have a drone?"

Faye couldn't believe that she hadn't already thought of using Ossie to help with the investigation. Nothing would make Joe happier than doing something concrete for the captain.

"It certainly would. We've got a couple of them, but we're

using them on that missing persons case. You can see why I wouldn't want to take them off that job. Can I tell Lieutenant Baker to get in touch with you when she's finished with the captain's house and car? She can meet you here, and you two can see what your drone might uncover."

Joe was so proud that his Ossie was practically a deputized officer of the law that his "Yes!" was immediate and enthusiastic.

Chapter Thirteen

"If you say so."

Faye winced when Amande tossed this snide comment over her shoulder as she walked with Joe and Michael toward the boat that would take them home. The unoriginality of those four words was evidence of her distress. If Amande's mind had been functioning on all cylinders, she would have done a more interesting job of rebelling.

Faye had been getting back talk ever since she decided to send Amande home and make the supply run herself. Any fool could see that the young woman was too upset to be behind the wheel. Faye wasn't in any shape to drive, either, but she was the mother and Amande was the daughter, so she had pulled rank. And she didn't take no for an answer.

Nor did she take whining for an answer. She'd helped Joe get both kids into the boat, and he'd taken them home. Joe would have to come back to the marina to help Lieutenant Baker look for the captain's boat, but the lieutenant was going to be busy for a while and he needed to go home and get Ossie. And Faye needed to get food and water to hungry, thirsty people.

She drove Joe's car to the pickup point in Crawfordville and loaded it up. After that, Thad's Surf and Dive Shop was beckoning, so she pulled into its parking lot and went in.

She had known the current Thad's late father, Thad Sr., but she only knew Thad Jr. by reputation. The first Thad had opened the dive shop in the late seventies and had been a fixture in the Crawfordville business community until his death thirty years later. His son was now in his late twenties, and the best thing that people could say about him was that he'd managed to keep the store open. Most of the time.

Young Thad was up front about his desire to sock away enough money to fund a life that was all surfing and no working. His pursuit of that goal had been singularly businesslike for a man who chafed at the very idea of having a job. The first thing he'd done after he inherited the business had been to sell his father's modest home and convert the dive shop's storage rooms into a small apartment. Now he had a cheap roof over his head and money for his early retirement fund. The second thing he'd done was to become a capitalist, investing the money in the stock market.

Thad's emotional life was now measured by the motion of the Dow Jones and the NASDAQ, which he checked compulsively whenever he looked at his phone. When Thad judged that his portfolio was big enough, he would shake the sand of Crawfordville off his sandals and head for Puerto Escondido or Tamarin Bay or wherever he thought his dollars would stretch far enough to set him up for a life of surfing and diving and nothing else.

Thad Jr. wasn't the type to join the Chamber of Commerce or the Rotary Club. He was the type to cut the store's hours to the bare minimum so that he could have more time to dive. He'd close the store on a whim to surf, whenever he heard the waves were right, although trying to surf on the coast off Wakulla and

Micco Counties was an act of optimism. The senior Thad had known that, but the junior Thad had added the word "Surf" to his store's name anyway, as if doing so would change geography and geology themselves.

Two young men with similar dreams stood in the shop, wearing *Surf Micco!* shirts and admiring a pale-green surfboard. Their heads turned when they heard Faye push open the door.

Thad gave her a small wave, as if to say, "Welcome to my store. Glad you're here," but he kept trying to sell the surfboard. Despite his slacker reputation, he seemed to be decent at sales.

"A lot of times," Thad said, "beginners make the mistake of buying a board that's too short, so you don't want to do that. But whatever you get, make sure you've got a car or truck that can transport it before you buy one that's too big. I made that mistake once. I had to sell it to my buddy, and he got the deal of his life. I totally lost my shirt."

Thad lifted the biggest board easily and his T-shirt tightened around his biceps. Faye had handled a few surfboards in her day, so she knew that this one wasn't heavy, maybe twelve or fifteen pounds. Still, handling a seven-foot-long hunk of polystyrene without raking his merchandise off every nearby shelf showed Thad's strength and dexterity.

He managed the board with a shake of his shaggy brunette hair that said, "This is no big deal for me, but it might be tricky for you newbies." He had Manny's gift of making people want to buy his stuff so that they could maybe be as cool as he was. Almost.

The customers looked like brothers. Both were stocky enough to need the sizable board that Thad was bandying about.

"We're long on big trucks, but we're short on money," one brother said as the two sidled toward the door. "If we could afford these, we could move them. But we're broke. Maybe some other time."

When they were gone, Thad turned his attention to Faye. His jawline was strong and his eyes were as brown as Faye's.

Faye introduced herself, and he recognized her name.

"Manny called to say that you were coming. Hey, I'm real sorry to hear about your friend. Manny told me that the man who died lived right near here."

"Over there," Faye said, pointing across the street and down a half-block.

"Him? He's the one that died? Oh, man. He seemed like such a good guy. Everybody around here knew that his house was the place to go when you were between jobs. Yard work, house painting, floor waxing, whatever. Sometimes he even hired people down on their luck to work in his library. Me? I'd rather work outside, even when it's hot. But when you're flat out of money, you go where the work is and not where you wanna be."

He looked around his store. "You see what I do? I sell stuff to people so's they can go out on the water and leave me here, working inside. It's a living, I guess, but I miss the sunshine."

Thad's Surf and Dive Shop was housed in a modest mid-century building, all stucco and glass inside and out. It had a practical terrazzo floor and an overachieving air conditioning unit that was making Faye forget that it was July. There was plenty of floor space for Thad's merchandise and for the tank-filling station. Thad was lucky to have inherited such a nice facility, and it must have come with a built-in clientele that his dad had built up over decades.

None of this meant that he enjoyed his work, and it was obvious that the current Thad did not. Not at all.

Thad affected the so-relaxed-as-to-be-lazy demeanor of surfers in Hollywood movies, despite the fact that he didn't look like them. His very dark hair seemed resistant to bleaching by the sun, and his light skin looked like he used sunblock consistently, at least on his face. His arms and upper chest were exposed by a short-sleeved V-neck T-shirt. They were deeply tanned, which proved that he had more time to go outside than he wanted to admit.

"I'm glad you know who Captain Eubank was," Faye said, "because I thought you might be able to answer some questions I have. You may have heard that he was killed in a diving accident. Except I've never once heard him mention scuba diving. Did he shop here?"

"Not while I was working. It's not like I keep a big staff. If I don't know him, he probably didn't come in here at all. I don't know that I ever even spoke to him, except for saying 'Hey,' when I passed him on the sidewalk. I just know that nobody deserves to die that way. When you spend as much time in the water as I do, you can't help thinking about what it would be like to drown."

Faye felt a chill in her gut when she imagined being far, far from the surface, knowing that the air in her lungs couldn't last until she got there. That feeling had gripped her from the moment she first saw the captain's body, and it hadn't left yet.

She waited silently, watching Thad. He looked uncomfortable with the silence, but no more than anybody else she knew. Most Americans didn't do real well with silence. Joe was the rare person who was willing to let it be.

"Seems funny," she said. "If a man's confident enough in his skills to dive by himself, don't you think he did it a lot? And wouldn't such a dedicated diver do business at the shop down the street?"

"Maybe he shopped with my dad and took his business elsewhere when he died, but I never saw him here. And I worked afternoon shifts from the time I was thirteen."

"He never in all those years even just struck up a conversation with you, as a neighbor, one diver to another? That's what most people do when they have a hobby they love. They go looking for people to talk to about it."

"You got that right. Some of my customers—they just talk and talk. Sometimes I don't think they'll ever leave."

And then he dropped the conversational ball and just stood there, silent.

Was he telling her to go? In a sense, she was wasting his time, but the store was empty. Was it really a burden to spend a few minutes shooting the breeze with someone who might turn into a customer? Maybe she should have mentioned her boats or asked if he had any snorkeling gear. Could a man with no customers in sight really afford to be rude to someone who might become one?

But these weren't the reasons he wanted her to leave. At least she didn't think so. More likely, this was a simple case of a man who didn't want to get involved. It was screamingly obvious that he hated everything that kept him out of the water, even this store that paid his bills.

Thad had told her what he knew about Captain Eubank, and he didn't owe her any more of his time. His body language said that he wasn't going to give it to her.

Faye instinctively took a single step away from this heavily muscled man who clearly wanted her gone. He responded with a single step of his own, crowding her in the direction of the door.

He really didn't want to talk about the captain.

"Thanks for talking to me about my friend," she said, taking another step back and watching him crowd her toward the door by taking a bigger step forward. "I've got a car full of supplies that I need to get to some hungry and thirsty people, so I'd best be on my way."

He did nothing to stop her from going, nor to give her a warm and fuzzy feeling that might make her want to return with money to spend. He didn't even say "Have a nice day." He just went back to organizing his stock.

As she walked to her car, she couldn't stop thinking about something she herself had said. Sometimes she didn't know what she thought until she heard herself say it out loud.

While she was saying to Thad that the captain must have been a confident diver because he was willing to dive by himself, the words had jangled her nerves a bit. Now that she had a moment to think about those words, it wasn't hard to figure out why they had jangled. She was presuming that the captain had been alone because nobody had reported an accident. But what if he hadn't been alone?

She considered that question, turning it over and over in her head as she sat in the parking lot of Thad's store, too dispirited to drive the car full of supplies to the people who were waiting for her. She could think of no innocent scenario that involved the captain having a companion when he went out on the Gulf. Yeah, maybe a friend in another boat had been there when he entered the water and then left before he surfaced, but that seemed far-fetched and, frankly, irresponsible.

There were really only two realistic options. Either the captain had been alone on his last dive, or he hadn't been alone and his companion had died with him. This scenario left his boat out there somewhere, and there might well be another corpse floating alongside it.

No. There was still another option. A second person might have gone out on the water with the captain and failed to call for help when he didn't reappear from his dive.

That would have been impossibly irresponsible. Unforgivable. Illegal. And deeply disturbing.

Chapter Fourteen

After ten minutes of sitting immobilized in the car, Faye was finally able to make herself drive out of the parking lot. During all that time, Thad had never walked out to ask what in the heck she was doing.

She'd spent those ten minutes watching cars pass by on a street that she'd driven too many times to count. The traffic was steady, which was weird because she'd never seen enough vehicles on this street at any one time to even merit the word "traffic." This was just another way that the hurricane had knocked down her world and built a new one that she didn't like.

The little town was full of strangers wandering around in cars—insurance adjusters, FEMA personnel, roofers, volunteers, tree removal companies, contractors. She knew that some were there to help, and some were there to make a buck, and some were there to cheat people whose lives were in ruins. Unfortunately, it was impossible to tell them apart.

She wanted everybody to go away. She wanted to be safe at home with her husband and children, confident that none of them would ever leave her. She wanted the trees to stand back up, and she wanted the beaches to clean themselves of dead and dying things. She wanted to go back to a time when she'd never seen her friend's body, wrapped in unfamiliar driving gear and floating dead in the water.

As she drove past Captain Eubank's house, she noticed a car in the driveway. Thinking that his invalid sister, Jeanine, had gotten somebody to drive her into town to begin the sad task of cleaning out the house, Faye pulled in behind the gray SUV. She got a lump in her throat just walking around the side yard to the captain's kitchen door, as she'd done so many times, but she didn't want to miss the chance to tell his sister how sorry she was. It had been a while since she'd seen Jeanine, but Faye would know her anywhere. Her gray hair and slim form looked like her brother in drag. Spending a few minutes with somebody who reminded her so much of her friend seemed like a comforting thing to do.

As it turned out, the woman wandering in the captain's back yard was emphatically not Jeanine Eubank. This woman was stick-thin and forty-ish. Her jaw-length, platinum blond hair was stick-straight and meticulously flipped under all the way round. Not a single hair escaped her perfect pageboy cut. Faye recognized this woman and her hair. Greta Haines had always made her uneasy in ways that she could not explain.

Faye didn't know Greta well, but she knew that the woman was an insurance adjuster. Faye had seen her recently when she stopped by Emma's house to talk about her homeowner's insurance claim. It had been an unpleasant encounter, because Faye had instinctively doubted every word out of the woman's mouth. Even the way she introduced herself and handed over a business card had felt slimy and underhanded.

There was no nice way to say it. If Greta was the person deciding how much Emma's insurance company was going to pay her to rebuild her life, Faye had serious doubts about how fair the decision would be. Was the captain's homeowner's insurance also with Greta's company? What about Jeanine? The captain had said her house was badly damaged, so she could be just as dependent as Emma was on a check from that company. More so, since Emma was a wealthy woman and Jeanine was not.

Faye was self-aware enough to know that she wasn't being completely fair to Greta. She had her own deep prejudices against insurance companies and their adjusters, based on sad life experience. Anyone who had lived through a natural disaster had hair-raising stories to tell about insurance companies wiggling out of claims that any reasonable person would agree that they owed.

She knew that it wasn't fair to judge Greta solely on what she did for a living. Insurance companies served a purpose or they wouldn't exist. Nevertheless, being fair didn't mean that she had to be okay with Greta wandering around a dead man's back yard without permission. She gave the woman a "What are you doing here?" look and waited to see what she had to say for herself.

"Dr. Longchamp-Mantooth," Greta said, extending a hand, "it's so good to see you again."

So she remembered Faye's name. This was probably because she had cut her visit to Emma's house short because she hadn't been able to make a move without Faye or Joe giving her a baleful look. Skimping on Emma's reimbursement was no way to treat an elderly widow, but Faye and Joe didn't know how to make sure nobody did it. They'd settled for following Greta around like hunting dogs on the trail of a squirrel. This, at least, was within their power.

Faye skipped echoing Greta's "So good to see you," and got straight to the point. "Who called you? Maybe you haven't heard, but the captain has passed away. Besides, I was here two days ago and the house was fine. The yard, too. Who's making a claim?"

"His sister, Jeanine, is a dear friend, but she lives more than hour away and she's too ill to come look at the house. I know she'll want to sell it, so I wanted to help out by making sure it was in good shape to sell. I'm not so sure you're right that there's no damage, though. Some of the siding around on the other side looks iffy to me."

Faye thought of how lovingly the captain had cared for this house. She hadn't even started trying to imagine somebody else living in it. They wouldn't understand that the heart of the captain's house was his library. How many years and dollars had he poured into those books and documents? His sister would probably just pay someone to empty it. They'd sell what was salable and send the rest of his collection to the dump. The thought made Faye queasy.

A deep voice boomed from around the corner of the house. "Do you think we should—"

Greta interrupted to say, "Come over here and meet Dr. Longchamp-Mantooth."

A lean figure in loose khaki work pants and a gray T-shirt strode around the corner, extending a hand. Short chestnut hair, heavily streaked with gray, framed a darkly tanned face and a pair of bright blue eyes.

"I'm Cyndee Stamp," she said, shaking Faye's hand. According to her T-shirt, she worked for Stamp Tree Service. Cindy confirmed this by saying, "My business is trees. Greta here thought I oughta check these out." She waved a hand at the pines and oaks surrounding the captain's house in the back and on the far side.

Faye eyeballed the trees. She didn't see any twigs or branches on the ground. The trees weren't leaning and they hadn't been toppled. "They're looking pretty good, right?"

"Well, actually," Cyndee began, but Greta interrupted her

again to say, "We're still checking things out." Then she stopped talking and stood there, just like Thad had, and waited for Faye to walk away.

Faye didn't have a lot to say to Greta, but she wasn't in the mood to give the woman what she wanted, either. Silently standing her ground on the captain's neatly mowed and perfectly edged back yard, Faye knew that the grass would be shaggy within days without him there to care for it. She watched Greta move away from her to tap on white-painted siding that seemed perfectly fine to Faye. There was no rot in that wood, but there would be. Rot would come soon, unless someone else took on the job of pressure washing and painting the siding. Wood doesn't last forever, no more than people do.

Cyndee hadn't gotten the memo that they were giving Faye the silent treatment, so she got right down to business. "Lotta people got trees and branches down in their yards since the hurricane. You got anything you need me and my crew to take care of? Or maybe some of your friends've got tree work that needs doing?"

Faye shook her head. "You can't really use the word 'yard' when you talk about my house. I live on an island, and we've let most of the property stay natural."

"That's what I do," Cyndee said. "I've got forty acres that I'm trying to put back the way God made it. I burn it—keeps the brush down, y'know—and I can't tell ya how many long-leaf pine seedlings I put in the ground over the last ten years. It'll take a lot more years than that to bring back a chunk of old Florida, but I can wait."

Faye immediately felt warmer toward Cyndee, which was dumb. Joe had once told her that she'd like an ax-murderer who hugged trees as hard as she did.

"We definitely have a lot of trees down on Joyeuse Island, but they're not hurting anything where they are. Joe will chop some of them up as we need firewood. We'll just let the rest of them lie. They make good wildlife habitat."

Cyndee looked her up and down for a second before saying, "Snakes is wildlife. You tryin' to make a good home for them?"

So Cyndee thought Faye looked too citified to put up with a few more snakes here and there? Well, she could think again.

"God gave us snakes to take care of mice," Faye said, giving Cyndee an appraising glance of her own.

"Well, now, so He did." Cyndee cracked a smile. "If the storm broke off any trees and left the trunks standing up, you can let 'em stay there. If they're in a place where it won't hurt nothing when they do come down, that is. Woodpeckers love snags like that. And if the tree's hollow, some owls might nest in there. They'll help you with them mice. Owls eat snakes, too, if they get outta hand."

Faye figured that she'd passed Cyndee's "Are you too prissy for snakes?" test. She went back to standing silent, waiting for Greta to make a move. Would she leave or would she stand her ground until Faye left?

Faye waited, fighting the urge to grin like the possums who would soon be moving into the hollow snags left by the hurricane. She was a patient woman, and her patience was rewarded when Greta finally said, "We've got some other houses to check on, Cyndee. I have lots of clients, and they have lots of trees on their roofs. Let's go."

Faye waved goodbye and watched Greta settle herself behind the wheel of her SUV, smoothing the hem of her tunic under her as she sat. Cyndee lifted herself into the passenger door and dropped into the seat in a single fluid motion. Faye could imagine Greta's slender foot in its elegant flat pump resting on the brake as the car door swung shut. It must be a heavy foot, since the engine revved loudly. Greta gave it enough gas to make it roar as she drove swiftly out of the driveway.

Greta and her revving engine were letting Faye know that she was perturbed by her interference. Faye did not care. She was glad to see the woman go. She didn't trust Greta around Jeanine's property without supervision.

After the insurance adjuster and her friend—or maybe "business associate" was a better description of what Cyndee was to Greta?—had disappeared around the corner, Faye drove away from Greta and from the other insurance adjusters clogging up Crawfordville's traffic. She fled a town filled with roaming roofers and tree removal contractors, hungry for work.

Mostly, she was running away from people hoping to make a buck off other people who had lost everything. The food and water in her back seat was completely inadequate to fill the needs of people whose lives had been blown away, but it was what she had to give. She pressed the accelerator a little bit harder and got the hell out of town.

She didn't notice the man leaning against a tree across the street from the captain's house with his phone to his ear. He was dressed in a bright red golf shirt and khakis, like the late middle-aged man that he was, but people who were aware of such things would have known that these were extraordinarily expensive middle-aged men's clothes. Just as Faye passed him, he held the phone out in front of him and snapped a series of photos of both Faye's and Greta's cars, taking care to capture their license plates.

Then he hurried across the street and did the very same thing that Greta had, the same thing that had enraged Faye. He trespassed on the property of a dead man.

Moving quickly, he slipped into the captain's back yard, giving the house and trees a good hard look. But instead of tapping on the siding, like Greta, or testing the strength of tree limbs, like Cyndee, he kept his distance. He spent a few minutes snapping photos of the house, the trees, and the yard, and then he was gone.

Within moments, yet another person stepped onto the captain's close-cropped grass. The young woman pushed her long auburn hair out of her eyes as she cast a longing look at the broad window that lit the captain's living room, moving instead to the side of the house where she could stand, partially hidden, outside a second, smaller window that opened into that same room. For a long moment, she did nothing but stand there looking at the books inside. Then, she shook herself a little and slipped her phone out of her back pocket.

Working quickly, she methodically snapped photos of every bookshelf that could be seen from her vantage point. In less than a minute, the phone was back in her jeans pocket, and she had faded into the shadows cast by the captain's azalea bushes. A few heartbeats later, she was back on the sidewalk, moving swiftly away.

Chapter Fifteen

Joe had hurried back to the marina to meet Lieutenant Baker, but their meeting time was hours in his rearview mirror, and she still hadn't showed. He'd gotten a text from her half an hour after she was due, saying that she should be there soon. And then he'd gotten another text and another, delaying their meeting again and again. He wished she'd just admitted that she didn't have time to fly Ossie with him, looking for the captain's boat. His family had been through hell that morning, and he'd rather be home with his kids than twiddling his thumbs while he waited for her.

He'd spent a little time with the kids on the beach when he got them home because Joe was convinced that there was no better cure for grief than the wind and waves. He'd have kept them out there longer, if he'd known the lieutenant would be this late. Instead, he'd hurried them indoors, bathed the sand off Michael, given Amande a goodbye hug, and taken Ossie back to the marina to wait for Lieutenant Baker. And wait. And wait.

He'd done his time-killing on social media. Everybody in Micco and Wakulla Counties now knew where he was, so it was no surprise to see Nate Peterson drop onto the bar stool next to him. Nate's dad, Ray, a local big shot who owned the newspaper and a whole lot more, sat down on Nate's other side.

"I saw your posts about being stuck at Manny's with nobody to talk to," Nate said. "Here I am, at your service. And Dad, too, of course."

Joe shook hands with both men and said, "Have the cherry pie. I'm about to order my third slice."

The Peterson men took his advice. Ray didn't have much to say, but Nate got busy quizzing Joe about where the fish were biting. This was Joe's favorite subject, except maybe Ossie. When he'd run out of fishing news, he started filling Nate's ears about his new favorite toy.

"There's a filter I want that'll make my pictures do a better job of showing how clear the water is in the shallows," he said.

"Buy it!" Nate said. "Get me some more pictures that meet my old man's standards for the front page."

Ray was looking at his phone while the two younger men talked, but Joe saw him cut his eyes in Nate's direction. He laid the phone down on the bar, took a bite of cherry pie, and said, "Maybe I should just hire Joe to take all my pictures."

Joe thought this statement sounded pretty innocuous, but Nate reacted like a man whose father had pushed his last button.

"I wrote the story for your all-important newspaper, Dad. You know the one. It went viral. As for who needs to be taking your pictures, I've done all your sports photography since I was in high school. You know what? I think I'll buy a drone myself, and I'll bring you front-page-quality shots within a week. Guaranteed."

Ray slid his eyes back to his phone, and Nate swiveled his stool toward Joe and away from his father.

Around them, the bar and grill was buzzing with gossip. Joe usually enjoyed eavesdropping on the conversations around him, but not so much on a day like today when people were antsy over whether they could afford the cheap burgers in front of them. The financial reality of the hurricane was starting to set in.

Some of these people had been eating out for more than a week because their kitchens were torn up, and those restaurant meals were eating holes in their budgets. Some of them were missing work to clean up their property, so their paychecks were going to be short. Some of them worked for businesses that were closed for cleanup, and enforced time off without pay was going to sting. Worst of all, some businesses were closed for good. Those paychecks were never coming back.

People were paying out of pocket for tarps to keep their homes dry, for propane to cook their food while they waited for electricity, for the cost of hauling away debris. They might get some relief from their insurance companies or the government, but it was laughable to think that they would ever be made whole. With every day that passed, Joe could feel the worry mounting for nearly everyone around him.

The two men at the table behind Joe looked particularly stressed. One of them, forty-ish and stocky with rabbit eyes, said, "You know, the insurance companies have only got thirty days to pay or deny. The clock's ticking, but I can't hardly afford the gas for my generator till then. Nine or ten gallons a day and that's not running it all the time, but I've gotta keep it on so my brother's oxygen machine can charge. And he can't get around unless I charge his wheelchair, too."

"Don't count on getting a cent," said his gray-haired companion. "My insurance company sent somebody out to look at my house. She had the guts to say that the repair costs won't even meet my deductible. If that's so, then I won't collect a dime. My family can't keep living in that house, not in the condition it's in, and I can't afford to fix it."

A woman from another table leaned over and asked, "You ever hear of anybody getting anything out of FEMA except the shaft?"

The laughter spread outward from those two tables until half the room was chuckling at something that really wasn't funny.

Ray spoke to his son, but he never stopped tapping on his phone. "I heard tell that there's been some break-ins west of here."

Nate didn't give him any eye contact, either, just whipped out his own phone to take notes. "Anybody see the robbers? Were they armed? Anybody hurt?"

"Not that I've heard. But people are wondering about those two folks that have been missing since the storm. Their house was destroyed. Her husband says he hasn't seen them since the roof came off. Their neighbor waded out into the floodwaters to try to save them, or so he says, but couldn't manage it. I say that the neighbor's story smells, because how did he know they were out there? He claims that he was standing at his window when they got washed away, but I don't buy it. Maybe the husband ran off and left his wife and kid to deal with the storm all by themselves."

"I'll get on it."

Joe liked seeing Nate in reporter mode. He had a reputation as a spoiled rich boy. To be honest, he'd earned that reputation and a lot of people didn't like him the way Joe did. Even Joe had to admit that Nate was a lot more appealing as a crusader for truth than as a man whose father paid his bills.

Joe saw the sheriff walk in and he wished Lieutenant Baker was walking in with him. He was long past being bored, but he also nurtured a dream that Ossie would rise up in the air and find the captain's boat right away. Finding that boat would be a first step toward setting the world right. It would be the first step toward justice for the captain.

Joe wanted to ask the sheriff if he knew where Baker was, but the man was focused on ordering his veggie omelet. Well, almost. He was obviously eavesdropping while he ate. Somebody hollered, "What does FEMA stand for?" and the sheriff raised his head, waiting for the joke's punchline.

When Ray bellowed back, "That's easy! It means Frowing Everybody's Money Away!", the sheriff laughed like the local that he was. Still laughing, he beckoned to Ray, who brushed piecrust crumbs off his expensive and tomato-red golf shirt before standing up. He grabbed his pie and coffee and went to sit with the sheriff.

Nate looked relieved to see his dad go, taking his dumb jokes and his boring dad-style clothes with him. He leaned over Joe's shoulder to get a look at his phone. "Got any more gorgeous pictures to show me? I'm counting on you to help me learn how to use the extremely expensive drone that I'm about to buy with Dad's credit card."

Joe answered with his mouth full. "Been a little busy. Ossie's getting antsy for me to get her back up in the sky, though. Like I tweeted, I'm getting ready to send her up. Just waiting on somebody who wants to be there when I do it. She's late."

"Well, *I* want to be there when you do it. Got a few minutes to show me how she works before your friend gets here? Maybe take a few pictures while we're at it, so we can put a piece in the paper that shows what a week's worth of cleanup looks like?"

"It don't look like much. I can tell you that," said the gray-haired man at the table behind Joe. "There's only so much that people can do with their chain saws and pickup trucks. We need heavy equipment like the government can send, but they ain't done it yet."

"Well, then," said Nate. "I'll show people. That's what newspapers are for."

"Ossie can help. Let's go put her in the air," Joe said. "But we'll need to be quick about it, before—"

Joe tried to be quiet about law enforcement matters, but he was way too honest to be comfortable with that. He finished his sentence with an awkward "—before my friend gets here." He swallowed the last part of what he wanted to say, which was, "Because I've gotta help the sheriff's lieutenant look for the captain's boat." He was very proud of himself for not spilling his guts about law enforcement secrets.

———

Joe watched Ossie rise in the air as Nate grinned and said, "Would you look at that?"

They'd chosen a grassy spot that Manny used for overflow parking, right at the water's edge. This location gave them a clear view over the Gulf, and a decently unobstructed view of the rest of the sky.

It was easy to tell that Nate was a reporter and the son of a reporter, because he'd asked a truckload of questions since they left the marina's restaurant.

Nate wanted to know how much Ossie had cost, which Joe didn't know since she'd been a gift. He couldn't shut up about buying one for the newspaper. "I've been telling the old man we needed one, but he's been too damn cheap."

Since Nate was a newspaper guy, he was really interested in how the drone's photos were stored and transferred. Joe was not so into computers, so he'd described his bare-bones method as best he could. "Ossie has a memory card, and I just bring her back to me when it gets full. I've got a card reader I use to transfer stuff from her card onto my computer at home. I take a lot more photos than videos, mostly because I like them better but also because they don't take up as much space on the card."

"Even so, that computer's hard drive is gonna fill up if you keep taking pictures. You could store them in the cloud, you know."

"The cloud makes me nervous. It's invisible and I like to be able to hold my files and pictures in my hand. I'm saving for an external drive."

"They're not that expensive. You should get one before you lose something you wish you hadn't," Nate said with the confidence of a man who had never wanted something that he didn't have enough money to buy right that minute.

Joe could tell that Nate particularly admired the way the controller used Joe's cell phone as a visual display. He let Nate watch over his shoulder while he put Ossie through her paces. Nate was champing at the bit to fly her, so Joe handed him the controller and showed him how it worked.

"The left joystick moves it away from the ground and back down, like this." Joe pushed the stick forward and Ossie went up. He pulled it back and she moved lower. "If you push the same joystick left or right, she'll spin in that direction."

Then he showed Nate how to turn the drone. "The right joystick moves her forward or back or spins her right and left. If you grew up playing video games, and I bet you did—"

Nate laughed out loud. "If video games handed out college credit, I'd have a PhD."

"I ain't much of a gamer," Joe admitted, "so it took me longer to get comfortable with the controls than it should've. But somebody like you? You'll be able to make her fly anywhere, and on your first try. No problem at all. She's got a ton of safety features, so you pretty much can't crash her."

He held the controller out, and Nate took it. For a few moments, Ossie moved around in the air close to where they stood, up and down and side to side, while Nate tried out the controls. Then he made her spin in place and she looked for all the world to Joe like a prop from an old science fiction movie that Faye had made him watch.

Joe half-expected Ossie to say, "I come in peace. Take me to your leader," and that made him think about how the best possible upgrade for Ossie would be making her talk. Or, even better, what if somebody figured out how to train her like a real falcon? If he could fly her with just a vocal command or whistle, like a living bird. Faye might never get him to come indoors again.

Nate couldn't take his eyes off the hovering drone, and he couldn't stop grinning. Joe was pretty sure that's what he himself looked like when he was flying Ossie. He was really glad his friend enjoyed putting the little drone through her paces.

"Hey, Nate. Want to take your own front-page picture? Send her straight up and you'll be able to get a real good shot right here where we stand. If you keep coming up with news photos that your old man likes, you know he'll buy you a drone. You won't have to piss him off by just slapping one on his credit card."

"I'd settle for hearing him say that I'm good at what I do."

Joe didn't ever want to be the kind of father who made his children wonder where they stood with him. "You're gonna take pictures that are so good that he'll send somebody else to cover all those high school basketball games. He'll have you doing all the important stories. I promise."

Joe had never heard such a bitter laugh from Nate.

"I'll need to take her really high to get the shot I need for the front page. And I need to send her out a ways, so I can point the camera back toward shore and get the longest possible stretch of shoreline. Like you did for that picture Dad printed on the front page. Can I do that? I mean *really* take her out for a spin?"

"You'll lose a lot of detail, but you bet. Take her up there. I'll help you get her positioned just right."

As Ossie rose high above their heads, Joe watched the controller's display over Nate's shoulder. He could see the tops of their heads, so he looked up toward the little drone and watched the display out of the corner of his eye to get a glimpse of his upturned face. Then Nate nudged both joysticks and she began to rise and move toward the marina.

Joe could see the familiar irregular contour of the coastline, broken by the broad creek. Beside it, the straight lines of the marina's docks and seawalls and boat slips were obvious. He could see the cut in the seawall where the marina's boat ramp sloped into the creek.

Nearby was the sprawling, tin-roofed building where Manny's bar and grill and his convenience store were housed. Beyond that building were the smaller outbuildings that Manny needed to run his business, clustered around the big barn that held a boat maintenance shop and rack after rack of stored boats.

Now Nate brought Ossie over their heads, leaving Manny's Marina behind and rising above a stretch of trees in front of them. The trees ran along the edge of a cypress swamp that marked the far side of the clearing where they stood. Far beyond that was Joyeuse Island, waiting quietly for Joe and his wife to return. And, on the gulf side of Joyeuse Island, there was a mysterious place that Faye had named The Cold Spot.

Joe knew that Ossie could see these things as she moved farther and farther away, but he couldn't see a lot because it was awkward trying to look over Nate's shoulder as he manipulated the controls. The drone was just barely visible in the eastern distance when Joe said, "You're supposed to keep her within your line of sight. It's a rule."

Nate answered, "Sure thing," and jiggled the right joystick, but he jiggled it the wrong way and Ossie moved a little farther away from them.

"Sorry!" he said. "Sorry, I'm not very good at this yet. I'll just bring her home."

He fiddled with the left joystick and managed to get the drone to turn toward them, but not quite enough. She swung inland, losing altitude fast.

"Here, let me handle it," Joe said, grasping the controller, but Nate didn't relinquish it.

"No, I can do it. I just need to practice a little more," he insisted, but the drone was still losing altitude and the safety features hadn't kicked in yet.

Joe had both hands on the controller and was opening his mouth to demand that Nate hand it over when a tremendous noise, loud as a nearby thunderclap, struck his ears. Since Joe's hearing were sensitive enough to hear the wind change at dawn, this sound was painfully loud. He let the controller go and clapped both hands over his ears.

Spinning in place, he searched for Ossie. When he found her, she was falling from the cloudless blue sky like a stricken bird. A second shot rang out, and Ossie exploded into a million pieces, right before Joe's eyes.

Chapter Sixteen

Ossie wasn't a bird. She wasn't even a butterfly or a dragonfly. She wasn't alive, and Joe absolutely knew that. Perhaps it was shock that made him act like he'd just seen a beloved living creature shot dead and falling to the ground.

Nate looked as startled as Joe was. He stood at the water's edge, shouting, "Joe, wait! Where are you going?"

Joe heard him, but he couldn't answer and he couldn't keep himself from running along the shoreline toward the unseen spot where Ossie had fallen.

Nate still hadn't moved. "Joe, what are you doing? Somebody's standing over there with a gun and they're mean enough to shoot a flying toy. You can't—Joe, are you nuts?"

Joe heard his friend's voice but not his words. Or perhaps his ears heard the words but they didn't register in his mind. He was already nearing the thicket of trees where the person who shot Ossie must be hiding when he heard Nate holler, "Dammit, Joe. I'm not gonna let you do this," as he took off running after him.

Joe had the long, lean legs of a distance runner. Nate wasn't quite as tall as Joe, so his legs weren't as long, but he was almost as fit. Under some circumstances, Nate might have been able to win a footrace between them, but Joe had a head start. And also, Nate was a native Floridian and thus he was wearing flip-flops.

Joe looked back and saw Nate shuck the shoes and take off running in his bare feet, so he ran faster to keep ahead of Nate. Joe's work boots weren't exactly made for running, but they were better than running shoeless, especially as he neared the swamp where foot-bruising cypress knees protruded from the ground. Even without proper shoes, Nate was able to close the gap between them slightly before Joe reached the trees.

"Joe, what are you thinking?" he called out. "You've got a family. That person has a gun. Are you trying to get yourself killed? Think about your kids. Think about Faye."

Joe had been able to ignore everything else Nate had said, but he heard these words. The mention of his family penetrated the haze of anger that was driving him, and he stopped so short that he stumbled and nearly fell. When Nate reached him, Joe was crouched with both hands on his thighs, shaking his head as if the motion would make the world make sense.

Nate clapped a hand on his back. "Glad you decided to stop being stupid."

"You ran after me. That wasn't a little bit stupid?"

"You're my friend. I couldn't let you die of being stupid. Well, I could, but I wouldn't." He used the hand on Joe's back to turn him around. "I would ordinarily buy you a drink to calm your nerves, but you've got a lot of water to travel before you get home. Let's go back to the marina, and I'll buy you some coffee instead."

Joe wasn't actually stupid, although he occasionally acted that way, so he knew exactly why Nate had a firm hand between his shoulder blades. If there was indeed somebody with a gun hiding in those trees, they were not safe where they were. Nate was frog-marching him toward safety, and he was doing it with some speed. He pushed Joe straight across the clearing, rather than along the curving shoreline, taking the straightest route back to the marina, and their pace was more of a sprint than a march. Joe understood the reason for this, so he let Nate set the speed.

This didn't mean that Joe stopped talking. "Why would somebody shoot Ossie?"

"Could've been a kid that wanted to try skeet shooting."

This was true.

"Also could've been a psychopath, who only shot your drone because there weren't any people handy."

This was also true.

Nate was starting to pant a little, but he kept talking. "Wasn't about to let you find out which one it was."

Joe tried to laugh, but he was getting out of breath, too. Nothing came out of his mouth but "Heh."

He noticed Nate looking over his shoulder as he hustled Joe toward the marina, like a man who was trying to calm his friend but was still pretty weirded out about what had just happened. As the patch of trees receded behind them, Joe could feel the hand on his back start to relax. He was just starting to realize how close he'd come to real trouble, and he had Nate to thank for getting him out of it. He might have Nate to thank for being alive.

It took a real friend to run into danger to keep his buddy from doing something idiotic. Joe had known Nate for a few years now. They'd fished together. Every now and then, they'd drunk a few beers at the marina while they watched pelicans dive for their dinner. He wouldn't have counted the man as one of his closest friends, not like Sheriff Mike, Magda, and Emma, but he liked him. Considering what Nate had just done for him, he might need to reevaluate this attitude. There were few things that Joe valued more than having friends he could trust.

As they neared the marina parking lot, they slowed to a walk, as if they had crossed a magical border into a place where the shooter couldn't come for them. Or wouldn't come for them. Now that Nate could breathe again, he seemed to have gone straight back to guessing who shot Ossie and why.

"Maybe it was just somebody who really hates drones and the people who fly them. Maybe shooting that gun was a way to say, 'How dare you fly a camera over my head and invade my privacy? Get out of my sky!'"

Joe shook his head. "I don't do that. I respect people's privacy. I try to only fly Ossie over public places. And I get permission to take pictures of people and their stuff. Mostly, I just fly her over the water, which is what you were doing. Well, I used to fly her and I used to get permission to take those pictures. I guess there's nothing left of Ossie for me to fly now. I'm really going to miss her."

"You're talking about a machine, Joe. You can buy another one just like her. Heck. I can buy you another one just like her, and I'll do that. I was the one flying her when she got shot."

Joe shook his head. "It wasn't your fault. Could've happened to anybody. Besides, I can buy another drone. No problem."

Joe knew that Nate was no ordinary newspaper reporter and his dad was no ordinary editor. They had inherited money, serious money. If he was going to be friends with a rich man, he couldn't let Nate spend money on him all the time. It wouldn't be good for their friendship, and it wouldn't be good for Joe's pride.

"Actually," he said, "our business can buy it. Faye and I have been talking about how aerial photos are always a big help when we're working a site. With a drone, we can take our own, and we won't have to make do with library photos that are a year old. Or twenty years old. They'll be up to the minute."

As they stepped from the patchy, weedy grass onto the marina parking lot, it felt to Joe like he was waking up from a nightmare.

Nate, too, seemed to relax a bit. He shook his head as if to clear it, saying, "Hey, this thing has had me too rattled to think straight. We need to call Sheriff Rainey. Should've already done it, actually."

"Um, weren't we hightailing it from a crazy person with a gun?"

"Coulda been. But we can call the sheriff now. Even if it was just a kid who pulled that trigger, the sheriff needs to know about it."

Joe reached in his pocket for his phone. "We should probably call Sheriff Mike. He's old school. Mike will naturally more put the fear of God into that kid."

"I hear you. But Sheriff Rainey's the one wearing the badge these days."

Joe was still groping for his phone. "I can't find my...oh, yeah. My phone's attached to the controller for Ossie. You got it?"

"I had it." Nate looked blankly at his hands. "I haven't given it a second's thought since that gun went off. I must have—" He turned around and scanned the open area between the spot where they stood and the trees. "Maybe I dropped it when I kicked off my flip-flops? I am so sorry, Joe. I'll go back and look for it."

Joe looked down and saw that his friend was picking his way across the gravel-strewn and broken pavement of Manny's parking lot in his bare feet. It was his turn to grab Nate and stop him.

"Don't be an idiot. The person who shot Ossie could still be hiding behind any of those trees. We're gonna go inside and you're gonna call the sheriff, since you've still got a phone. He can send out some people who know how to take care of situations like this. They'll find the controller and my phone."

"Neither one of us is thinking straight. The sheriff's in the marina. Remember? We don't need my cell phone to call him. Yours, either."

Joe turned around to see if he could spy the controller. He saw nothing between him and the tree but grass and weeds. Right near the water, he could see two small, flat objects that must have been Nate's flip-flops, but he didn't see anything that could be an electronic device. This made him think of the downed drone. He supposed that the shore and water on the other side of the trees could be littered with pieces of Ossie.

"Leave it where you dropped it," Joe said. "It's just a controller for a busted drone."

"And your phone."

"I can get another one. Besides, maybe the sheriff will find my phone."

"Please tell me it was backed up."

Joe cleared his throat, embarrassed. "Faye's always after me to do that. She uses the cloud, whatever that is. I was planning to get serious about backing things up when I got that external drive for storing my pictures. I'm guessing it would have had enough space to back up my phone and my computer, too."

Nate's mouth was hanging open. "You don't back up your devices? My whole life's in my phone. And my computer. I back them up in triplicate, religiously. It's worth it, just so I never have to worry about losing a story when the paper's going to print."

"That's the difference between you and me. My whole life's on Joyeuse Island, where my kids are. And in my car, too, since my wife's driving it around the county right now. Faye makes sure our business stuff is backed up, and she takes care of our family pictures. Until I started taking pictures with Ossie, I just didn't care about anything on my phone or my computer bad enough to worry about losing it. And also I really hate fussing with passwords."

If Joe hadn't been so upset about losing Ossie, the horrified look on Nate's face would have made him laugh until he cried.

Chapter Seventeen

Sheriff Rainey didn't have much to say other than, "This is a small town. Heck, the area around the marina ain't even a town. It's just a wide spot in the road with a few businesses and a church. Not to mention that I know pretty much everybody in these parts. It's really hard to hide in Micco County. We'll find out who did it, Joe."

His words were encouraging. His facial expression? Not so much. Joe knew that the man's resources were limited, and he preferred that the sheriff spend them on finding out what happened to Captain Eubank.

"I don't even know what the law says about shooting a drone. It's not like Ossie was a person, and there wasn't a person anywhere close," Joe said.

"Willful destruction of property ain't murder," Sheriff Rainey said, "but it's surely criminal mischief. It's no felony unless that was a right expensive piece of equipment, like maybe a thousand dollars or more—"

Joe shook his head. He said, "Ossie couldn't have been that expensive. She was a Christmas present. Sheriff Mike and Magda wouldn't have spent that much," then he felt bad about saying "Sheriff Mike" in front of the real sheriff.

"So shooting it down wasn't a felony. It was still a misdemeanor, though. Maximum sentence for that is a year in jail. That ain't nothing to sneeze at. Discharging a firearm in a public place is another misdemeanor," the sheriff said, "and it can also bring as much as a year behind bars."

Joe could see that Sheriff Rainey was trying to make him feel better, but nothing he'd said indicated that he had enough evidence to even find out who did the shooting. His deputies had turned up almost no sign of the shooter. They'd found some indistinct footprints among the trees at the edge of the cypress swamp, but the prints had led into a small clearing carpeted in unkempt weeds. This is where they petered out.

There was no obvious evidence of a parked car nearby, but the shooter had gotten away somehow. Most likely the car had been parked in one of three parking lots within a half-mile of the spot where Ossie had gone down. There were tire tracks from any number of cars and trucks in those lots, but it was going to be hard to link any of them to the shooter. The sheriff had assigned someone to find security camera footage from the entities associated with the lots—a restaurant, a church, and an RV park—but none of them looked especially prosperous. Joe wouldn't be surprised to hear that none of them had been able to afford the expense of a security system.

"I guess Ossie was busted into a million pieces," Joe said. "If you found the card, though, I guess I might be able to recover some pictures I took with her."

The sheriff shook his head. "We didn't find the card or even the main body of the drone where the card would be. To tell you the truth, we didn't find much of Ossie at all. At first, we thought she went down over the water."

It did not escape Joe's attention that the sheriff had picked up his habit of talking about the drone as if it were alive. Well, good. Maybe this quirk would have an effect on the sheriff and the people he had working the case. If they felt the emotional connection to Ossie that they would have felt for a person or an animal that had been ambushed and killed, then maybe they'd feel driven to find the culprit.

"Why don't you think she went down over the water?" Joe asked.

"After a lot of looking, we found a few little bits of plastic and a couple of pieces of the battery on the ground. The more interesting thing is that we found them right around where we found those few footprints. If I had to guess, the shooter took the time to pick up the biggest pieces and carry them away. There wasn't time to get them all, because the shooter knew it was important to get to the car and get away, but the big pieces? Yeah. They're gone. And so's the controller and your phone. We even tried calling it and listening for the ring. Nothing. Either it's in the water and shorted out or somebody took it. And even if it's in the water, that still means that somebody—probably the shooter—threw it out there. You would have noticed if Nate had overhanded it into the Gulf."

"Seems a little weird to me for somebody to spend time picking up my phone and the pieces of Ossie, when they knew that somebody'd probably called the cops," Joe said. "But I don't understand where else my phone could have gone, unless Nate accidentally dropped it in the water. The boats at the marina keep it stirred up there, so it ain't real clear. My phone could be right there at the edge under a layer of silt, and it would be the devil to find it. Or maybe he dropped it when we were standing at the edge of the woods and the person that murdered Ossie was able to get to it without us seeing."

"Well, that's just one of the things I'll be asking this person who goes around shooting a gun where guns shouldn't be shot.

I'm looking forward to being face-to-face in the questioning room."

Joe noticed that he planned to do the questioning himself. He doubted that sheriffs made a habit of scheduling face-time with misdemeanor suspects, so he was taking this thing seriously. This was good, although Joe didn't have a clue why he'd do that. For all their talk about Ossie as if she was a recently murdered human being, she wasn't. She was just a hunk of plastic with a camera and a memory card, powered by a battery pack.

Captain Eubank, however, had been a human being. He'd had a sister and friends who loved him, and he'd loved life. Nobody could look at his library and believe that he wasn't fascinated with the world and the people in it. Joe hoped that his death had been a terrible accident, but he wasn't sure. And he needed to be sure.

"Do you think this crime has anything to do with what happened to the captain?"

He expected a blank look, but he got a guarded one instead.

"I can't think of a single thing to link them, other than that they happened close to each other geographically. I'm sure you know that 'These things happened close to each other, Your Honor!' is not something that will hold up in a court of law. Still, there's nothing to stop me from investigating them both a lot more closely than is strictly required."

"And you're doing that?" Joe didn't know Sheriff Rainey quite well enough to know how he would respond to this kind of pushback, but he was in the mood to test him. It's what Faye would have done. He wished she were standing there beside him.

"With no crime scene and no physical evidence other than the captain's body, there's not much more I can do, other than wait for that autopsy. But, no, I have not written his death off to an accident or natural causes. Not yet. Unless we find some shred of evidence that it was foul play, though, I'll have to do that soon enough. Right now, I'm just listening to the creepy feeling in the back of my brain saying that something's not right."

Sheriff Rainey fiddled with the change in his pocket like a man whose nerves were nagging at him. Then he went back to talking. "And I guess that's true of this Ossie-shooting incident. There's nothing to say that it's anything more than simple vandalism and there's nothing to say that it's linked to the captain's death, but I've still got that creepy feeling that things aren't right. When I get that feeling, I listen to it. Does that approach meet with your approval, sir?"

At first, Joe recoiled at his use of "sir." It seemed like a sarcastic way to answer him. When he saw that there was no sarcasm on the sheriff's face, he heard the "sir" differently, as a signal that Sheriff Rainey respected his opinion enough to answer him, but he also wanted to keep the conversation light. Since Joe wasn't sure he could walk that same conversational tightrope, he just nodded.

Chapter Eighteen

It had taken Faye forever to run Amande's delivery route, and she'd spent that time in parts of Wakulla County that were still without a functional cell tower. This had become obvious when she finally edged out of the hurricane zone, because her phone had lit up with notifications. She'd had calls and texts from Joe, Amande, Magda, and Emma, and none of them made sense.

Even Manny had shot her some messages that were meant to be reassuring:

Dont freak out

Joes telling the truth

He's ok

Then, as soon as she'd read the messages and listened to the voicemails, she'd lost service again. This forced her to drive for another quarter-hour wondering what people were talking about. Why on earth would somebody shoot Ossie?

Also, despite what everybody said, somebody had been firing a gun in her husband's vicinity, so she felt completely entitled to freak out. And she did, within reason. She held herself together enough to handle the car, but the inside of her brain was a mess.

When she got Joe on the phone, he sounded fine. He was already home with the kids. This gave her permission to finally fall apart. She found a stretch of road where the shoulder wasn't heaped with hurricane debris, parked her car, and indulged in some hysterics while he kept saying that there was no reason for her to do that.

"You keep saying you're fine," she said between hiccuping sobs, "but the things you're telling me don't sound fine. I'll be home as quick as this car can get me there. And my boat… which isn't at the marina, is it?"

Joe tried to say that he'd come get her, but she interrupted him. "You've been through enough today, and so have the kids. I'll use Amande's boat. I'm sure she won't mind, but I'll ask her. She thinks I don't respect her space. I don't want to make her right about that."

As soon as she ended the call, her phone rang again. It was Amande, trying to sound like she hadn't been crying about the captain or Ossie or the pain of being nineteen. All she said was, "Please use my boat to get home as soon as you can," and then she was gone.

———

Faye was finally, finally home. She buried her face in Joe's chest, grateful for the feel of his heartbeat against her cheek. "I was so scared."

Michael was sandwiched between them, yelping for air.

"What happened?" she asked. "Why would somebody be shooting at you?"

Joe shook his head, saying, "They weren't shooting at Nate and me. They were shooting at Ossie. She'd been out over the water and was just coming inland when we heard the shots, two of them. As soon as Ossie was on her way down, there weren't any more."

"Mission accomplished," Amande said. "A perfectly harmless machine was dead, so they stopped shooting. I'm sure this makes perfect sense to somebody, but not to me."

And now the children were crying over Ossie, forcing Joe to say, "She was just a machine. I mean, *it* was just a machine. We can save up our money and buy another one just like her. I mean, just like *it*."

Faye came to his rescue. "Ossie can be replaced. Your dad can't. Everything turned out for the best. And if the sheriff can find the person who's shooting a gun when they're way too close to people, that'll be even better."

———

When Joe had seen Faye trudge into their house at the end of a terrible day, he'd had a feeling about what she was going to say. And he'd been right.

"I'm not sure Sheriff Rainey is taking the captain's death seriously enough," were the first words out of her mouth when the children were out of earshot, and Joe wasn't at all surprised. And her next words weren't unexpected, either. "We're supposed to be happy that he hasn't closed the case and called it a day, but I don't sense that he's as hell-bent on solving it as he should be. I'm gonna call Sheriff Mike."

He felt obligated to point out the obvious. "He ain't the sheriff anymore. He's just Mike."

"Don't give me that. You still call him 'Sheriff Mike,' too."

This was true, so Joe was now out of half-hearted arguments. "Then call the man. It'll make you feel better."

———

"What exactly do you think I can to do to help? I'm retired."

Sheriff Mike even sounded retired to his own ears. In earlier years there would have been a sarcastic edge to his voice. Now, he sounded almost mellow, and "mellow" was not a word that anyone had ever associated with Mike McKenzie before he married, had a late-in-life kid, and walked away from law enforcement for good.

Faye was not easily dissuaded.

"You still know people. You still know the law. When somebody dies mysteriously, you know how to work the case. I think maybe Sheriff Rainey's still a little green."

Mike knew that this was what Faye sounded like when she was trying to be diplomatic. God help him if she decided to just come out with the unvarnished truth. If he didn't address her concerns one way or another, she would escalate all the way up to undiplomatic straight-shooter and inform him that she was pretty sure the new sheriff was incompetent.

Sheriff Mike knew that Sheriff Rainey wasn't incompetent. He was a good, steady, hardworking officer of the law. It might be possible, though, that he lacked the tendency toward treachery that made a good investigator great. If you weren't capable of treachery, then how would you recognize it when you saw it? Sheriff Mike was immodest enough to admit that he was born a little treacherous. Brushing elbows with criminals for decades had honed this trait a little more with each passing year. This was why retirement had been so good for his soul. He didn't deal with criminals every day, and this removed the temptation for him to be a little more like them.

"Tell me what's bothering you, Faye."

"The new sheriff seems willing to take Captain Eubank's death at face value. Yeah, he's going through the motions of doing an investigation, but he's handed a lot of the work off to somebody named Lieutenant Baker—"

"The man is dealing with the aftermath of a hurricane. People died. Some are still missing. His attention is divided."

"I know that. I do. I'm out there looking at what's left of my friends' homes every day that rolls. And you know it." She heard herself and stopped. "I'm sorry for yelling."

"Faye, honey, if you can't yell at your friends, who can you yell at?"

"Yeah, well, sometimes I want to yell at the new sheriff. He thinks the captain got so carried away by excitement when he thought he'd located a treasure ship that he took his boat out and hopped right in the water. Alone. And then he died. The end."

Mike knew that a good investigator tried not to talk much when he was talking to somebody who was just burning to tell him something, so he said nothing but, "You knew the captain well. What do you think?"

"When I last saw him, he was excited about maybe finding a shipwreck. I'll grant you that. Maybe that explains why he did something so dumb, but I don't know. Nobody would ever have called the captain dumb. You knew him. Do you think he would have risked scuba diving by himself? Especially since I don't think he had a lot of experience. Have you ever even heard him mention scuba diving?"

This question had been bothering Mike ever since he heard about the captain's death. "No, I've never heard him mention it, but that don't prove much. I do believe that if the captain was ever going to do something crazy, it would happen when he was all excited about something historical. And you yourself have said that he thought he was on the trail of a shipwreck. That would have made our good friend fairly well giddy."

"He would have waded into a gun battle if it meant that he would learn something." Faye's usually no-nonsense voice was wistful. "I know that. Only…"

Sheriff Mike's instincts were suddenly on alert. When someone as analytical as Faye Longchamp-Mantooth stopped herself in the middle of an emotional rant, it usually meant something. He knew Faye well, and he knew what this hesitation meant for her. It meant that she'd had a logical thought that contradicted what she was saying. Faye's logical thoughts were consistently worth exploring.

"Only what?"

"That's the thing. I don't think he needed scuba gear. Not to check out the spot we were talking about. The tide was pretty low yesterday afternoon. Early evening, too, and I just can't imagine the captain going night diving by himself, so I think he was dead by nightfall. I know it didn't happen this morning, because that's when he was planning to go see Jeanine. You know he wouldn't put anything ahead of her, not even a fabulous shipwreck."

"Now, that's true."

"I'm pretty sure the tide was low enough yesterday evening for him to land the boat on Joyeuse Island and walk all the way out there. Even if he didn't think to do that, he could have gotten there with a snorkel. Using scuba gear was overkill, especially since nobody has said anything yet to make me believe that the captain even owned any. And don't forget that he lived near the Gulf all his life. He knew he needed to watch the tides, and he almost certainly swam like a fish."

Oh, yeah. The captain could swim. Sheriff Mike remembered a time, maybe fifteen years back, when the man swam out to a tourist caught in a riptide and hauled her to shore single-handedly. Captain Edward Eubank most certainly didn't drown because he couldn't handle himself in the water. Nevertheless, people made mistakes and sometimes they had terrible, awful luck.

But was that really what happened? The captain had been serious about his passions. He had talked Sheriff Mike's ear off about fishing many times. He could also deliver an hour-long monologue on nineteenth-century fish canneries in Micco County that was actually pretty interesting if you were in the right frame of mind. It helped if you had a cup of coffee in your hand. But never once had Mike heard him deliver one of those monologues on scuba diving.

Faye was right to harp on this fact like a dog worrying a bone. And she was right to wonder about why he was scuba diving in water that was really pretty shallow.

"Think about it," she said. "If he'd gone out at another time, the tide would have been higher, but we're still not talking about unfathomable ocean depths. You could drown in that water, but you'd almost have to work at it."

She was right, but she was ignoring a very real possibility. "It ain't all that hard to drown if you've had a heart attack," Sheriff Mike said his voice gentle. "Or a stroke or something like that. The captain was my age or better, and stuff like that happens to old dudes like us. Surely there will be an autopsy."

Her voice was quiet, barely audible. "Yeah. It's probably happening right now, if it's not already done. Not that I expect the sheriff to stumble all over himself to tell me what it says."

"I'll talk to some people and see if there's been any chatter on the street. If I hear anything, I'll call you. I promise. But Faye, honey, sometimes terrible things happen and it ain't nobody's fault."

She didn't say anything.

"Honey," Mike said, knowing that he was really concerned about Faye if he was calling her "Honey" in back-to-back sentences. "Magda's real worried about you. She's sitting right here beside me, telling me to tell you that you should pick up your phone once in a while."

Faye must have seen the calls from her best friend. They'd been coming in all the damn day, ever since word got out about the captain's death. With his connections, Sheriff Mike was among the first to know such things. Magda, as his wife, was the next. She'd been dialing Faye's number ever since.

"I saw the messages. Tell Magda—"

Faye went silent.

So what was Mike supposed to tell his worried wife? That her friend was just too sad to talk?

Magda knew that. That's why she was blowing up Faye's phone, because she knew that letting her stew in that misery wouldn't end well.

"Tell her what? Please say that I should tell her you'll call her soon."

He got a quiet "Yeah" out of her, and he figured that was the best he was going to do when loyal Faye was hurting over a friend.

Chapter Nineteen

After Faye had read Michael his bedtime story and Amande had retreated to her room, Joe came to her and said, "Before I went back to the marina…before Ossie got shot…I sent her out to do some reconnaissance here on the island. Got something to show you. I think you're gonna like it."

She followed him into his office in the aboveground basement of their old home. The late afternoon light slanted in through a small window in the tabby cement walls, molded by enslaved people out of sand, oyster shells, ash, and sweat. Those walls were covered in many layers of whitewash, worn by time. Over their heads, the vast plantation house shifted as the sea wind breathed through its porches and around its cupola. It creaked, as old wooden things tend to do. A loose shutter slammed rhythmically against an exterior wall, telling Faye that she needed to add yet another task to her never-ending list of maintenance chores. This was the price of living in a house that was two hundred years old. Well, parts of it were.

Joe's desk was littered with coffee mugs, maps, and books about vegetable gardening. On his computer display was a slide show of pictures Ossie had taken, flashing on the screen one after another. Or, rather, with pictures that Joe had used Ossie to take. Just because Joe had forgotten that the late Ossie was a machine didn't mean that Faye should join him in his fantasy world.

His fancy new printer sat on a stand next to the desk, and it made Faye think of Captain Eubank. The last time they were together, he'd shown her pictures that Joe had printed just for him.

Joe, despite being a generation or two younger than the captain, was only a little better with technical things. He could email because their business required it. He could operate search engines, not just because their business required it but because he was as curious about the world as Faye was. Joe had learned to use Ossie because she intrigued him, and he'd learned to download the drone's photos onto this desktop computer just because he loved to look at them.

Honestly, though, he was still stuck in the twentieth century in a lot of ways. One of them was his love for physical photos. He had spent a pretty penny for this printer, just so he could hold Ossie's images in his hands.

"So, like I was saying, I took some pictures for you today, Faye. After I brought the kids back here, I took them out on the beach and we flew Ossie for a while. They watched while I sent her way out over the Gulf, south of here."

He was grinning, so she knew what he'd done.

"You sent Ossie out to look at The Cold Spot?"

"Yup. Those were the last pictures she ever took. I think they would have come out better if I'd waited a little later in the day. The sun wouldn't have been so harsh, for sure. And the tide would've been lower, so maybe Ossie could've seen the bottom better, but I needed to put Michael down for a nap before I left home again."

"Smart move. What could you see?"

He handed her an eight-by-ten glossy so brightly colored that Faye wondered what Joe's ink bill looked like. It had been taken when Ossie was flying high. "First, I sent her way up, so I could see the shape of Joyeuse Island and the coastline. Kinda like that other picture, the one that went in the paper. See? There's the house. That's Seagreen Island. And that's us."

Faye thought she might be able to see three person-shaped blobs on the beach.

"This high-up picture helped me get a notion of how things were laid out."

The blotch of darkness was hard to see at this scale, but she was pretty sure it was there.

"Next, I brought Ossie down a little, like a zoom lens. Speaking of which, if we decide we need to get another drone for the business, I want to get a zoom lens, too." He gave her an appraising look, as spouses do when they want to spend money on something fun. "When we've got a little extra money, I mean. Whatcha think?"

Distracted by the photos, she gave him an absent nod. And boom. The family budget had a new line item.

Next, Joe handed her a sequence of five photos taken at successively lower altitudes. The top one, like the one the captain had given her, showed the colorful biminis of pleasure boats, this time in deep red and shades of blue.

She flipped through the photos one by one. It was obvious by the way the center shifted with each new photo that Joe was focusing in on a particular location, the shaded area that grew more defined with each shot. By the time she reached the fourth photo, the boats were off-screen and so was land. There was nothing left to see but open water. Her heart quickened to see a small dark spot, sharply demarcated and almost circular, at the center of the last two photographs in the stack.

Because Joe was a sucker for drama, he had held the last photo in reserve. He handed it to her, then he sat back and waited for her squawk.

And she did squawk. Then she said, "That's not a sunken ship," with full confidence.

"Nope. I don't think so, either."

In the middle of the dark circle was something long, dark and narrow, with crisp edges. "It looks…geological. I guess that's the right word."

"Yeah. It looks like a hole in the ground."

She laughed and gave him a playful swat on the shoulder. "That's what I want it to be. A deep watery hole in the ground."

"Yeah, I know." He took the photo back and studied it. "You still can't tell much. Too much reflection off the water. Not enough color contrast between your hole in the ground and the seabed. I've been reading up on post-production editing, though. I think I could clean it up, if the file hadn't been blown up along with Ossie, and if I had the right software. I could scan this print on a really good scanner and maybe still be able to clean it up some."

"Well, aren't you tech-y?" asked Faye, who had no idea what post-production editing could and couldn't do.

He grinned. "I can be if I buy that software. I've been checking into filters for drone lenses, too."

Joe wasn't one to spend much money. If he was willing to even consider buying something so expensive, Faye knew they'd be getting that software and another drone to go with it. And the zoom lens and the filter, too. Maybe he could hold off on some of it until Christmas. Or his birthday, which was almost as far away because it was Christmas Eve. She suspected that every present with Joe's name on it was going to be drone-related this year. She had to admit that she loved Joe's pictures and the joy it gave him to make them.

She put on her reading glasses to make the image a little crisper to her eyes, but this tactic wasn't showing her any more detail than she'd already seen. "When we can send another drone out there, you should try to get some pictures from a low, oblique angle," she said. "If the hurricane opened up a big spring vent, there might be enough water coming out to make a bulge in the surface of the water over it. It might even bubble, like the springs we see when we go kayaking in Spring Creek. A boil like that might show in pictures, if you took them when the drone wasn't right overhead."

"The right lens and filters will help with that."

"You're hoping my obsession with this…" She waved her hand at the photos. "…this underwater crater thingie…will convince me that you need to buy some more toys. Right?"

"You got it. But Faye, don't you think we can use a drone in our work? I've been reading about how other archaeologists are finding all kinds of cool stuff. You can even see things that are all the way underground, because the plants grow different in the ground on top of them. Foundations. Gardens. Walls. Mounds. Roads. You can't see 'em when you're standing on the ground, but you can sure see 'em from the sky. Just think what we might uncover right here on our own island if we outfitted a drone with really good lenses and stuff. Not to mention for our clients. And it would all be tax-deductible."

"He's doing tax planning," Faye said to the air. "He's not just tech-y today. He's business-y."

Joe said nothing. He just waggled his eyebrows at her.

"Buy your toys," she said. "And keep your receipts for our tax returns. The IRS is finicky about helping people buy toys."

Chapter Twenty

When morning came, it took Faye a full minute to remember that her friend had drowned and a hurricane had blown her surviving friends' lives apart. During that minute, she enjoyed the sunshine through the window and the sound of Joe breathing at her side. She was glad for the roof over her sleeping children and for the unending sound of the waves on the shore of her island. And then she remembered that bad things had happened and that there would always be more coming.

She hauled herself out of bed, trying to ignore the shoulder that hurt all the time. It was time to wake the kids and get ready to go ashore. She moved quietly, so that Joe could sleep a little later while she made breakfast. The kids would complain because Joe's cooking was sublime and Faye's was merely adequate, but they'd survive. Her scrambled eggs weren't that bad.

The kids ate her substandard eggs, then Joe appeared with his long black hair still wet from the shower. They all loaded themselves onto two boats. Amande was in hers because Faye had come home in it the night before, and families who lived on islands needed to choreograph their boats' movements to avoid stranding somebody. Amande took off for shore without a look back.

Faye, Joe, and Michael piled into Faye's oyster skiff and followed her. They all headed to the marina where their cars waited. And where Manny waited, too.

Sometimes Faye felt like Manny enjoyed having her family as a captive audience. They saw him way too often to suit her, but they also didn't have many other options for traveling between home and shore. She'd kept a boat slip at the marina long before he bought it. Before she met Joe, in fact. Over the years, she'd done business with Wally, Liz, Wilma, and now Manny. Based on history, she had every likelihood of outlasting Manny, so there was no point in looking for another place to keep her boat.

Short of finding a place on Alligator Point or, even worse, going around it to get to Panacea, there were no commercial marinas within a reasonable distance. The hurricane had taken the only other reasonable alternative when it destroyed Emma's dock. Faye and Joe had steadfastly refused to keep a car parked at Emma's house so that they could save a few bucks on slip rental and parking. It was important to them to pay their own way.

Now that Emma was getting older, Faye had begun to rethink that position. Maybe it would help her to have them around more. Also, Faye was pretty sure that Emma would agree that it wasn't a good thing for Amande to spend too much time with Manny. These points were moot since Emma's dock was completely gone, along with her back deck and a big chunk of her roof. The only thing keeping rain off Emma's concert grand piano was a blue tarp that Joe and Faye had spread over the missing shingles.

Thus, for the foreseeable future, Faye was forced to make pleasant conversation with Manny whenever she took a boat to the mainland, which had been every day since the storm. She had spent a little time feeling sheepish about her dislike for him after he was so kind in the immediate aftermath of Captain Eubank's death, but twenty-four hours had passed. She'd had time to remember why he bugged her.

And now they were at the marina and Manny was seriously bugging her right at the moment. Here he was, greeting Amande dockside with the fancy coffee she liked. Faye could feel her attitude shift instantly from, "Maybe Manny is okay," to "This man is going to ruin my daughter's life."

Whenever she felt this fear, she opened her mouth and stupid came out. Today, it was, "There was some interesting college mail for you yesterday, Amande. The Ivy League must have gotten a look at your SATs."

Amande's withering look said *You're going to start in on me before I've even had my coffee?*

Faye knew that she'd said the wrong thing, but she also knew that she was right. An island was no place for a young adult like Amande, especially when nobody lived there but her immediate family. Her daughter liked to tell her how much she was learning from her online classes, but a brick-and-mortar college was about more than schooling. Young people needed friends and, yes, they needed love lives. Faye was terrified that Amande would get involved with Manny just because he was single and handy.

Nevertheless, behaving like an overbearing mother was not going to stop that from happening. She really needed to get a grip.

Amande stalked away from her and disappeared into the bar and grill. Joe did his usual conflict-avoidance thing of focusing his entire attention on tying up the boat. Wondering what to do next, Faye hauled herself out of the boat, hoisted a fussy Michael onto her hip, and got him out of his life jacket. Then she noticed that Manny was still standing there. He had a second cup of coffee, and he was holding it out in her direction.

"Sorry, Joe. I'd have brought you one, too, but I only have two hands." He reached into a pocket, then stopped himself. "I have a B-A-N-A-N-A in here, if it's okay for Michael to have it."

Faye had one arm around Michael, but she totally had a free hand for coffee. Feeling like the worst possible hypocrite, she reached for the cup and wished she weren't so suspicious of the man offering it. "Oh, absolutely. He loves bananas. Thank you! And thanks for this."

"Look," he said, "I get it that you're protective of Amande. I am, too. I've known her since she wasn't much bigger than this guy."

If he was hoping to establish some kind of pecking order in Amande's heart by reminding them that he'd met her first, Faye wasn't going to stand for it.

Maybe Manny saw the thundercloud on her face, but he didn't let on. He just kept talking. "I want the same things for her that you do. Honest, I do. She's too smart and too hardworking to sell herself short. Any college would be lucky to get her, and she should absolutely go to one of them and get a degree. Two degrees. Three, maybe, like you. I remember taking her to the library when she was a little kid and watching her pick out books that were almost too big for her to carry. She was born to go to college."

Faye couldn't quite tell what the man was trying to say. Yeah, Amande was born to go to college. Any fool could see that, but nothing in his little speech said "I have no romantic interest in your daughter." And if he did have that interest, then reminding Faye that he'd known Amande since she was a child just made everything ickier.

As she grappled with these thoughts, a stricken look crossed his face. "You think I'm...you think I want...oh no no no. No. When I look at Amande, I still see a little girl. Dirty face. Pigtails and all that jazz. I used to pretend like she was my little girl sometimes."

Faye tried not to let her emotions show on her face. Jealousy was an ugly word for what she was feeling, but it was accurate.

"Why do you think I sold everything and moved here?" Manny asked. "When she left, there was nothing to distract me from the fact that my life was going nowhere. I looked at the losers all around me, and I knew I needed a new start. When she told me this place was for sale, I decided that it looked like as good a place as any. Business is better here, for sure, and there's a community college right down the road. Maybe I'm not as smart as Amande, but there's no reason I couldn't take some business classes. And maybe some art classes for fun. Who wouldn't want to paint this?"

He gestured at the sky, the birds, the boats, the watery horizon, everything.

"This is a place where my life can be different. And, yeah, I picked a place where I could see Amande, because I missed her. That's all. I just missed her. And I wanted to make sure her new family was making her happy. Is any of that a crime?"

Faye didn't know how to respond as she stood there holding Manny's gift of coffee, but Joe did. He looked up from his task, stood up straight, and extended a hand to shake Manny's. "I hope we're making her happy. We're trying."

Faye found that she actually wanted to believe Manny. She had the coffee in one hand and the other arm was wrapped around the child at her side, but she was struggling to shift things around so that she, too, could shake Manny's hand. Unfortunately, she didn't manage it before she looked up and saw Amande, who was standing so close that she must have heard Manny defending himself from an accusation of being inappropriately interested in her. The fact that Faye hadn't actually made that accusation—at least, not out loud—did not matter a bit.

The expression on Faye's daughter's face was a painful mix of mortification and blinding anger. She reached out, snatched Michael off his mother's hip, and sat him on her own.

As she turned on her heel and stalked away, she spoke to nobody but him. "C'mon, Bubba. Thirsty people are out there waiting for me to bring them some water while you go play with Magda, Mike, and Rachel." And then they had gone too far away for Faye to see them.

Chapter Twenty-One

Steering her car down winding roads to the homes of people too sick to leave the house satisfied Amande's sense of adventure, and the massive chunks of downed trees in the rights-of-way made it all feel even more exotic. Even better, when she was out making deliveries, she was free of her mother's fears and demands.

Michael was a cheerful kid, so he sat behind her in his car seat all the way to Mike and Magda's house, narrating their journey.

"There's a tree! There's 'nother tree. Why'd the trees fall down, Sissy? There's 'nother tree. Look, that lady has a chain saw like Daddy's!"

Fortunately for them both, they enjoyed the same music, so the soundtrack for their adventures always consisted entirely of hip-hop and '70s soul. When the occasional Isaac Hayes number surfaced from her playlist, though, Amande hit the skip button immediately, not because she didn't like his music but because her mother did. Michael had not yet differentiated his musical tastes from his parents', so he squawked when she did that. To keep him cheerful, she always made an exception and let the theme from *Shaft* play in full.

Michael was now playing happily with his best friend, Rachel, so Amande was free to listen to music that was dark. Angry, even. Today, she wanted music that sounded uglier than the way she felt inside.

Looking at the damage left by the hurricane broke Amande's heart. It made her feel helpless, useless. There was no quicker way to become a hero than to hand a bottle of water to a Floridian who had been without air conditioning for a July week, but Amande didn't want to be a hero. She was looking at a torn-apart world, and she wanted a different one.

She didn't want to live in a world where thirteen-year-olds died when the car they were riding in slammed into a fallen tree. She didn't want to live in a world where a person's worth was measured by a piece of paper from a university. She didn't want to live in a world where people who worked all day and all night at two jobs—three jobs, maybe—couldn't afford a comfortable life with a few small pleasures. She didn't want to live in a world where good and gentle men like Captain Eubank met ugly deaths.

Amande didn't reach Jeanine Eubank's house until midday, because the captain's sister lived as far from the Crawfordville supply pickup site as it was possible to be while still being in Micco County. This was her first food-and-water run to Miss Jeanine, because it had taken all this time to clear the country road leading to her house from a horizontal forest of fallen trees.

She wasn't sure what she would say to Miss Jeanine. This was the first time she'd seen the old lady since her brother died. It wasn't that Amande had no experience with grief. She'd lost the grandmother who raised her when she was only sixteen. She remembered her empty certainty that nothing would ever be right again. It was just that she had no experience with comforting other people who had lost loved ones.

As she pulled into the driveway, she saw that Miss Jeanine's roof was littered with heavy tree limbs, and whole sections of shingles were gone. If Captain Eubank had lived, he would have taken care of those things for his sister. Amande knew that her parents would find a way to come help her. That made her feel better, but only a little.

The thing that kept Amande awake at night was the sheer mindboggling scale of the disaster. Her parents could help Miss Emma and her neighbors and now Miss Jeanine. They could keep helping people, one after another, and they would. People were counting on the government and insurance companies and charities and churches. All those institutions should come help, and maybe they would, but Amande saw a lot of people shaking their heads at the thought.

They'd lived through hurricanes before, and they knew how things were. Micco County was sparsely populated. The hurricane was "only" a Category 3. The news channels had already moved on to something new and fascinating. The weather channels were reporting on the next hurricane, which had drawn a bead on the Texas coast. Nobody remembered that there were people still digging out from the last one.

Even cheerful Emma expected to be forgotten. Amande had heard her say, "We have to presume that we're on our own. It has happened before and it will happen again," as she handed Amande's parents money to buy tarps for the roofs of people who couldn't afford them.

And what about these trees lying flat or leaning precariously against each other? If they were in the road or on somebody's house or in somebody's yard, then yeah, somebody would get rid of them. But what about the ones lying in the woods, their rootballs reaching for the sky? They would stay right where they were for years and years.

Most days, Amande was pretty sure she was a grown-up, then she found herself smack up against something like this old woman who had lost her cherished brother. She wanted so much to help, but she felt overwhelmed and awkward. Truthfully, she felt like a little kid.

A massive pine tree had crushed the full length of the front porch of Miss Jeanine's lifelong home. Yes, it was a blessing that it had missed the house itself by two feet—maybe less—but that didn't take an old woman's memories into account. Amande knew how much time she'd spent on the porches of the big old house on Joyeuse Island, sitting with Michael on her lap, or playing rummy with her parents, or just enjoying the breeze while she killed time playing stupid games on her phone.

A fallen tree couldn't take away Amande's memories, but it would break her heart to see those old boards splintered. How much worse would it feel to lose a porch if, at the very same time, you lost the brother who had sat there with you?

Amande decided she'd better stop thinking about that stuff. Otherwise, she was going to start crying, and that wouldn't help her street cred as a grown-up at all.

She paid no attention to the fact that there were two cars in the driveway, a sky-blue 1990s Cadillac and a new gray SUV, when there was only one person living in the house. She knew that people sometimes got attached to cars and kept them around. As it turned out, the second car didn't belong to Miss Jeanine. It belonged to her guest, a woman named Greta Haines who answered the door when Amande knocked.

Ms. Haines shook Amande's hand with the excessive warmth of somebody trying to sell her something. "Thank you for being so good to my friend Jeanine," she said. "I just couldn't stand to think of her out here all by herself, so I drove out to check on her as soon as the road was clear."

She ushered Amande into the dining room, where a big display of fruit cut to look like a bouquet of flowers sat on the long maple table. Next to it sat a basket of fancy cheeses wrapped up in cellophane and two bottles of wine, one red and one white. Amande looked at what she herself was carrying—bottled water, raisin bran, dry milk, and a few cans of tuna—and wondered why she'd bothered to drive all the way out there. Greta's gifts were fancier and finer. More exciting, for sure.

Miss Jeanine was sitting in an upholstered chair tucked in a corner, beside a window with cardboard covering two busted-out panes. A third woman sat next to her in an identical chair. After a couple of false starts, Jeanine was able to struggle out of the chair.

She tottered toward Amande on spindly legs. "You are so lovely to bring me food. And water! I never thought I'd want to see more water after the hurricane filled most of my house right up. But you can't drink floodwater, and I'm pretty thirsty these days. Now you've brought me water to drink, and my cell phone has service again. I think I'll probably get my electricity back in time to keep it from dying, and that's a good thing. Things are getting better every day."

Amande was at a loss. This woman had lost her brother and her house was falling apart around her ears. What was she supposed to say to her?

She went with a cliché, saying "I'm so sorry for your loss." Then she kicked herself for not thinking of something better.

It was hotter inside the house than outside, so steamy that Amande could hardly breathe. The curls around Miss Jeanine's face were damp with sweat. Her thinning hair was almost as gray as the captain's had been, but with a beige tinge that made Amande think she'd once been blond.

This made Amande realize that she didn't even know what

color the captain's hair had been when he was young. He'd gone gray before she met him. It felt weird that she didn't know that. She looked around the room for pictures of him and saw none. The house smelled of must and mold, so the odds were good that any photos Miss Jeanine had owned were ruined by the storm.

The dining room might be the only livable portion of the entire house, because it looked like Miss Jeanine had moved her entire life there. Plastic bags overflowing with clothes were lined up along the walls. Assorted china knickknacks on the sideboard had been shoved aside to make room for a pile of canned food and a can opener.

Miss Jeanine pointed at the canned goods and said, "You can unload the things you brought right there on the sideboard, Amande, and I thank you so much for them. I'm keeping food in here until there's a solid roof over the pantry again."

Leaning hard on her cane, she gestured toward a chair at the dining room table, inviting Amande to sit next to Greta. When her guests were settled, she sank back into her chair.

"I'm so sorry. I forgot to introduce you to Cyndee Stamp." She gestured at the woman in the chair next to hers. "She's a friend of Greta's, and she's a tree contractor. I just love meeting women who do things that people said weren't for me when I was a little girl—women like your mother, Amande, and her archaeology business. She impresses me a lot."

This made Amande very proud, and also a little bit resentful that her mother couldn't leave her alone when she wasn't even in the room.

Jeanine was still talking about the good old days, which didn't sound very good to Amande. "I don't think my parents thought about what the life they chose for me really meant. When I didn't marry, I lived here with them. I earned my keep by taking care of the house and garden, because they were afraid to think of me on my own. We were happy—very happy!—but what did they think was going to happen to me when they were gone?"

The idea of being so vulnerable and dependent horrified Amande.

"I guess they knew that dear, sweet Edward would step into their shoes. They just had no way of knowing that he would pass before me or that he wouldn't have children to take me on as their burden. Times were different for women then, and I'm so glad to see things change."

Amande had a flash of memory—her grandmother stooped over a table full of envelopes with windows on the front. Beside them lay her slim blue checkbook full of checks that had no money to back them up. She knew what life was like for old people who couldn't always pay their bills.

She blurted out, "Are you going to be okay? Now that he's gone, I mean." And then she wanted to sink through the floor, because it was probably really rude to talk about money, especially in front of guests. And, even worse, to remind Miss Jeanine that her dear, sweet Edward was dead.

Jeanine took both of Amande's hands and said, "God bless you, child. Not many people your age would give my worries a single thought. Not because they're not good people, but because they haven't seen much of the world. I'm thinking you have."

She squeezed Amande's hands a bit, and her own hands were stronger than they looked. Then Jeanine said, "Edward took care of me, even in death. He lived on his military pension, so he didn't have a lot of money to leave me, but he paid faithfully on a life insurance policy with me as the beneficiary. And the sale of his house will bring in some money. I can stay here in my home. I'm grateful to my brother for that."

She raised her cane and pointed it at the sideboard where Amande had stacked the food and water. "And I'm grateful for people like you who bring me gifts like those. Edward's in heaven now and he knows what you're doing for me."

"Well, it's not like I brought brie and pineapple," Amande said, perched on the edge of the dining chair and acutely aware of Greta's fancy food.

The strong bird-like hand grasped hers again. "You brought me practical gifts, dear, and Greta brought me luxurious ones. Both of you make me feel like you care." Then she plucked a chunk of cantaloupe off Greta's arrangement and handed it to her.

Then Amande remembered that Miss Jeanine hadn't had electricity since the storm. There was no way that one person could eat pounds of unrefrigerated cut fruit before it started to turn brown and smell. And once that hunk of brie was cut, it would spoil faster than the fruit.

Also, Amande knew for a fact that people who lived where Miss Jeanine did got their water from a well. Her electric pump wouldn't be working until the electric company got her lights back on. She had a feeling that Miss Jeanine was a lot happier to see her bottled water than Greta Haines's wine.

Somehow, the frail old woman had let Amande know that she shouldn't feel bad for not bringing caviar and champagne, yet she'd done it without insulting Greta's gifts. Amande figured that on the day she was smooth enough to do that, she would truly be grown up.

When Miss Jeanine urged her to have some fruit and to help herself to a hunk of cheese while she was at it, Amande ate heartily, like a fellow adult who was in on the secret that these things needed to be eaten before they decayed. She steadfastly refused to accept anything nonperishable, though, not even a bottle of water.

When Amande rose to leave, Miss Jeanine said, "Come back to see me, dear, and don't think you have to bring anything with you. Well, you can bring your brother. His sweet smile reminds me of Edward at that age. We were like the two of you. I was much older and he was like my living baby doll. I think he spent the first five years of his life on this hip." She smacked a hand on her loose cotton skirt. "I can't believe…well, I just can't believe he's gone."

Again, Amande stood there feeling stupid and wondering what her parents would say if they were standing there. She decided to cheat and let them do the talking.

"My parents send you their sympathy. We all loved Captain Eubank, and we're just heartbroken to lose him."

Greta echoed her. "Yeah, me too."

Cyndee said, "I know how I'd feel if I lost any of my brothers."

Now Amande was completely out of things to say. She was saved by a knock at the door. Hustling to get to her feet before Greta did, she almost ran to let the visitor in.

Opening the door, she saw an auburn-haired woman with blue eyes peeking out from under long bangs. She didn't look much older than Amande.

The young woman held out a hand, shook Amande's, and said, "I'm a friend of the captain's, and I have something for his sister."

Jeanine called out, "A friend of Edward's? Oh, my. Please bring her in here so I can say hello."

Amande did that. Jeanine's most recent guest introduced herself as Samantha Kennedy as she held out a book bound in worn brown linen. "The captain lent me this book on the history of the lumber industry in Florida, and I wanted to return it," she said. "It was a big help while I was writing my dissertation. There aren't many copies left, and the other ones are held in archives too far away for me to even think about visiting on a graduate student's budget. I can't tell you how grateful I am to him, and I wanted you to know."

"Have you finished your dissertation, dear?" Jeanine asked. "Are you Dr. Kennedy now?"

Samantha nodded shyly. "Yes, and I'm teaching, just like I've always dreamed—two courses at Micco County Community College plus a course at Florida State. With the captain's help, I've put together a book manuscript that just might get me a tenure-track job, once I find a publisher. I couldn't have done it without him."

Samantha was still holding out the book, but Jeanine waved it away. "Keep it, dear. If it helps you in your work, it will be keeping my dear brother's memory alive. Please sit down and tell me about yourself."

Amande jumped up to give Samantha her chair, despite the fact that there were still two empty ones in the room. Then she fled, because she just couldn't bear to be where she was any longer. Jeanine's grief just might break her if she stayed.

Also, Samantha seemed very sweet, perhaps even someone who could be a friend, but Greta Haines and Cyndee Stamp made her skin crawl. Amande couldn't say why she felt that way, but she did.

Amande knew that when she told her parents about her day, her dad would say he was glad Miss Jeanine had friends to visit her. Amande's dad loved everybody in the whole wide world. It would never occur to him that anybody might have bad motives, because he'd never had one in his life.

Her mother, however, would share Amande's instinctive response to Greta and Cyndee, which was to roll her eyes and watch her back. She didn't know exactly why Miss Jeanine would need to watch her back, but Amande had seen some hard years. Her grandmother had always been able to make sure that she ate, but it hadn't always been enough to fill her up and make her feel safe. Amande had the impression that Faye's mother and grandmother had worked just as hard to make sure she had what she needed, most of the time. Joe's family had been poor, too, but poverty hadn't marked him the way it had marked Amande and her mom.

To Amande and Faye, money was a buffer against a hard world. Neither of them would steal to build up a pile of money big enough to make them feel safe forever, but Amande had no doubt that some people would. This gave her a suspicious streak and she wasn't proud of it. It had taken years for the notion to sink in, but Amande was now realizing that she and her mother were a lot alike. This did not make her especially happy.

She shoved that thought away to think about something else, like what gifts she could bring to Miss Jeanine that would outshine Greta's stupid luxury items. Maybe a photo to remember her brother by?

Amande had taken a picture of Captain Eubank that she liked. It was nothing special, just something she'd snapped with a phone camera when he'd come back to the marina with a really big fish. She'd insisted that he hold that cobia up next to a yardstick, because it was just so darn big. His grin lit the whole picture.

She knew that her parents would come help Miss Jeanine. Her dad would climb up on the roof to make sure the tarps up there were doing what tarps were supposed to do. Her mother had been patching the roof on their Joyeuse Island house since she was in grade school, so she could help him, but she'd be more useful in the house. Miss Jeanine was going to need help filling out the big pile of insurance paperwork sitting on her kitchen table, and her mom was way better than her dad at that kind of thing.

Amande was confident in the fact that her parents were good people, even the mother whom she often wanted to throttle. She just wasn't sure that she could live with them.

Chapter Twenty-Two

Faye was exhausted from a morning spent with people who were still trying to patch their lives together. She and Joe had just finished helping a young couple sweep broken window glass out of their house. They'd loaded a dumpster with those shards, and then they'd stacked busted boards with protruding nails on top of them. The goal was to get the house safe enough for their toddlers, who were all three staying with their grandparents. The nearer the couple came to being reunited with their kids, the perkier they got.

Now Faye sat with Emma, trying to work up an appetite for another peanut-butter-and-honey lunch. This was hard to do in a house that felt like a sauna. No wonder Emma looked so weary and so sweaty. Faye knew intellectually that her friend was in her seventies, but she worked hard to stay in denial about it. Faye planned to have Emma around until she herself was seventy. At least.

Emma ate well, she exercised, and she was finicky about her clothes and makeup, so her youthful looks made it easy for Faye to stay in denial. Today, though, one of the people Faye cherished most finally looked old. Faye was shocked by how much this rocked her world.

"If you could just cool off, you'd feel better, Emma. At least let us get you a generator and an air conditioner. Just a window unit. Joe will drive to Georgia if that's what it takes to find one."

"No, thank you. Do you know how many years of my life I spent in Florida before I could afford air conditioning? I'm tougher than I look."

Faye didn't doubt this, but she also knew how long it had been since Emma weathered a Florida summer without artificially cooled air. The temperature in her house was nearing the one hundred mark. This was the kind of weather that killed people. There was a reason that she'd had no takers from the neighbors she'd urged to come stay with her. They were more comfortable in their tents.

Emma wasn't finished arguing. "Do you know how many children live in the houses around me? I can't have them listening to my generator whine all day and all night while they sit in the heat."

"Then invite them over."

Emma looked at her as if she were just too tired to say, "How many people do you think I can fit in my living room? This problem isn't solvable for everybody, so don't try to solve it for me."

Faye wasn't finished arguing, but she decided to take a break from it and try to be useful. The dining room table was loaded with papers that were mostly pretty dry, because Emma had thrown a plastic tablecloth over them until Faye got the roof leak patched.

Faye pulled back the tablecloth and heard Emma say, "Oh, don't do that. I keep that stuff covered up because I can't stand to look at it. I've got insurance paperwork to do and FEMA paperwork to file. The documents I need to fill out all those forms were stored in a filing cabinet that leaked. Now they're moldy and mildewed. I can't even find my regular bills, and it's way past time to pay them. It's all just awful. Leave that pile of misery alone, please. Let me just sit here and fret about it."

Faye pretended like she didn't hear a word as she poked around in the damp paper. Then she found a form that brought her to her feet, spouting language that she ordinarily didn't use in front of her substitute mother.

"What is this shit? You didn't sign it, did you? Emma? Tell me you didn't sign it."

"Does it look signed?" Emma was too exhausted to even scold her for cursing. "What's got you so upset, Faye?"

"Upset" was a very pale word for the way Faye was feeling. "Enraged" might begin to cover it. Maybe. "Apoplectic" was better.

"This is a power of attorney. If you sign it…well, I'm not a lawyer, but if I read it right, signing it will give away your rights to any money your insurance company gives you to get this house fixed."

Emma's house was luxurious, because her late husband Douglass may have started life as a sharecropper's son but he'd ended it as a very rich man. The hurricane had ripped some of that luxury away and dumped a ton of rain on what was left. It was going to take a big pile of money to make Emma's house the way it used to be. Faye firmly believed that Douglass would haunt her if she didn't make that happen. The idea that Emma could have been tricked into letting somebody steal the money she needed to repair her home made Faye want to beat her head against the wall.

Emma tried to speak, but she only got out "Greta said—" before Faye interrupted her.

"Greta Haines? Greta works for your insurance company. She's an insurance adjuster. She's supposed to decide how much her company owes you and then she's supposed to tell them to cut you a check. That's all. She's not supposed to have any control over your money."

Faye was pretty sure she was oversimplifying the situation, but she thought this explanation was close enough.

"Oh, no. She doesn't work for my insurance company. She's what they call a public adjuster. You hire her to be your independent advocate, like you'd hire a lawyer. It only makes sense, Faye. Why should I trust my insurance company to volunteer to give me what I'm due? That's the way Greta puts it. I feel like I need somebody like her on my side, making sure the insurance people do what they're supposed to do."

"No no no no no, not somebody like Greta." Faye made a big show of tearing up the power of attorney. "We will help you with this paperwork."

"We? I doubt Joe's any better at paperwork than I am."

Faye tried to imagine Joe gathering the information to file a bunch of insurance claims, then filling them out and filing them, and then following up when the company threw up roadblocks to getting them paid. She couldn't do it. There was a reason that Faye ran the business side of their lives.

"Okay. Not we. Me," Faye said. "I'll take care of the paperwork."

"When? Faye, you always try to do too much, but this hurricane has made everything worse. All of it. You can't fix everything for everybody. I thought that maybe hiring Greta to help me would take some pressure off of you."

"Okay, so I can't fix everything for everybody, but let me try to fix things for you. You, Joe, and the kids. And maybe the sheriff and Magda, if they run into trouble."

"Is that everybody you plan to load on your back and carry? You're going to break, Faye."

"I've been doing it a long time and I haven't broken yet. I'll get through today. We'll worry about tomorrow later. Just please don't even talk to Greta Haines, not ever again. Don't let her in your door. Don't let her step foot on your property. Promise me."

———

Faye did her best thinking alone in the car. Damaged roads near the coast meant that she'd had to take a roundabout way to Crawfordville and back for her afternoon supply run, but the extra minutes gave her time to clear her head. She needed to sort through the sick feeling that the captain's death had left in her stomach. She also needed time to stew over the damp papers steaming gently in her back seat, topped by the torn-up pieces of the odious power of attorney. By the time she'd driven ten miles, she had a plan.

Unless the captain's autopsy turned up something unexpected, there was a real chance that his death would be declared an accident. Faye wasn't ready for that, not yet, and she didn't feel the need to wait any longer to try to learn more. There was a way to do some investigating that didn't require the sheriff's permission. And it was even legal.

When she entered the land of satisfactory cell service, she called her daughter and said, "Will you see Jeanine Eubank this afternoon?"

Amande said, "Yes," so Faye immediately said, "I've got a favor to ask."

Chapter Twenty-Three

At the end of a long Wednesday, Faye put her car in park and looked around the marina parking lot for Amande's car. No luck. The young woman was still out making her rounds. Or maybe she was picking up Michael, strapping him in his car seat, and bringing him home. It was well past five, so they both must be exhausted. Faye certainly was.

She saw Joe waiting for her on the deck with a cold drink, and she tried to remember where their boats were. If Amande's boat was here, then she and Joe could get in the one that had brought them ashore and make tracks for home. If Amande's boat was back at Joyeuse Island, then they'd need to wait. It would be really embarrassing to get a call and hear her say, "Mom? Do you want to come get us? Or do you want Michael and me to sleep in the car?"

Oh, yeah. They'd figured this all out over breakfast. Amande's boat was here. Faye and Joe could go on home in her oyster skiff, because Amande kept a tiny little life jacket for Michael on her boat at all times.

She cut across the parking lot, waving at Joe to meet her at the boat ramp, because she was just too tired to walk out of her

way. And also because she was too bone-tired to make idle conversation with Manny.

Then she saw Manny standing by the boat ramp, chatting
with Joe's buddy, Nate Peterson, and she knew that she wasn't
going to be able to avoid him. From this distance, even Manny
looked a little worse for wear, and that was notable because his
personal brand was to be utterly chill. She wasn't sure that twists
and curls as bouncy as Manny's could be said to droop, but his
were hanging closer to his sweaty face and neck.

As Faye drew near, she heard Manny and Nate talking,
mostly about the price of gas and the heat, which was still a sti-
fling ninety-five with only an hour or two left before sundown.

"Nice new paint job on that sweet, sweet boat," Manny said.
He appeared to be speaking of a sleek twenty-four-footer with
twin engines big enough to make a boat that size really go.
Nate's boat must have cost a fortune, and it must move like a
bat out of hell. Not coincidentally, that was its name. *Bat Out
of Hell* was stenciled in black across its platinum gray stern, and
matching black pinstripes swooped down its sides. It sat on a
trailer behind a charcoal-gray pickup truck big enough to haul
this boat that was almost too big to trailer. Even the truck had
black pinstripes. Faye thought that the gray-and-black color pal-
ette totally suited Nate's floating bat-boat.

"Thanks. Cody did it. He's a real pro."

"I only hire the best. Hey, that was a nice article about the
hurricane cleanup, man. It tells it like it is," Manny was saying.
"I mean, I always read your fishing column, but it's time your
old man let you do some real reporting. He was right to put that
article on the front page."

"It was Joe's picture that sold him the article. I did the reporting first. Talked to a bunch of people. Got their stories about living through the storm. Made sure to pack the piece with plenty

of human interest stuff. Then I took it to Dad, but I made sure he got a good look at that picture before he started reading. He said I did a good job on the article, but what he really wanted was that photo for the website. He thought it might go viral and get a lot of clicks, and that's exactly what it did. It's a weird way to do business, but that's how the newspaper biz works these days."

"Is Joe getting paid by the click?"

"No, he gave it to me. No charge."

Manny grunted, but he didn't say anything at first. Faye wanted to butt in and say, "Is that how you treat your friends?"

After that initial grunt and after a moment to think over the situation, Manny said exactly what Faye had been thinking. "You stiffed Joe for a picture that got you on the front page?"

"And all over the internet."

"Yeah. The internet. I guess that's where the money is these days. Is that how you treat your friends?"

Nate laughed it off, and Manny didn't push the issue any further.

Late afternoon was a busy time at the ramp. Some people were coming in off the water, but people with day jobs were rushing out to spend the end of the day enjoying the boats they'd worked so hard to buy. Nate was clearly one of the day job crowd. He was literally unbuttoning a dress shirt while he and Manny talked. His chestnut hair was trimmed razor-sharp, so sharp that a fine white line of untanned skin along his hairline proved that he'd seen his barber within the past twenty-four hours.

After shedding the shirt, Nate removed his dress pants to reveal a light beige bathing suit that was surely chosen to be close to his skin color, so that it wouldn't show through the fabric of his work clothes. One of his buddies, whom Faye recognized as

Cody, was yelling good-naturedly out of Nate's truck window as he confidently maneuvered the truck and the trailered boat behind it down the boat ramp.

Within minutes, Cody had gotten *Bat Out of Hell* afloat and was driving the truck back up the ramp. Somebody else, another of Nate's friends, based on the trash talk being thrown his way, was piloting the boat, easing it up near the dock where they stood. When the boat pilot turned his shaggy brunette head Faye's way, she recognized Thad from the dive shop.

As if the entire procedure were choreographed and rehearsed—and perhaps it was, since these men probably did this several times a week in the summertime—Nate tossed the dress shirt, the pants, a belt, and a tie over his shoulder into the boat. Based on his carelessness with his dress clothes, Faye inferred that a dry cleaner took care of them for him. Reaching down to grab the dress shoes sitting beside his bare feet, Nate flung them into the boat without looking to see where they fell. Faye wondered how long a pair of dress shoes lasted him. Thad, who seemed like a fastidious boat captain, stashed Nate's discarded clothes and shoes in a compartment near his feet.

Now that he was stripped down to his bathing suit, Nate was dressed just like Manny, but his I-work-behind-a-desk pallor distinguished them. Stepping easily into the boat, he lifted a hand in Manny's direction and said, "Later, man. I can hear the fish talking and they say they miss me."

Cody parked the truck that was pulling the empty boat trailer and hustled back to the ramp, wading out toward the boat and hauling himself up the ladder. Thad had just finished raising a black bimini that set off the boat's crisp black pinstripes. He held up a bottle of something unidentifiable, wrapped tight in a plastic bag, calling out, "Nate and Cody! Time to celebrate!"

Nate slapped Manny on the shoulder, said, "Later, man," and

stepped into the boat. He took the captain's seat as Thad handed Cody and Nate each a plastic cup.

"What are we celebrating?" asked Cody as Thad poured something golden-brown into his cup.

"We're celebrating making it through another day, dudes! And we're celebrating this afternoon on the beautiful water. It's been…well, it's been at least a couple days since we were all together. We'll toast…um…we'll toast Nate's dad for buying Nate the boat that's making this fine moment possible. How 'bout that?"

Nate seemed about as happy with his father as Amande was with Faye, most days. He held his empty cup in his lap until Thad snatched it up and sloshed an oversized shot into it.

"You don't wanna toast your dad?" Thad asked. "You should try running the business your dad built, every day that rolls, like I do. He's dead and I'll still never measure up. If I make it big and take home millions, it's just because he handed me the business and conveniently died. But if I fail, the whole town will say I disrespected his memory by running his business into the ground. I can't win."

Nate and Thad looked at Cody, as if hoping he'd unload some daddy issues, too. And he surely had them, because he said, "I showed my old man my back on the day I turned eighteen," but he didn't tell them why.

Faye cringed at the thought of these guys being miles from shore and drunk, but Florida had no open-container law to keep passengers from drinking. As long as the person piloting the boat stayed sober, these men were perfectly within their rights. And Nate wasn't drinking yet. He had let Thad pour him a drink, then surreptitiously set it on the deck, holding it upright between his feet.

Thad held the boat in place, holding the bottle in one hand

while he kept the dock at arm's length like a man determined to protect Nate's flashy paint job. He gave a hard shove. As the boat floated away from the dock, he lifted the bottle to his lips for a long swig. "Just a pick-me-up, y'all, nothing that'll impair my ability to help Nate captain his ship like the pirate captain that he is! Yo ho!"

As the boat moved slowly away, it passed Amande's oyster skiff, tied up in its usual place. So Faye's weary brain had been right that she and Joe could take Faye's skiff home now.

She was ready. More than ready.

Chapter Twenty-Four

Manny turned toward Faye. She hadn't realized that he knew she was there.

"I saw you looking at Nate and his boat."

"That thing's huge. Why does he trailer it? If he can afford that boat, surely he can afford to keep it here in a slip."

"Well, rich folks are cheap. But to be fair to Nate, he lives on a lake, and you can't blame him for wanting to keep it at home. He trailers it down here when he wants to kick back with his dude bros."

"If it was a single inch bigger, he'd have a hard time doing that, even with his big ol' truck," Faye said.

"Yeah. And if he wore those swim trunks a single inch lower, I'd have to call the sheriff to come haul him in for indecent exposure."

Now Faye was embarrassed to be caught watching Nate take off his clothes.

"I wasn't eavesdropping on purpose." She blushed and Manny noticed. "It's a little distracting when a man unexpectedly strips down while he's standing a few feet away from me, that's all."

As the word "distracting" came out of her mouth, something else distracting cropped up in her peripheral vision. When she turned her head, she saw Greta Haines backing a center console cruiser down the ramp. The long blue boat was as big as Nate's, or close to it, and she too was pushing her luck when she hauled it around on a trailer. Greta's boat was so sleek that it looked fast while it was still sitting on the trailer. Faye wouldn't have thought that insurance companies paid their adjusters that well, but now she knew that Greta was self-employed as a public adjuster. She also knew that Greta just might be supplementing her fees with money pilfered from the old and the sick.

Manny was still talking about Nate's strip-tease act. "More days than not, Nate's standing in just that spot at just this time, taking his clothes off. I've been thinking of charging admission. And maybe taking out a few ads. 'Handsome, rich man takes it all off!' I could set up a cooler right about here," he pointed in the general vicinity of his feet, "and sell beers. People would come."

Faye laughed. She'd never denied that Manny was charming and funny. The problem was that he put way too much effort into charming her daughter.

"I think you'd turn a profit," she said. "I wonder how he'd take it if you made money off of him without at least giving him a cut."

Manny shrugged. "I'm not sure he'd notice. Rich people are funny about money. One minute, they're squeezing you for every cent. The next minute, they want to act like money rains out of the sky for them and they never have to give it a single thought. You can't talk to them about the way things really are for most people. They don't have a clue, or they like to pretend that they don't."

"But you did say something to him about how he treated Joe."

"No, I never said straight out that he was wrong. That's what it takes to get the attention of somebody like Nate. If I did, it would be real interesting to see if he realized what he'd done and ponied up the money. He's certainly got it. His daddy runs the newspaper because he likes to stay busy, but he makes his real money from real estate. A hundred years ago, probably more, his great-granddaddy had the great good sense to buy up a big chunk of Micco County. I bet it never once crossed Nate's mind that he was taking advantage of Joe when the paper printed that picture for free. You know, I think I *will* say something to him about it. I wanna see what happens. Maybe I'll sell tickets to that, too."

"Oh, now I get it. Nate's one of *those* Petersons. The only person around here who ever had more of a knack for making money than the Peterson clan was my friend Douglass, Emma's late husband."

"So I hear," Manny said. "But there's a big difference between him and Nate. Emma's husband started out from nothing, and he earned his own money. No Peterson alive has done that."

"What about the newspaper?"

"I doubt it breaks even. Nate's daddy feels strongly about the free press. It seems that he's read the First Amendment. The paper's a rich man's project, for sure, because he doesn't care if it makes a cent, but it gives him something useful to do. To tell you the truth, I respect that. Many's the week that he wrote every word in it. Or so I hear. Now that Nate's home from college and helping out, the old man's able to kick back a little. He loves to fish. Used to go fishing with the captain from time to time."

"Sounds like letting Nate do more at the paper is good for Nate and good for his old man, too," Faye said.

"Yeah, but Nate's pay probably covers the upkeep on that boat we just saw. Maybe. He has a trust fund that covers his bills. He never paid a cent for college, not even out of the paycheck he got for covering high school football for his daddy's newspaper. He ain't never gone on a job interview. Ain't never wanted a job he didn't get. I ain't sure he's ever wanted a woman he didn't get. Nate's not a bad guy, but he's not quite a grown-up. Life's gotta knock you around some before you really grow up. If you know what I mean."

Faye did. It seemed to her that Thad, another of Nate's friends, had been handed a successful business that he didn't appreciate, so he wasn't much of a grown-up, either.

Cody? She wasn't sure about Cody. He did a good job of fitting in with his mildly jerkish buddies, but her heart went out to a man that young who was making his own way in the world without the benefit of a dad who gave him a great big head start.

Manny had clearly spent some time stewing about how lucky Nate was. He couldn't stop talking about the man.

"Nobody alive in Nate's family remembers what it was like to be short on money," Manny's hand moved, probably unconsciously, toward the bathing suit pocket where he kept his cash in a plastic bag. "I don't know how many ways they've found to make money off that land. The captain told me that their family bought it just so they could clear-cut the virgin longleaf pines. Then they grew more trees and more trees, so they could spend the next hundred years selling logs to the paper companies. Over time, they diversified into whatever was profitable— lumber, cotton, tobacco, soybeans, sorghum, corn, whatever. The captain said that the Petersons and all their industries have run the Micco County economy for a century or more. These days, they build property developments on their land, so that more people can move down here and wreck what's left of the place."

Faye cocked an eyebrow at him.

"Yeah, I know I just moved here. But I took over a business

that was already here and I live in an apartment that was already here. It's not like I'm tearing things up just to make a place for myself."

On this point, Faye had to side with Manny.

"Me living in my little old apartment isn't a bit different from you and your family living in your big old house that somebody else built a long time ago. Which I hear is very nice, by the way, so thank you for giving my girl Amande a cool place to live. Speaking of your family, didja know that Nate's been trying to get a date with Amande?"

Faye had not known that, and she didn't know how to respond.

"Asks her every day if he can buy her a drink, usually after he's stripped down to a bathing suit and flip-flops so he can show off his pecs."

Faye cringed and Manny saw.

"Yeah. I feel the same way about Nate and his manly chest. They don't belong in the same room as Amande. Every day, before she tells him she's not old enough to drink and walks away, he runs down the list of things he wants to buy her. A Coke, dinner, a bag of chips, a pair of sunglasses, a fine bottle of champagne. If I sell it in the store, he's tried to buy it for your daughter. Well, I guess he was planning to go to Tallahassee to get the fancy champagne, but all the rest of it was stuff he planned to give her on the spot."

"She hasn't let him?"

"Nope. Don't know why. He's maybe five years older than her, which isn't so bad. She's got him on maturity, though. He's probably pretty cute, if you're into the frat boy look. Apparently, Amande isn't. Or else she's playing hard to get, but that doesn't seem like her style."

Now Faye was wondering whether Manny was jealous of

the man's money or jealous that he wanted to spend time with Amande.

Manny wasn't finished tweaking her maternal anxiety. "Nate's not alone, you know."

"What?"

"This marina stays full of men who'd like to buy your daughter a drink. All three of the guys on that boat, matter of fact. Frat boy Nate. Surfer dude Thad. And then there's Cody, who is, to be fair, a hardworking individual. I wouldn't pay him to work in my store, and I wouldn't rent him barn space, if I didn't think it was true. As far as I know, she's told them all no, and there's no arguing with her taste. There's not a one of 'em that I'd like to see spending time with her."

Faye was speechless. How could this be true when Amande was usually standing right there next to her? Or next to Joe, who was six-and-a-half-feet tall and mildly terrifying to people who didn't know him?

Manny laughed at her confusion. "If young people didn't know how to sneak around behind their parents' backs, the human race woulda died out a real long time ago. I thought you should know what was going on."

"Tell me more about Cody. He works for you. You have to know something about him."

"It's a real part-time thing, mostly in the mornings before he starts fixing boats for his own clients. And off and on through the day, when I need help at the fuel pump."

"Is he a frat boy like Nate? Or ex-frat boy? How old is he?"

"Naw. Don't think he went to college. Don't know how old he is. I'm getting old enough that it's hard to tell the difference between an eighteen-year-old and a twenty-four-year-old. I don't see any sign that the daddy he ran away from was rich, that's for sure. Lives by himself upstream a ways."

He gestured up the creek that his marina fronted.

"Cody has got himself a little bitty place. His dang boat's longer than his house. The folks that rent it to him used it for a fishing shack, but he lives there year-round. The farther you go up the creek, the easier it is for a boat mechanic to afford waterfront property."

"But he can afford a big boat?"

"Think about what the man does for a living. Some people can't afford to pay for repairs so they leave their boat at his shop forever. Then Cody keeps it or he sells it or he fixes it up and sells it. Other people want a better boat and they like that fixed-up boat, so they trade up and Cody makes money on the deal. And then he pours that money into a better boat for himself, maybe one that he can get cheap 'cause it ain't running. Run through that cycle a few times, and a poor man can absolutely be the proud owner of a rich man's boat. The only way Cody will ever live in a house that's better than his boat will be if somebody trades him a houseboat."

Faye thought that there were worse things than living on a houseboat. She'd done it for a while. Amande had grown up on one. Her hat was off to Cody for his entrepreneurial talent. No wonder Manny trusted him with his own business. They understood each other.

"Anyhow," Manny was saying, "Cody thinks your daughter is the hottest thing around."

Faye wasn't surprised to hear this. He'd given Amande a miniature candy bar that said it was true.

"So does Nate. And Thad. They're all hot for Amande."

Faye wished she could wash out her ears. And her brain.

"I keep an eye out for her," Manny said. "Been doing that for longer than you've known her."

Faye was getting tired of being reminded how long Manny

had known her daughter. Four words escaped her mouth before she could choke them back.

"Not jealous, are you?"

"Of the little frat boys? Not a bit. Not jealous of you, either, if that's what you mean."

Manny's eyes left Amande's hopeful suitors, riding away on a big boat that was receding into the distance, and they met Faye's. Faye wasn't sure she'd ever made sustained eye contact with the man and she found it disconcerting, because there was no denying how good-looking he was. And there was no denying that Manny was her husband's age, so she couldn't hide behind any claim that he was too young to be attractive to her.

In the sunlight, Manny's eyes were a warm brown that matched the dyed tips of his hair. He was wearing it a little shorter than he had in Louisiana, sporting an up-to-the minute style with long-ish freestyle twists sprouting from the crown of his head and a close-dropped fade on the sides. It looked like an expensive style for a man who had just bought a struggling business and was working hard to get it back on its feet.

In Manny's defense, the marina's success or failure had always been directly tied to the charm of its owner. People had loved Liz for her long bottle-red hair and her willingness to say whatever was necessary as long as it was the truth. And everyone, even Faye, had loved the scalawag Wally for reasons that passed understanding, because he had possessed very few redeeming qualities.

The entire southern half of Micco County had grieved for Liz and Wally. If Manny was trying to craft a personal brand that said he was warm and hip and funny, he might well be headed for success. This seemed to be what his customers liked. Maybe that awesome hairdo would do it for him.

"I'm not after your daughter, you know," he said. "I know you think I am, but I'm not."

Faye didn't know how to respond now that he had bluntly stated something that everyone close to her knew to be true.

Her mouth gaped while she floundered for something to say. Manny was a lifelong fisherman, so she knew she must look to him like a just-landed catfish gasping for air. Joe, too, was a life-long fisherman, and she hoped he never saw her looking like that.

"Actually, I prefer older women, so I'm truthfully just a little jealous of Joe. There's nothing like a pretty woman who's smart and knows her own mind."

Manny's even white teeth flashed in his dark face, and Faye lost her train of thought. What had she been planning to say?

The only thought she could dredge up was an incoherent hope that he was being honest about his feelings for Amande, or lack thereof, because Manny's charm was potent. Faye wouldn't have been able to resist it at Amande's age. Even at her age, she found that Manny was doing a very good job at chipping away at her defenses.

"If I were Joe, I'd spend less time fishing and hunting and more time with my gorgeous wife."

Then he turned away, a move calculated to make a woman miss those mesmerizing eyes. Faye had been around long enough to see what he was doing, even as she felt its effects. A woman her daughter's age wouldn't have a chance of resisting Manny.

Chapter Twenty-Five

Amande loved her boat even more than she loved her car. It was just an old oyster skiff, not much different from the ancient oyster skiff that her mother had owned and loved since before Amande was born. Like her mother's boat, Amande's looked just awful but its motor sang like an angel, because Faye had taught her how to make it do that.

When that thought crossed Amande's mind, she adjusted it to be more truthful and also to preserve her self-esteem. She reminded herself that she had been pretty handy with a wrench long before she came to live with her mom and dad, but she had to admit that Faye deserved some credit for helping her fine-tune her skills.

Amande loved that boat because it represented freedom, the same reason that most Americans worshiped their cars, but the difference between her and a run-of-the-mill teenage driver was that she'd gotten her first boat before she was twelve. Amande felt like she'd always been free. She loved her home and she loved her family, but she stayed with them because she wanted to be there, not because she wasn't free to go. Her parents understood this, because they approached the world in the same way. This was the reason they hadn't already killed each other.

No, that was too dark. They would never have killed each other, but Amande might well have left by now if she hadn't believed there was a chance that her parents would eventually understand her. And if she didn't believe that once they did understand her, they'd still love her for who she was.

It always made her happy to pilot that junky boat out into the wild blue somewhere. Weirdly, she couldn't do that right now, because something was on her seat. She deftly snapped Michael into his life jacket and settled him in his usual spot on the deck beside her seat. Then she took a second to study the small box that was sitting where her butt should be.

The evening was late and the sun was low. Its rays struck the shiny object at a shallow angle, but they illuminated it well enough. A frilly white bow adorned the package's cobalt-blue wrapping paper. Somebody had left her a present. Was it weird that she wasn't even sure who it was from?

It could be from Nate, but he seemed to limit himself to trying to buy her drinks and dinner. She might have said yes to dinner, but he was altogether too focused on buying her liquor, as if buying a woman alcohol was the coolest thing you could do when she wasn't old enough to buy it for herself.

Thad had flashed some concert tickets at her just a day before, when Nate wasn't looking. And what if she'd said yes? How long would it take him to admit to his richer and cooler friend that he'd cut him out of a date with the girl he liked?

It peeved her that Thad was trying to get her to say yes to a date by showing her the tickets, but he was too cowardly to actually taking the risk of saying, "Will you go out with me?" Wrapping them up and leaving them for her to find—or for them to get lost in a howling thunderstorm—seemed to be about right for chicken-livered Thad.

No, she would not be going out with a man so afraid of

rejection that he couldn't spit out the words, "I like you. Want to spend some time together?"

Cody, whose light hair, blue eyes, and deeply tanned skin made him memorable, even compared to the good-looking Nate and Thad, was even less straightforward than they were. But maybe she should cut him some slack because he was the youngest of the three. She had a vague idea that Nate was maybe twenty-five or twenty-six, and Thad was a few years older than that. This meant that Thad was closer to Manny's age than hers. (And maybe to her father's. *Ew.*) And Nate wasn't far behind.

This thought did nothing to jump-start her libido. Cody, though, wasn't much over twenty. They could have known each other in high school, if they'd lived in the same state and if she had actually gone to a high school that wasn't online.

She picked up the long, narrow package and sat down. Michael, who was pretty sure that her gift belonged to him, was easily staved off with the frilly bow and the bag of peanuts in her pocket. Sliding a finger under a meticulously applied piece of tape, she stopped to consider the gift's wrapping. Heavy foil paper. Precise folds. Straight-edged seam. This thing, whatever it was, had been wrapped by a professional.

The paper fell away, revealing a white box embossed with the golden logo of a Tallahassee jewelry store. The sight of it put a lump in Amande's throat, but not in the way that the giver probably hoped. There was nobody in her life that she would reasonably expect to buy her jewelry out of the blue. Her parents would never do that. Neither would Manny. If Sheriff Mike and Magda wanted to spend big money on her, they'd put it in her college fund. If Emma wanted her to have jewelry, she'd give her something meaningful from her own jewelry box. And nobody in her life would take the risk of leaving something valuable on a boat, unattended.

She opened the box and found a bracelet crafted of heavy gold links, closed by a clasp that was set with small rubies and shaped like a heart. Tucked into the box was a small card that said nothing but "Cody." She knew how he wanted her to feel, but he had missed the mark because the only thing she felt was pissed off.

She was so mad that she started talking to herself while she maneuvered the boat out of the marina and into open water. "So you can't talk to me. And you can't even write down whatever it is you have to say. You've got nothing to say to me but your name, which is pretty freakin' self-centered, if you ask me. And now what am I going to do with this? If I want to give it back, I have to talk to you. That's more than you were willing to do for me. This is too expensive to throw away, but I'm damned if I'll wear it."

"That's an ugly word, Sissy," said Michael, his mouth still full of peanuts.

"I'm feeling pretty ugly right now, Bubba."

She gunned the motor and headed to Joyeuse Island.

———

Amande was so tired when she came home that she said almost nothing, and Faye noticed. More and more, she spent a lot of time wondering what her daughter was thinking. This evening, she learned nothing about Amande's thoughts as the young woman handed Michael over to Faye, ate the grilled cheese sandwich and tomato soup that Joe had made for her, and then retreated to her bedroom.

Michael had gone to bed, so now Faye sat in her office, listening to her daughter's feet on the stairs taking her up to her room. She could hear Amande's jeans creak and the faint sigh of her breaths. These were the sounds she would miss when Amande went away to college.

A loose-leaf document lay on the desk in front of Faye. It was a photocopy of a mimeographed copy of an oral history collected in the 1930s. The story it told was one of Faye's greatest treasures. These pages recorded the memories of Faye's great-great-grandmother, Cally Stanton. Ever since she'd talked to Captain Eubank about the wreck of the *Philomela*, she'd been waiting for a chance to see if Cally might have had something to say about it.

Faye had read the pages so many times and so closely that she'd nearly memorized them. She was dead certain that the word "*Philomela*" never appeared in Cally's memoirs, but she did remember something about a mysterious ship that visited Joyeuse Island and was never seen again. Cally may even have used the words "blockade runner," though Faye wasn't sure about that. Now she was wondering whether Cally's mysterious ship might have led Captain Eubank to his death.

———

Excerpt from the oral history of Cally Stanton,

Recorded in 1935 and preserved as part of the WPA Slave Narratives.

> *Nobody that's been hungry has ever forgot what it's like. And I've been hungry. When I was a girl, my first master would make us all hungry on purpose. Maybe it was because he'd got a chance to sell every last kernel of corn we grew that year on Joyeuse Island, and at such a good price that he didn't see any sense in holding back enough to feed to the folks that*

planted it, hoed it, and picked it. Or maybe it was because one of the field hands said something to the overseer about being tired and he decided to teach us all a lesson by cutting our rations. Sometimes, he didn't even have a single excuse for starving us, not unless you want to call pure meanness an excuse.

After my first master died and went straight to hell, things got better. For one thing, the second master, Mister Courtney, freed everybody at the beginning of the war, right before he died. That made things a helluva lot better, if you'll excuse my language. After that, it was just us on Joyeuse Island. We'd been farming it all our lives. Farming it for ourselves was better. And I was in charge, because Mister Courtney had left the whole place to me and to our daughter, Courtney.

When there was food, and there usually was, we ate. This island's a big place, so there's room to grow a lot of food. But then it takes a whole lot of food to keep a hundred people alive, don't it? One time, it rained for a solid month and everything rotted in the ground. We planted again and the fields made enough to keep us alive, just barely, but everybody was naturally more skin and bones at the end of it all.

The worst year of all came toward the end of the war. The blight got the beans, and the cutworms got the corn. I don't know what it was that ate all the collards, but I thought we'd surely all die. By that time, Mister Courtney was dead, everybody on the place was free, and I was running things, so every soul that died would've been on my head and on my heart. How could I let my people suffer?

And if you're a-wondering why we didn't just take a boat to someplace where we could get food, remember that there was a war on. Didn't nobody on land have any extra food to sell, and I didn't have any notion of reminding hungry folks about us living out here on Joyeuse Island. They would've been out here by nightfall to take what little we had to eat and I almost wouldn't have blamed them. Almost.

I wished hard for a supply boat, but I might as well have been wishing for the moon. To tell you the truth, living on Joyeuse Island in those days was about like living on the moon. Months would pass when we saw nary a soul. Not a passing boat. Nobody. Well, except maybe a war ship now and again. We did our best to pray those away, and we must've been pretty good at praying.

And then the day came when I would've been glad to see even a war ship if it was carrying food. It was the day when I knew in my heart that everybody on the place was hungry, and everybody was going to stay hungry and probably die, if I didn't fix it. Winter was out there a-waiting for us, and it was only going to get harder to put food on the table.

I'd run out of prayers. Hope, too, and it takes a lot to put me in a corner where I can't see any way to get out. I always find a way. On that day, I couldn't see how I was going to manage it.

I had sent everybody who could hold a pole out to fish. Every boat we had was on the water, full of people with shrimp nets, and the rest of us stood fishing from land. I even sent the little children out digging for worms and checking crab traps. Come dark, when the shrimpers rowed their boats in with their catch, I was gonna send 'em right back out with lanterns and frog gigs. That was my plan. Like I said, it's a lot of work to feed a hundred mouths.

I had high hopes for the frog-gigging. The tide was low. That meant you could count on the creeks along that swampy stretch of mainland just north of the island to be working *alive with frogs. And the moon was new, so there wouldn't be no light but the lanterns to make shadows that could scare the frogs. Fried frogs' legs will put you right straight in heaven when you're hungry. Even when you ain't hungry, if you're me.*

Well, one little rowboat went out frog-gigging one night and come right straight back in. I run out onto the dock ready to shake my fist in some faces. They needed to be out there finding food.

Turned out that they'd spied a ship snugged up against the shore, a-hiding from something.

"Union?" I asked. "Or Confederate?"

I wasn't sure it mattered. Soldiers in either color of jacket would be more'n happy to take the last of our food.

"Couldn't tell. But it was a big 'un, a steamship all covered with iron and running with two side wheels."

When I heard that, I hiked my skirts up past my knees, stepped into that boat, and told them to take me to that ship as fast as they could row. I thought there was a decent chance that this ship was carrying people who didn't want our food. They wanted money. I didn't have any of that, either, but maybe I had something to trade.

Chapter Twenty-Six

Faye took a moment to absorb what she'd read. It was far from the first time that she'd read this story, but she'd always been focused on the near-starvation of a hundred people. Hunger held a horrible fascination for Faye. She had been poor. At times, she'd been really poor, but she'd never been truly hungry.

She picked up Cally's oral history and carried it into Joe's office. He knew this part of Cally's story well. He liked her to read to him in the evenings, so she'd read the whole oral history out loud to him more than once, but he particularly liked this part. Joe loved to go frog-gigging along those same creeks Cally had described, so her story put him right into the past.

From a hunter's point of view, frog-gigging was fun on a primitive level—no gun, no bow, just a long-handled fork for spearing prey. And what could be better than a nice evening on the water that ended with an all-fried-food midnight meal? Distracted by Cally's gripping tale of hunger and by the frog-gigging, neither of them had ever given much thought to the steel-sided boat outfitted with two paddlewheels that Cally had seen.

With Joe sitting in a chair pulled up beside her, she pointed at

Cally's description of the ship and said, "During the war, there were a ton of reasons for a ship to lay low like that. Both navies had ships floating all along American coastlines."

"Yep," Joe said. "No matter who you were, half of those ships you saw—give or take—would have been happy to blast you out of the water."

"Exactly. And if you were a blockade runner like, say, the *Philomela*, and if it was as late in the war as Cally described, then the people who wanted to blow you out of the water were the ones who were winning."

"Also, they were the ones who still had bullets. And cannons."

"Yeah, that's a good point. But look here." Faye pointed to the part where Cally said that the ship was "snugged up against the shore" and said, "Even its location is suggestive. Think about it. A ship that could lurk in tidal wetlands would have had an extraordinarily shallow draft."

"That's something that a blockade runner would surely need. It's not like they could waltz into a big port to do their buying and selling."

Now Faye laughed out loud. "Can you imagine them sailing right past the Union Navy into Mobile Bay? I can just hear the captain saying 'Never mind us. We're just here to buy and sell some contraband. We'll be on our way after we finish trading with your enemy.'"

She opened a browser window on Joe's desktop computer and said, "Let's take a look at some ships like the one Cally saw." Then she typed in a search string.

iron-hulled steamship

She clicked on "Images," and they sat back and looked at a bunch of cool old ships. When she tweaked the search by adding "blockade runners," the screen filled with sleek, low craft. Most had masts as well as paddlewheels, because the world was barely a half-century into the steamboat era when the Civil War began. Steam engines weren't always reliable, but neither was the wind. Shipbuilders in those days liked to hedge their bets.

"Here goes nothing," she said as she added two words to the search terms:

twin sidewheels

Nothing on the screen changed and Joe said, "Well, crud. I thought that would help."

"Oh, it helped," Faye said. "It told us that iron-hulled, blockade-running ships with twin steam engines weren't all that common. The internet can't even dredge up a picture of one, at least not on this first page."

She changed the search from "Images" to "All," and she was rewarded with a list of links to articles on iron-hulled side-wheeled steamships with twin engines that made her yell "Oh, yeah!"

Joe silently fastened his green eyes on her. He might as well have said what he was thinking right out loud: *Are you planning to explain to me why you're so excited?*

"First of all, there are only two ships on this first page. One of them is the *SS Syren*. She's famous for running the Union blockade thirty-three times, more than any other ship, so her twin-engine design clearly did what it was designed to do. It made the ship fast. The *Syren* is so famous that she has crowded almost every other ship remotely like her off the first page of the search."

Joe pointed at a line about halfway down the screen. "Except for that one."

Faye gave a satisfied sigh. "Yes. Except for that one. Except for the *Philomela*."

The *Syren* had survived all those blockade runs, only to be captured in Charleston Harbor just a few months before the war was over. The *Philomela*, too, had continued shuttling goods and money in and out of the Confederacy until very late in 1864, but she was never captured. Nor was she sunk by a Union ship. She presumably sank in a fierce storm, somewhere near Apalachicola, Florida, where she was last seen. Apalachicola wasn't all that far from Joyeuse Island, not in the grand scheme of things, and the wreck could be even closer to their island. Nobody had ever known exactly where she went down.

Except, perhaps, for Captain Edward Eubank, who believed he'd found her. The captain might have spent his last moments diving on the *Philomela*. Or on some other nameless ship that the internet didn't know about. But Cally had seen a ship toward the end of the war—say, 1864 or 1865—and the *Philomela* sank late in 1864. There was a very real chance that this was the ship that Cally saw. It wasn't out of the bounds of possibility that the captain had been hot on her trail when he died.

Faye turned back to Cally Stanton's oral history and began reading it out loud, so she could share it with Joe.

———

Excerpt from the oral history of Cally Stanton,

Recorded in 1935 and preserved as part of the WPA Slave Narratives.

The evening was almost full dark, with hardly any moon and the stars hiding behind the clouds. I sat in that boat a-listening to the night wind. The singing of the crickets got louder and louder as we got closer and closer to shore. The frog-gigging lanterns were all the light we had. Soon enough they lit up the iron sides of a big, big ship.

I had ahold of a frog gig, in case I needed to defend myself, but I put it down when I got an eye full of that ship. No one person could defend theirself against something that size, not to mention the people that it carried. I certainly couldn't do it, sitting in a little boat way down at the water-line. I sat there and looked up...up...up. The hull stretched so far to my left and right that it looked a million miles long.

You can't know how big it was unless you could be there with me, sitting in a rowboat and just floating. I can still hear the lapping of the water on the sides of our little boat as we sat in the little bay where the ship was anchored.

The lantern light shone down into the water and lit the backs of fish skittering into the shadow of our boat. The frogs I'd been a-hoping to eat were making big plops all along the shore, hopping into the water. I remember how the fish and the frogs took my eyes away from the big iron boat, just for a second, because they reminded me how bad I wanted something to eat.

It's been a lot of years since then and I've forgot a lot of things, but I know this: When I climbed into that rowboat, I hadn't put a bite of food in my mouth all day long.

If I'd been a-planning to sneak up on the ship, then I would've put the lanterns out, but that wasn't what I wanted to do. I sat in that boat hoping against hope that somebody was on watch that night who would see us and our lanterns a-coming. And they did.

One man after another came up on the deck and looked down at us. I could hear them talking amongst theirselves, but I couldn't hear a word they said. I couldn't count 'em, but there wasn't a bit of doubt that they outnumbered the five of us in the rowboat.

When we got close enough that I thought they could hear me, I picked up a lantern and held it high, yelling, "Ahoy the ship!"

I held its light close to our faces so they could see who we were, not Union nor Confederate sailors but people who had been born in bondage. "Ahoy the ship!" I hollered. "We need your help."

They threw down a rope ladder. It wasn't any small job to get up it in my long skirts and petticoats and button-top shoes. I almost didn't have the strength. I had to tell myself, "There's food on this ship and you're here to find a way to get some."

The captain had a kind face, and I hoped that meant that he wasn't planning to kill me or the men who brought me. He found me a place to sit down before I fell over. Then he handed me a cup and said, "You say you need our help. Tell me what it is you need, but first drink up. You look like death on two legs."

I didn't have to be told twice to drink my tea. It was well-sugared and I was weak from not eating, so it tasted like melted gold to me.

It's funny how something simple like a cup of tea can make you trust somebody. What did I know about him? There I sat, the only woman on a ship full of lonely men. What was to keep them from lifting anchor and taking me someplace where I'd never see my home again?

Well, that might happen and I couldn't stop them, so I put it out of my head. I had an important thing to say and I had to trust that the captain was as kind as he looked. I told him how it was with us. I was living every day with hungry men, hungry women, hungry children, and not nearly enough food stored up to get us all through the winter, which was a-coming sooner than I wanted it to.

He turned to a man standing beside him and said, "Go fix this woman a plate and pile it high. Don't forget to bring her a piece of that rum cake we ate this evening." Seeing the look on my face, he said, "Make sure the men who brought her here are fed, too."

When that man talked, people listened, because I had a plate in front of me before I'd taken another good sip of tea. He waited until I'd chewed through a few bites before he asked me to tell him more about myself, but he got around to it. By the time I was working my way through the rum cake, my story had all came out in a rush. I ain't usually so free with my words, especially not back then. Being under the thumb of a man who calls himself your master will do that to you. I must have been half out of my mind with gratitude to see all that food in front of me.

I told him that my people had been taken out of Africa to work on Joyeuse Island for a terrible man, but he was dead and all of us on Joyeuse Island did our own work now. I had papers to show him if he wanted proof.

"Oh, my dear," he said. "President Lincoln freed you all a year or more ago."

Maybe I shouldn't have let my tongue get salty, but I did. I told him that I talked Mister Courtney into freeing us a long time before that. And I told him that we'd been fending for ourselves since Mister Courtney died, using nothing but our strong backs and good minds and not a cent of cash money. I made sure he knew that we could grow our own food, but we couldn't make money out of thin air. We didn't have no *other way to get it, so we couldn't buy supplies. We had to make do with what we grew in the ground. Still and all, we'd done right fine until the cutworms ate the corn, thank you very much.*

I did a lot of talking, feeling guilty about my full stom-ach, since I still didn't know whether he had any food in the cargo hold for me to take back to everybody else. I knew that blockade runners—and I was pretty sure that's what he was—mostly ran cash crops out of the Gulf of Mexico and brought food back in. If he was on his way out, he might not have much onboard to eat. And maybe that didn't make no never mind, because I didn't have a cent of money to buy it with, anyway.

But I did know one thing about blockade runners that might save us. They didn't just bring food back through the blockade. They brought fine, expensive things for rich folks who'd managed somehow not to lose all their money in the war—things like wine, silk, jewels, liquor, and spices. That's where they made their real money, selling fancy things to rich people who thought they was suffering because they was having to live without them.

I didn't have any of them things to sell him, but I did have a library full of Mister Courtney's fine books, leatherbound with golden edges on their thin, smooth pages. Rich people liked to have pretty books on their shelves. I knew that. I certainly dusted enough of the first master's books.

I also knew that they didn't always read them. Mister Courtney had read all his books, but his mama? And her husband, the first master? Oh, hell no.

Me? I loved those books. They kept me company on the long nights when everybody else on the island had gone to sleep and left me to do their worrying for them. I would miss those books, but I could live without 'em. None of us could live without food.

I offered him the books and he laughed in my face. That's when I thought we would all be starved to death by springtime.

And then he told me that he could spare twenty barrels of supplies for us. He said, "I'd give you more, but I'm carrying no food for sale, just supplies for my crew. Fortunately, we've got more than we need. Even without the twenty barrels I'm giving you, we'll have enough to make Havana. I can restock there."

The word "giving" was echoing around in my head. I wasn't sure I'd heard right. I was afraid to believe that he was going to give us what we needed to stay alive, not asking for a thing in return.

"I have some beautiful first editions. They would for sure bring you a fine price, if you have agents who can get them someplace like Richmond or Montgomery," I said.

He pulled a bottle out of a cabinet behind him and poured a good splash of brandy in my tea. "Drink up, Miss Cally. I don't want your books. Well, perhaps just one, if you will inscribe it as a gift to me."

After we were finished talking, the captain's men stood on the deck and handed down enough food to fill the boat, leaving just enough room for me and the men to sit. They emptied their kitchen larder, so we carried a big load of whatever-you-got back to the island for a midnight feast, knowing that twenty barrels of supplies would be coming the next day.

I can still see the food being handed down to the folks in the boat that night. They gave us the carcasses of three chickens left from their evening dinner, heavy with meat *somebody left on the bones. Loaves of stale bread. Bags of cold boiled potatoes. A tray of biscuits. A vat of cornmeal mush and another one of boiled cabbage. To tell you true, most all of it probably came out of a slop bucket where the cook had dumped that day's leavings and maybe the leavings from a couple of days before that, but it looked to me like a gift from heaven. I divvied it all up among a hundred people and nobody got full, but nobody went to sleep that night with a stomach that was empty and hurting.*

The next day, the captain himself came to Joyeuse Island with the men that he'd tasked with bringing the barrels of food to us, some of 'em full of cornmeal and some of 'em full of flour. Two was full of salt pork and we made that pork last a month, at least. One was full of lard. Twenty barrels won't keep a hundred people alive all winter, that's for sure. But put it together with fish and frogs and oysters and crabs, plus the pitiful little bit we grew that year, and we all came through all right. Stronger. Tougher. Maybe a little meaner, but still alive.

The captain took his leave of me by lifting his hat and bowing over it a little. He treated me like the lady that I have always believed myself to be, and that made him uncommon.

"It will be spring before we come back through this part of the Gulf. With your permission, I would like to stop to learn how you and all your people fared during the winter."

I thought of the barrels of food stored safely in the basement of the big white house where I slept upstairs in the master's old bedroom, and I said, "I expect we will fare very well, but we would be most proud to be able to thank you again."

"I expect you will fare very well, too. As a man who has spent many years with people under his command and in his care, I have a great deal of trust that no one in your care need

ever fear that you will shirk your duty to them. Nevertheless, I will make a stop here come spring to see after your welfare and to pay my respects." Then he tucked the book I gave him tight under his arm like it was a treasure, and he lifted his hat again before he walked away, exactly as gentlemen do in books when they take a lady's leave on a city street.

But he didn't make that stop in the spring or ever, and that worried me for a time. To tell the God's honest truth, it worries me still. He was not the kind of man to break his word.

Word was slow getting to us, but we did eventually hear about Appomattox. As that year dragged on, I supposed that the surrender had put an end to the need for blockade runners. Maybe this was why the captain never made the stop he said he'd make.

I hoped so. I hoped he and his crew had slipped back into their old lives after the war, whatever those old lives were. I certainly hoped that they didn't wind up in jail or at the bottom of the ocean.

That's the trouble with living on an island, far from the world. People pass in and out of your life and you never find out what happened to them after they leave you.

Chapter Twenty-Seven

Faye slept lightly, and at first her dreams were full of cornmeal and bullfrogs with fat, juicy legs. Then they shifted to images of her friend alone, floating, helpless, with nothing to breathe but cold seawater. Until she knew what had happened to the captain, this nightmare would be a soft, black spot of rot at her center. She would never really rest while it was there.

Faye lay awake in the gray light of dawn and saw that Joe wasn't sleeping either.

He met her eyes and said, "Tide's low and getting lower."

Within minutes they were in their bathing suits. It would have been unkind and borderline immoral to skip out on helping hurricane victims, just so they could take a swim and explore the bottom of the Gulf of Mexico. But who would judge them for enjoying the water for a couple of hours early on a Thursday morning before they came ashore and got to work?

"Let's go for a snorkel," she said.

Light was seeping from beneath Amande's door, making Faye wonder whether her daughter ever slept. When Michael reached Amande's age, she would know what his habits had been for his entire lifetime. She'd notice when his sleeping patterns changed or his appetite ebbed, and thus she'd have a reasonable shot at knowing when her son was depressed or struggling. Amande had arrived in her life at sixteen, nearly grown. Faye felt like she was parenting in the dark.

She tapped on the door, and Amande opened it.

"Do you mind keeping an ear out for Michael? We'll be back in a bit. If he's hungry, give him a little bite, but don't worry about breakfast. We'll fix something when we get back. Or maybe we'll just eat at the marina."

In a boat, they could have gotten out to the The Cold Spot in the time it took them to walk from the house to the water's edge, but Faye didn't want to take a boat. She didn't want to drop an anchor and risk damaging whatever was down there.

A shipwreck? A Paleolithic occupation site? Faye almost didn't care, because either of them would be pretty cool. With the water this low, even the motor's wake could disrupt fragile archaeological remnants. Wading, with occasional stretches of swimming, was a far safer way to get out there than boating.

A plummeting anchor could also destroy evidence from Captain Eubank's last moments. She ached to know what had happened to him.

It was entirely possible that she and Joe were making their way out to the very spot where he had died. Faye was walking outdoors at dawn in a bathing suit, so she was already a little cold, but this image sent a chill creeping up her spine.

Change was in the nature of water. The water that drowned the captain had moved on, dispersed by currents in all directions. One of those currents had carried his body to the marina. Those currents might also have carried away everything he left behind—strands of hair, DNA-carrying skin particles, maybe even a carabiner from his equipment bag. It wasn't likely that evidence remained from his death, but the odds weren't zero.

For example, she doubted that a current could carry a weight belt very far.

Joe reached into the storage shed that he'd built on their beach so that their equipment would always be handy. "What do we need? Masks and snorkels, but no fins?"

"Sounds about right. The water's so shallow that fins would just get in our way, especially if we need to stop swimming and walk. Let's just wade in."

The water was only cold on Faye's legs for a moment. The sun was rising so fast that she could see it move, and the color of the water was changing just as fast. As its rays reached the bright white sand beneath her bare feet, reflected light made the water glow electric green. By the time the water reached her knees, it was the color of the turquoise ring her grandmother had given her when she was thirteen. As it reached her hips, it was a clear, pure, uncomplicated blue, and Faye's happiness at being there in that moment was just as uncomplicated.

"I know about where The Cold Spot is," Joe said, "but I'm not a hundred percent sure I could walk straight out to it."

"Me neither," she said. "That's another reason I thought it made sense not to bring the boat. This way, we'll feel it when the water gets cold."

"Yeah," Joe said, and the look on his face said what he was thinking so plainly—*You know how bad I hate cold water*—that Faye couldn't help laughing.

"Look at me," she said. "This water's up to my shoulders and it hardly covers your navel. I don't want to hear anything about how cold you are."

He shifted the conversation back to the question of where in the heck they were going. "I know The Cold Spot isn't quite straight out from the beach. It's more to the west, getting toward the end of the island."

"Good thing the hurricane wasn't too bad here. If it changed the shape of the coastline too much, we may never figure out where we're going."

"Let's hope it didn't," he said, wading farther from shore.

It took ten minutes of walking for the water to reach her chin. Faye put on her mask, put her snorkel in her mouth, lowered her face into the calm water, and stretched out on top of it. Patches of dark seagrass dotted the sand below her. Brown-shelled scallops were tangled in them, each with a rim of bright-blue eyes. The rhythmic opening and closing of their shells seemed to Faye to drive the motion of the water around her.

As she paddled slowly forward, she passed a school of fish, each as small and silvery as a new dime. She could see the bottom falling away a bit, so she raised her face to tread water, reaching her toes for the bottom.

The sand was out of reach, deeper than she'd expected. Even Joe couldn't quite touch bottom while keeping his face out of the water. She put her snorkel back in her mouth, pointed her head downward and kicked hard for the bottom.

The sea grasses tickled her belly as she skimmed over them. If the *Philomela* had gone down near here, she sure didn't see any sign of it. It looked to her like Captain Eubank had risked his life for nothing, but she wasn't surprised that she saw no sign of the old steamship. If it had sunk here, so close to Joyeuse Island, Cally would surely have known and she would have talked about the wreck in her oral history. Faye knew for a fact that she didn't.

The sand beneath her continued to slope downward. Taking a moment to surface and grab a chest full of air, she dropped to the bottom again, beckoning to Joe as she swam. Everything looked as it should—seagrasses, shells, sand, fish—and that's not what she was hoping to see. She wanted to see something human-made and disruptive. Part of her wanted it to be a shipwreck at the end of a long debris field. A bigger part of her wanted to see stone tools, the black burn mark of a hearth, mastodon bones, and anything else that would prove her theory that The Cold Spot marked a Paleolithic occupation site.

She didn't actually want to find evidence that her friend had drowned here, but she had to admit to herself that seeing it would be a positive thing. It would make his death more real to her, and it might ease his sister's mind. Hard evidence might prove, once and for all, whether his drowning was really an accident.

She didn't know what kind of evidence to hope for. Maybe the captain had left behind a flashlight or some other piece of equipment that he'd dropped while struggling not to drown. And, of course, there was the missing weight belt. Surely the loss of a human life would have left a trace, no matter how small.

She surfaced for another breath. Joe surfaced next to her, blowing the water out of his snorkel before diving for the bottom again.

The water around her was chilly, much colder than it had been when she first got into the water. She hadn't even noticed it cooling off. It appeared that they'd found The Cold Spot, proving that Joe's navigational skills were as fearsome in the water as they were in the woods. She'd been to this place countless times, but something was different today. How could there be something different about an expanse of wide open water?

Treading water, Faye kept her face above the surface as she turned in a slow circle. It quickly became clear what the difference was. In all directions, small wind-driven waves rippled the water's surface, as they always did on a day when the waves were calm, but she and Joe hovered in a patch of water that was as smooth as ice. The area of calm water extended for twenty feet or more in all directions.

She'd seen this phenomenon many times in freshwater creeks but never in the Gulf. It marked a place where the flow of a constant, steady upwelling of water was strong enough to blunt the effects of the wind rippling the water's surface.

She caught Joe's eye and knew that he saw it, too.

"Do I feel water coming up from the bottom?" he asked.

"You do," Faye said.

They each dove for the sandy seafloor below.

The seagrass obscured her view of the seabed, but the feel of rising water on her skin took Faye where she wanted to go. As she got closer to its source, the moving water began to tickle her skin like bubbles in champagne. Her face was barely a yard from the bottom when she saw it.

There was a crack in the world. The bare white sand was interrupted by an almost-circular expanse of exposed tan-to-dark-brown rock, about seven feet across, which must have been the reason for the dark round area that Ossie had seen from so high in the air. In its center was a long narrow crack that had to be the thin black slash that Faye had seen in Joe's sharpest, closest photo. She could see through the crack into a dark void that was like a small cave.

Water flowed out of the crack with enough force to stir the green grasses surrounding the area of exposed rock. The hurricane had scoured away the sand and debris that had once filled it. Many, many years had probably gone by since the water had flowed freely, but it was doing that now.

Faye had been right about the spring, but this didn't necessarily mean that Captain Eubank had been wrong about a sunken ship. It wasn't impossible for the two things to exist in the same place.

She looked around for signs of anything man-made. There was no hull, no debris field, not even a torn section of the

Philomela's rusted iron sheathing. If Captain Eubank did drown in that spot, he had seen no shipwreck in his last moments.

She moved as close to the crack as she could, wishing she had her fins to help her make headway against the strong current belching out of it. Did Captain Eubank swim into the opening, trying to access a cave on the other side?

She had friends who couldn't have resisted the call of this crack in the earth. She worried that one of those friends might someday die from insatiable curiosity. Cave diving was one of the most dangerous sports in existence. Even a few skydivers had survived equipment failure, still alive after a long fall to the ground. A cave diver whose equipment fails dies, every single time.

Desperate for a breath of air, she lingered, exploring the lips of the opening with her fingers. The crack was big enough to admit both her hands to the wrist, just barely, if she'd been foolish enough to cram them in there.

Was it big enough for even one arm? Nope, not that she planned to try it. There was no way Captain Eubank could have thought this crack was big enough to swim through, even if he'd somehow been able to shed his equipment.

Joe dropped down beside her. Her lungs were bursting, so she left him staring into the slender opening and headed up for air. Shortly after she broke the surface, he followed.

"You see that?" he asked as soon as he could get his snorkel out of his mouth.

"The spring vent? I absolutely did. And the opening's not big enough for Captain Eubank to pass through."

"D'you think he might have gotten stuck somehow? My heart nearly stopped when you stuck your hands in there."

"My hands never passed through the opening. Not even the tips of my fingers. I might take some risks sometimes, but

I'm not stupid. But here's an important thing—I didn't see any signs of a struggle. Did you? It seems to me that if the captain was stuck in an opening like that one, you'd see evidence that he'd tried to get himself free. The area of exposed rock is small enough that his legs would totally have extended into the sand. You'd see marks where he struggled. And his weight belt would be somewhere nearby."

"You'd see torn-up seagrass, too."

"Exactly," Faye said. "I didn't notice any traces of a struggle at all. Did you? Honestly, everything I saw looked pristine, but let's go back down and look again, just to make sure."

She tried not to think about a man flailing around, trying to free a stuck foot or hand from that opening in the rock. Water would have been piled on top of him, waiting to silently end his life, and this image made Faye want to stay on dry land forever. She honestly didn't think the captain was foolish enough to jam any body parts into the crack, at least not hard enough to get stuck.

And if he wasn't trapped like that, how could he have drowned? The water was so shallow here that he could literally have bounced off the seabed and breached the surface over and over again, grabbing one breath after another while he worked to shed his gear. Then he could have walked or swam to shore as easily as they'd gotten to this spot.

Heck. He could have dog-paddled.

"This isn't the place," Faye said, surprising herself by how certain she was. "This isn't where the captain drowned. I'm sure of it."

"Me, too."

Chapter Twenty-Eight

Faye wished she liked Lieutenant Baker better. The young woman was probably a perfectly lovely human being, but weren't officers of the law supposed to know how to deal with the public?

Faye had left the lieutenant a voicemail as soon as she and Joe got back from their snorkeling expedition. She supposed that the woman's three-hour delay in responding was reasonable, but Faye was not a patient person. Baker's delay in meeting Joe on the day Ossie was shot had been rude, to say the least. This delay in returning Faye's call made the rudeness seem intentional.

By the time her phone rang, Faye and her family had taken both oyster skiffs to shore. They had consumed heaping plates of Manny's pancakes, and now they were splitting up for the day. She'd just finished buckling Michael into his car seat in Amande's car when her phone rang. As she pulled it out of her pocket, Amande pulled out of the parking lot, on her way to do her daily rounds.

"You wanted to speak to me?" The lieutenant's tone was cool and professional, but it would not have hurt her to say hello before launching into the conversation.

"I wanted to let you know that Joe and I swam out to the spot where we were thinking Captain Eubank might have been diving."

"Did he say he was planning to dive there? To you or to anybody else?"

"No, but he and I were talking about a possible shipwreck in that spot just hours before he—"

The lieutenant couldn't be bothered to let her finish her sentence. "But there's no physical evidence that places him at that spot. And no witnesses that say he planned to go there."

"No, but—"

"I'm interested in evidence, not supposition. I'm working with scarce resources and that means I have to target my activities. I can't run out into the Gulf on a hunch, not any more than I can randomly search all that water."

Faye was literally chewing on her tongue to keep from lashing out. There was no point in alienating one of the few people in a position to get justice for her friend.

She took a deep breath and spoke calmly. "I hear what you're saying, but I'm going to tell you what I know. You don't have to listen, but I don't have to stop trying to get you to listen. Even if you hang up on me, I'm going to write down what we saw and send it to you."

"You found some evidence that he'd been there? You found something that makes this spot different from the whole wide Gulf?"

"No, I didn't. That's the thing. I thought that there was a good chance he'd gone out there, but I found no trace. No weight belt, for sure. I found the spring vent that I think he might have been heading for, though. There's a chance that he could have caught a hand or foot in it and drowned, but I think we'd be able to see marks in the sand made by his legs as he fought for his life. And the vegetation in that area is undisturbed. The most important thing, though, is that the water there is very shallow. Yeah, you could drown there, but it wouldn't be easy."

"Well, if you want to send me an email and include a map showing this place where the victim didn't die, you can do that. That will make one less spot in the great big Gulf of Mexico for me to worry about. Right now, I need to get back to checking out the whole rest of the world. The autopsy is our best bet at finding something concrete. I also think that there's nothing concrete to find. I think the autopsy will show no signs of foul play at all."

Faye wanted to say, "Why did the sheriff order it then, if he thought it was pointless?" Instead, she kept it simple. "Will the report be in soon? It's been almost two days."

"Ma'am, I'm pretty sure that the autopsy is being done in a morgue that's still using a generator for power. But everybody on this case is a professional. If there's evidence of foul play on that body, it'll be found. Maybe it has been found. The sheriff has other things to do besides babysit this case that you just won't let go. But if the autopsy doesn't turn up anything suspicious, I can't see much reason to think this wasn't a simple and sad diving accident."

Faye took a breath, intending to answer her, but Baker interrupted even her quiet breath.

"I mean that. It *is* sad. Truly. But the time I spend trying to prove the obvious—which is that Captain Eubank's death was an accident—is time when I'm not using my resources to find two missing people. Or to track down the looters who shot a gas station attendant last night."

Faye had the sense that Lieutenant Baker wasn't always like this. She was coming off of a long string of nights without sleep and days full of never-ending work. Faye sympathized, so she didn't reflect Baker's anger back at her. She just said, "We're all tired these days."

"I'm not tired. I'm outraged. Did you see the picture of that mother? The one who's missing along with her little boy? I guarantee you that I've shed more tears over them than her husband has. There's no way that his fairy tale holds water. He is not the kind of man who wades out into a flood to save his family. And I don't believe the next-door neighbor, either. He knows something, and he won't say what it is. One of them knows what happened to that woman and child. Maybe both of them know. If you were wondering where I was while your husband was waiting for me, now you know. I was with the husband and then the neighbor—questioning them, pressing them, trying to get them to break."

Faye didn't know what to say, other than "I'm so sorry. I had no idea."

"Next time you want to think that I should be watching your husband fly his toy instead of trying to get the truth about that woman and her child, you go get a copy of the newspaper and take a look at their faces."

———

After another morning of boarding up broken windows, Faye took a break and called her daughter. She didn't have a lot of hope of getting through, but lunch was the time when Amande was most likely to be picking up her afternoon supplies in Crawfordville. This meant that there was a decent chance that she had cell service. And she did.

"You caught me just before I drove back out into the land of dead cell phones."

Amande sounded almost glad to hear from her. Faye hoped

that this attitude stuck around. She needed to remember how happy it made her daughter to feel needed.

"Did you do that favor for me?"

"Yep, I went to Miss Jeanine's house first, like you asked me to. Guess what's in my back seat?"

"A big, big pile of paperwork that includes a power of attorney made out to Greta Haines? Unsigned, I hope."

"Yep."

"Thank you, sweetie. You did something really important for Jeanine. What did she say about letting me check on the captain's house?"

"She said that you were more than welcome to do that. If you don't mind, it would be a big help if you'd air it out a little while you're there."

"It's the least I can do."

"She said something else, and this made me a little sad."

Everything about Jeanine Eubank's life was sad right now. "What did she say?"

"She said that she wanted you to take anything you wanted from his library. She doesn't want anything out of the house except family photos. She's going to hire somebody to do an estate sale, but she knows you appreciate all his books and maps and stuff. She'd rather give them to you for free than sell them to somebody who just wants them because the shiny gold printing on the spines looks good."

Faye wanted to pull the car over and cry. When that library was broken up, it would be as if the captain had never existed. He really would be dead.

"But you know what, Mom? There's at least one person who wants those books for the right reasons. Besides you and me, I mean."

"Who's that, sweetie?"

"Her name is Samantha Kennedy. I've seen her at Miss Jeanine's house twice now. She's there now."

"Samantha Kennedy? I know her. I interviewed her for a job."

The words, "But I didn't hire her," hung in the air asking to be said. Faye had a soft spot for young people trying to get a start in the world, so she didn't say them.

Amande said them for her, more or less. "There's got to be a reason you didn't hire her. You and Dad have some big contracts coming up soon. You're gonna need warm bodies to do all that fieldwork."

Faye heard what Amande didn't say, which was that she wasn't planning to be around to help. "That's why I didn't hire her. Samantha is very smart. You saw how young she is, but she's already got a PhD. And a Master of Library and Information Science, too. But she's just not a field archaeologist. Samantha has tons of intellectual stamina, but I need somebody with the physical stamina to dig all day with an actual trowel."

"That's what most people want from an entry-level archaeologist," Amande said.

This was true, but Faye was surprised that her daughter had given this much thought. Maybe she wasn't wrong to harbor a hope that she could hand the business down to Amande someday.

"You're right about that, sweetie. Samantha was born to be a professor, but the academic job market is in the pits these days for people who want full-time work. And by full-time work, I mean teaching jobs that pay a salary you can live on. Last I heard, she was teaching single classes here and there, making about a third of what she'd make teaching the same classes in a tenure-track job."

Amande said, "Well, that sucks," and her tone said that Faye had just dissuaded her from ever considering a life in academia, but her question was on a different topic entirely. "Is she from around here?"

Faye was surprised at this question. If there was one thing that Amande wasn't, it was provincial. "No. She's from somewhere up north. Indiana, I think. Why do you ask?"

"I'm just wondering how she knows Miss Jeanine. It's not like she gets out much."

"Did Samantha say why she was there?"

"Oh, yeah. Now I remember. The first time I saw her, she was there to return one of the captain's rare books. Maybe she and Miss Jeanine really hit it off and she came back just to keep her company. That's really sweet. Maybe Miss Jeanine wants to be around somebody who likes books as much as the captain did. I bet Samantha reminds her of her brother a little bit."

The lump in Faye's throat was back. It came back at odd times when she remembered Captain Eubank and really understood, deep down, that she would never again hear him enthuse over something cool that he'd just learned. Her silence broke the rhythm of the conversation, making it obvious to Amande that her mother wasn't doing very well.

"Mom? Are you okay?"

Faye prided herself on being the buffer between her children and a hard world, and now she'd failed at that. Again.

"I'm fine. Just fine. Did you get a key to his house like I asked you to?"

"Don't be silly. The captain lived in Crawfordville. I'm surprised that he locked the house at all. Miss Jeanine says there's a key in the garage. It's on a shelf over his workbench, under the third Sir Walter Raleigh can from the left. You can go on over there right now. You don't have to wait for me to bring you a key."

Now Faye remembered watching the captain scoop Sir Walter Raleigh pipe tobacco into cigarette papers, rolling his own smokes and carefully licking the paper to seal them into neat cylinders. With this memory, she was undone, but she still managed to say, "Well, that makes it easy to get in the place. And the garage isn't locked?"

"The garage key is under the doormat outside the side door of the house. The one that goes into the kitchen. I guess the captain liked the idea of a burglar standing on that doormat trying to figure out why the key he found under it didn't fit the door."

And now Captain Eubank felt alive to Faye again, smoking a roll-your-own and enjoying one last laugh against intruders who might want to steal his precious books.

———

The third Sir Walter Raleigh can from the left was heavy, because it was full of nuts and bolts instead of tobacco. So was the second Sir Walter Raleigh can from the left, but Faye was pretty sure that the nut and bolts in it were ever-so-slightly smaller. And the nuts and bolts in the first tobacco can from the left looked infinitesimally smaller still. Captain Eubank's workshop was as meticulously organized as his library, minus the Library of Congress numbers. None of the tobacco cans were labeled, but Faye felt sure that the captain had known exactly where his 5/16-inch hex bolts were.

She palmed the key and headed for the kitchen door. Once through it, she saw that everything in the captain's kitchen looked the same as always, except it didn't. A fine layer of dust dimmed the sheen of the countertops he had kept so brilliantly waxed. A faint sprinkle of black dots on the grout around the kitchen window showed the beginnings of mildew, because decay happens fast in a steamy climate. The captain would have hated seeing his kitchen look like this.

Faye's hair was beginning to stick to her sweaty neck, and she thought that she, too, might begin to mildew soon. A stack of opened mail sat on the corner of the captain's kitchen table, and the corners of the individual sheets of paper were beginning to curl in the humidity of a house where the air conditioning hadn't run for days.

This brought her up short. The captain wouldn't have turned off the central air just because he was going to be gone for a few hours. He probably wouldn't have turned it off if he was going to be gone for a week, because heat and humidity wouldn't have been good for his books and maps. As she listened to the quiet house, she realized that she had never been there when it was utterly silent. The captain's dehumidifiers had always been a humming counterpoint to every conversation.

Who had turned off the central air conditioner and the dehumidifiers? Jeanine?

No, wait. It couldn't have been Jeanine who shut off the A/C. She was housebound.

Would the deputies have done that when the sheriff sent them to check out the house? Maybe, if Jeanine had asked them. Faye didn't see any visible signs that they'd been there, so the sheriff had been serious when he'd called it just a walk-through.

Faye dialed Amande's number and had the great good luck to get through again. "Did Jeanine say if anybody else has been in the house since the captain died, other than the people from the sheriff's office?"

"She didn't have to say. I know at least one person who's been in there. Yesterday, I heard Greta volunteer to close things down for her. Shut off the water heater, empty the fridge, turn off the A/C, return the cable box...that kind of stuff. It was nice of her to think about those things, wasn't it?"

Faye mumbled an insincere, "Yeah."

"It's good thing she did, or else Miss Jeanine would have been stuck with a kitchen full of rotten food, not to mention bills for electricity and cable that she didn't even use. Greta said she would wait to shut off the water and electricity until after the house sold, because the estate sale people and the real estate agent would want them on, but the cable's off now. I never would have known what needed to be done. Sometimes I think I'll never be a real grown-up because there are just too many things to do. I'll never know how to do them all."

Faye thought that Amande would navigate adulthood just fine, but she did not like her daughter being on a first-name basis with a woman who seemed to be doing her best to cheat vulnerable people. She thought of the innocuous-looking power of attorney that Greta had given Emma, and she thought of all the ways it could help an evil person cheat somebody like Jeanine Eubank. Greta could offer to handle the estate sale and pilfer anything valuable she found in the house. She could lie about how much she made on the sale, giving Jeanine a pittance for all of her brother's worldly possessions. She could even sell the house and pocket the money, and the captain's own sister might never know.

That was the advantage of cheating somebody old and house-bound. After a few years of Jeanine asking, "Did my brother's house ever sell?" and Greta answering, "Not yet, dear," the older woman would eventually die. In her condition, she might never come into town again, and Greta could make that even more likely by doing Jeanine's shopping for her and urging her not to exert herself. When Jeanine died, her estate would be settled, Greta would wave her signed power of attorney at the estate attorney, and all the lying and cheating would be done. It would be wiped away as if it had never happened. All but the money in Greta's pocket, that is.

Faye got a sick feeling when she remembered the pile of paperwork that Amande had seen at Jeanine's house. Somebody evil could have slipped anything into that pile, where it now sat waiting for her signature. Faye needed to go through that paperwork, page by page, and help Jeanine get her affairs in order.

Faye was not ignorant of the fact that this was essentially what Greta had offered to do for Emma and probably for Jeanine, too. She ignored that quibble, because she knew that her motives were pure, and she had deep doubts about Greta's.

Chapter Twenty-Nine

Feeling like a ghoul, Faye stood in the captain's kitchen and flipped through his mail. She found nothing but bills and advertising circulars. Everything else in the kitchen looked exactly as it had during her last visit, so she moved on into the library. It, too, looked exactly as it had.

The library's walls were still lined with floor-to-ceiling bookshelves. A large worktable and the captain's personal desk still dominated the center of the room. The room still smelled like library ink and dust, but the acrid tang of mildew was beginning to intrude.

Amande's voice came out of Faye's phone. "Mom?"

"I'm here. Sorry. I got distracted by the captain's books. I forgot to ask you something when I called before. Did you give my message to Jeanine?"

"Sure did. I told Miss Jeanine that you wanted to help her with her paperwork. I made sure nobody was around when I asked. She was so so so grateful, Mom. I had a box with me, just like you said, so I loaded the papers all up. It was a really good idea for you to offer to take care of them for her."

"Thanks, sweetie. I think it's the right thing to do."

Standing in the middle of the captain's vast book collection, Faye spun in place. She saw any number of volumes that she'd love to have in her personal library, but she saw nothing out of the ordinary.

A teetering pile of books on the captain's desk caught her eye. Some of them had ragged linen covers and some were wrapped in cracked leather, but all of them were old. Had they been there before? Faye wasn't sure.

She leaned over sideways to read their spines. Some of them were too timeworn to have legible titles, but a few of them did. She saw early copies of Harriet Beecher Stowe's *Palmetto-Leaves* and Frank Parker Stockbridge's *Florida in the Making*, as well as an old promotional book aimed at bringing people to the Florida Panhandle to work in the lumber industry. Atop the stack was a Hammond's Complete Map of Florida from 1912. She knew these books and knew that their publication dates bracketed the late nineteenth and early twentieth century years when Micco County's longleaf forests were clear-cut by people like Nate Peterson's ancestors. She also knew somebody who would be interested in these particular books.

"Amande? Do you remember what book Samantha Kennedy was returning to Jeanine?"

"It was an atlas of railroads in the Southeast around the turn of the twentieth century."

Yep. That book fit perfectly with this stack of volumes that could have been hand-selected to appeal to Dr. Samantha Kennedy. And they probably had been hand-selected, because that was the way Captain Eubank treated his friends.

———

Faye had ended her call, then circled the captain's living room. She was looking for the shelves where he'd stored books with Library of Congress numbers beginning with F, which denoted books on local history in the Americas. She also scrutinized GE titles on environmental science and SD titles on forestry, arboriculture, and silviculture, all of which probably had Samantha Kennedy's fingerprints all over them.

On a hunch, she did a web search for Dr. Samantha Kennedy and Florida history. A sizable number of scholarly journal articles popped up, especially considering the woman's youth, and they were in some highly respected publications. Since it was the twenty-first century, the web search also turned up social media posts. Even in those, Dr. Kennedy was focused on her career.

> Do any of you people have access to documents that show railroad spurs in Micco County in the early 1900s? Not the permanent ones. I'm looking for the ones that served the temporary sawmills that moved on when the trees were all cut down. Surely somebody drew maps showing those but I can't find them. I'm also coming up dry in searches for photographs of those sawmills.

The post was a year old, but none of her Twitter friends had been able to help her. Maybe the book she'd returned to Jeanine had shown where the spurs were, but it wouldn't have had photos of the mills. Samantha might well be looking for documents that didn't exist any longer. This was the kind of wild goose chase that the captain would have loved.

Faye studied the shelves full of books in Samantha Kennedy's field. They were all neatly filled from end to end with books. If she—or anybody else—had taken and kept anything from those shelves, it wasn't obvious to Faye. And why should Faye think she'd done that? She knew that the woman had just returned a book voluntarily, when it was a reasonable bet that nobody would ever have known she had it.

Faye hated herself for being so suspicious. The absolute worst motivation that she could ascribe to Samantha Kennedy was that she might be kissing up to Jeanine Eubank so that the old woman might give her some rare books she wanted.

And what if Jeanine did give them to Samantha? They were her books now. She could burn them if she wanted to.

———

Samantha Kennedy crouched in Captain Eubank's azalea bushes, waiting. Traffic along the street in front of the captain's house had been nonstop for ten minutes. She couldn't risk being seen, so she resigned herself to wait for her chance.

Her phone was open to a photo she'd taken on the last occasion she'd crouched in these azalea bushes. It was hard to read the titles on the captain's books on this small screen, but her computer screen had been big enough to do what she needed. She knew now for certain that the captain's library held the books that could make her career.

Samantha had done everything she could think of to prompt Jeanine Eubank to offer her the pick of Captain Eubank's library. She'd had no luck.

The old lady had said that she dreamed of finding a home for her brother's collection where it could be available to anybody who was interested in it. Donating it to a university library wouldn't serve that goal, because university libraries were for the use of their students and professors, not the general public. But nobody else had the kind of money that it took to take care of all those fragile bits of paper.

Jeanine was Samantha's last hope, but she was no more cooperative than her brother had been. He, too, had wanted his library to be open to everybody, forever.

Samantha couldn't live with that. She didn't want everybody to have access to the books she had in mind. If everybody had access, then somebody might publish their findings before she was able to write them up. It was a slam dunk that a tenured professor would have more time to write those articles than Samantha would, running as she did from class to class and from college to college. These days, she was waiting tables, too, because the class she needed to make her income livable had been canceled at the last minute.

Samantha had her eye on three books and just three books. They were as rare as they could be, because she knew of no other copies, but they wouldn't bring much money on the open market. Nobody but Samantha and two rival academics had any interest in them whatsoever, but for the three of them those books could mean scholarly publications and respect. If she played her cards right, they could bring her a full-time job doing the work she loved. They could bring her a retirement account. They could bring her health insurance.

Samantha wanted them out of the captain's house and safely hidden in her own home. The captain had denied her this. So had his sister.

If this meant that she had to steal those books, then so be it.

———

Faye had spent too much time prowling among a dead man's treasures. She could so easily conjure up the living memory of her friend while she stood surrounded by his things, but the memories lasted only so long. When they dissipated, she was left with nothing but the memory of him floating facedown in the water.

That image made her shiver. She moved away from the shelves of books that Samantha Kennedy probably coveted—away from the all the books, actually—and she found a place to stand in the exact middle of the room.

Right next to her, so close that she couldn't move without bumping it, was the chair where she'd sat during her last talk with the captain. Unsure why she had ever thought that coming to his house was going to help anything, she dropped into that chair to think.

The newspaper with Joe's photo on the front page still sat where she and the captain had looked at it together. His green teacup, made with the clean art deco lines of the 1920s, sat across the worktable from her, right where he'd left it. It had belonged to the captain's grandmother, and it had been his favorite.

Faye could see him even now, sipping his tea and holding that newspaper. The image made her breath catch in her throat. She held the cup up to the light. Its porcelain was so thin and fine that the cup was translucent.

The fact that the captain's cup was still sitting here might mean that he had walked out to his car as soon as she left. It was possible that he had driven straight to the marina and gotten into his boat for the last time. If so, he could have drowned within an hour or two of seeing Faye. Or he might have sat in that chair, sipping tea and pondering the *Philomela*'s end for hours.

This train of thought presumed that he left alone. She saw no signs of a struggle, and it seemed far-fetched to imagine that someone would burst in, forcing him into the car, onto his boat, and into the scuba gear that he would wear to his death, without leaving some sign. She supposed that a hurried departure could be explained equally well by the sudden arrival of some friends who said "Hey! Let's go diving," but this explanation turned quickly dark when she asked why those friends didn't call for help when he drowned.

As her memory of their time together grew clearer, she remembered the stack of Joe's photographs that the captain had pulled from a drawer in the desk behind him. The idea came to her that she should take another look at those photos. It seemed so clearly the right thing to do that she set the cup down decisively, so hard that she reflexively checked it to see if it had broken. No, the fine porcelain was too tough for that.

The pictures weren't on the worktable where she thought he'd left them, so she checked the drawer. The photos weren't there, either, and they weren't in the kitchen or in his bedroom or in either of the bedrooms that he used as library annexes.

Had he taken them with him on that last boat ride? That seemed out of character for a man with the instincts and habits of an archivist, but she couldn't find them in any of the logical places where he might keep pictures.

Taking printed photos out on the Gulf of Mexico in a small fishing boat was a guarantee that they'd be sprayed with saltwater. This thought reminded her that the captain's boat hadn't been found. She wondered if it ever would be. He had loved that boat. She didn't like to think of it floating out into the Gulf or capsizing or sinking or running aground in a coastal swamp, taking another small remnant of her friend's life with it.

If the captain hadn't taken the photos with him, there weren't many ways to explain the fact that Faye couldn't find them. One scenario supposed that someone had come to the house before the captain died, he let them in, and he gave them the photos. Or perhaps that person or persons took him and his photos against his will but took nothing else. Another scenario said that an intruder had entered the house after the captain left, taking the photos and nothing else.

Faye knew for a fact that Greta had been in the house, so she was a prime candidate, but there was nothing to say that someone else hadn't done it. It really wasn't that hard to get into the captain's house. Anybody could have known which Sir Walter Raleigh can hid the key.

Was there anything else missing from the library, other than the photos? The room—the whole house, really—had always been so orderly that she couldn't imagine anything out of place. Lieutenant Baker must have found searching this home to be quick work.

But had she searched it, really? It didn't look like anyone had done things like empty the drawers and move the furniture around, as they would have done if they'd been working a murder investigation or a drug bust. Because it wasn't a murder investigation. She needed to remember that. Lieutenant Baker certainly wanted her to remember it.

Lieutenant Baker and her crime scene investigator had checked to see whether the captain had left a suicide note or whether there was some other clear sign that something in his life wasn't right, but that was all. And her tone during their recent phone call had left Faye no doubt about one thing. The lieutenant would not have gone a single step further than her assignment in investigating this case.

Faye wasn't even sure what a sign that the captain's life wasn't right would look like. Evidence of a break-in might do it, perhaps, or some sign that he was mentally ill, like hoarding or unsanitary living conditions. Lieutenant Baker hadn't found those things, so she had moved on.

In a way, Faye was grateful. She would have been so sad to see his library overturned and scrambled. There could have been no greater desecration of his memory. The captain had always sat patiently with each visitor to make sure that they got whatever they needed from his collection.

The thought of his library visitors made Faye's eyes turn involuntarily to the small table by the door where he had kept the sign-in sheet. He had maintained it faithfully, because he was proud that people used his collection and because those attendance records had helped him earn the grants that funded his historical work.

The sign-in sheet was gone.

Chapter Thirty

Dr. Samantha Kennedy crept along the side of Captain Eubank's house. She moved quickly, considering that her flimsy sandals weren't made for creeping through piles of pine straw and dead leaves. She needed to make it around the side of the house and slip into the back yard before somebody drove by and saw her.

And she must not be seen. Samantha was desperate for validation, for recognition, even for a job that met her minimal needs. To get those things, she needed those books, and she was more than willing to break a window, crawl through it, and take them.

She passed the window where she'd taken the photos, the all-important photos that she'd used to pinpoint exactly where the critical books were stored. There was no need to turn her head and look into the room again, but human beings do many things reflexively. The contents of that room's bookshelves were critically important to her, so she couldn't help herself. She looked.

There, her back to the window, sat a woman who had turned Samantha down for a job she desperately needed. She wanted to pick up a rock and throw it through the window at Dr. Faye Longchamp-Mantooth's head.

Instead, she dropped to all fours and backed quietly away

from the window. There was no sense in trying to get to the books until the intruding Dr. Longchamp-Mantooth was gone.

Samantha knew that she'd lost her chance at working for this woman because she was too cerebral and not outdoorsy enough. Or at least Faye Longchamp-Mantooth had judged that this was true. Now that she was moving on her hands and knees, rather than struggling with her inappropriate shoes, Samantha found that she was as agile as she needed to be.

Maybe the opinionated Dr. Longchamp-Mantooth, who had made her thoughts clear by the way she eyed Samantha's shell-pink nail polish, would have been more impressed if she could have seen how well she moved when the occasion required her to scrabble in the dirt. Maybe she would have understood that Samantha Kennedy was someone who could do whatever needed to be done.

Samantha crawled through the azaleas, bush by bush. When the coast was clear, she escaped to the sidewalk, where she had as much of a right to be as anybody.

If anybody had been paying Samantha any attention at all, they would have seen the brown stains on the knees of her beige pants and the green twigs in her auburn hair. But she wasn't the kind of person who attracted attention, so they didn't. She moved inexorably away from the house where Faye sat, but she would be back. Faye couldn't sit there forever.

Samantha faded into the distance, plotting her return.

———

Faye stared at the empty spot where the captain's sign-in sheet should be. Who would have taken it? Probably somebody who didn't want anybody to know that they'd spent time here with the captain.

Faye looked at the stack of books on the captain's desk, all of them dealing with Samantha Kennedy's research interests. Her name was almost certainly on that sign-in sheet. But so were the names of the people the captain had mentioned, the ones looking for the *Philomela* and other nearby shipwrecks. Amande's name was on it, since she said she'd been here recently to do a school project. Faye's was on the list, probably more than once, but she was certain that she hadn't stolen it. Other than that, there was simply no way to know who took it and why.

She slid her phone out of her pocket and dialed the sheriff directly. She was done with presuming that Lieutenant Baker considered this investigation to be worth her time.

"Did your people take anything when they came to Captain Eubank's house, Sheriff?"

"No. They didn't find anything out of the ordinary, so they left."

"And they haven't been back since that first day?"

His answer was quick and firm. "If we find something that indicates that the captain's death wasn't accidental, then we'll do a complete search of the house. Until that time, I see no reason for my people to be plundering through a dead man's things."

"Well, I'm at the captain's house at the moment, but I'm not plundering through his things. At least not much."

Faye could hear some testiness in the way he dragged in a breath and blew it out. "And you're there why? Do I need to come arrest you for breaking and entering? And are you touching anything? Stop touching things."

Faye jerked her hands away from the captain's beautiful books and stuffed them in her pockets. Then she remembered the timing of her last visit and said, "This house was already full of fingerprints I left behind just a couple of days ago. I'm here because his sister asked me to check on things. I have her permission, and I have a key, so I don't think this qualifies as breaking and entering. Is it unusual for a friend to help the family out when somebody dies suddenly?"

"No, but I don't usually get calls from people standing alone in a deserted house that ain't theirs. So why did you want to know if my people had been there?"

She noticed that he didn't ask why she was calling him instead of Lieutenant Baker. He had to know that she and Baker did not see eye-to-eye on the captain's death. Baker had probably told him exactly how annoying Faye was.

"I called because there are some things missing—a stack of photos and the sign-in sheet that kept track of his visitors."

"You're sure?"

"I saw them here the afternoon before Amande found his body, so yeah. I'm sure. If his last day was as simple as it should have been—he drove to the marina, got on his boat, and never came home—then everything in the house should be pretty much like it was when I last saw it. And it is, except for what I just told you."

"Some pictures and a piece of paper? What did the pictures show?"

"They were aerial views of the area damaged by the hurricane. Joe took them right after the storm passed. You saw one of the same batch. It was on the front page of the newspaper."

"Well, if it was in the newspaper, it ain't much of a secret. Could be that one of the other pictures showed something that the thief didn't want people to see, though. You got any idea who would want those things?'"

"The pictures? I don't know. But maybe somebody's name was on the sign-in sheet and they didn't want anybody to know they'd been here."

The sheriff's wordless grunt said, *I can't argue with that logic.*

"Was it a notepad? Did they take the top sheet and leave behind a sheet with impressions of the signatures made by the pencil point?"

"That would be handy, but no. It was a clipboard and the whole thing is gone."

"Well, damn."

Faye's eyes raked over the gilt-embossed spines of the captain's books. "We've been overlooking one motive for murder."

"I'm so glad I have you to tell me about my mistakes."

"No, this one's on me. I'm the one who spends a lot of time working with rare books. Any of the books in this room could be worth real money, and it could be shelved next to a worthless book that looks just like it. There's no way to tell just by looking. The leather-bound ones with gold lettering could be worthless. The ratty-looking ones with worn-out cloth bindings could be priceless."

"You think somebody wants to sell off his collection? Maybe they've already started. Can you tell if any of 'em are missing?"

"There can't be many books gone, because it would be obvious. The captain kept his shelves exactly full. No big gaps. Certainly no overcrowding, because that totally messes up a book's spine. If a thief has been here, it was somebody who knew what to look for. And it was somebody who knew how to cover their tracks by sliding a few books off their shelves but no more."

"Could you do that? And, no, I'm not accusing you. I just want to get a mental picture of who might be able to pull off something like that."

Faye shook her head as if he could see her. "No. Well, I could take a few books and make it look like I didn't. But I don't know his collection well enough to know which ones are valuable."

"What would it take for you to figure out which ones were worth a lot of money?"

"I'd need access to the captain's card catalog—and I do literally mean a card catalog. He maintained a physical catalog, so there would have been no way to access the information from anywhere but here. I'd still need an internet connection to check the prices of individual books, one at a time, and I'd need plenty of time spent right here in this room to check on their condition. Not to mention the other rooms where he kept his maps and such. It would take for-frickin'-ever, but it could be done."

She looked around the room and wished she had the time to give the captain's collection a good going-over.

"Maybe that's why somebody stole the visitor log," the sheriff said. "If they hadn't, it would have told us that somebody's been spending a lot of time in the captain's library. And the captain would certainly know who's been there. If any books went missing before he died, he might have been suspicious. Maybe he even confronted the person. That wouldn't have gone well for him, because criminals tend to be dangerous."

Faye was still studying the printing on the spines of a thousand books. Several thousand books, probably. "That's exactly right. But it's not like somebody killed him in a fight, shoved his body in a wetsuit, and dumped it in the Gulf. That would be obvious during autopsy."

"Heck," the sheriff said. "I'd have seen it on sight. You might even have seen it on sight. You saw the body."

Faye tried not to think about the way the captain had looked hanging in the water. When she was here with his books, it was almost like he wasn't dead.

"Maybe the thief thought it was better to get rid of the captain before stealing his stuff," she said. "We do know one other person who has been inside this house since the captain died. Besides your people, I mean. And besides me."

"Who would that be? And how do you know?"

"Greta Haines. I saw her standing outside in the yard just a few hours after we found him. I was just driving past the house and I saw a car I didn't recognize, so I stopped to check things out. I thought it might be Jeanine, and I wanted to pay my respects."

"Did she go in the house?"

The sheriff sounded interested. Well, good. Faye wouldn't be sorry for Greta Haines to get a little close attention from law enforcement.

"I know she's been inside sometime, because Amande says that Greta shut the captain's house down for Jeanine. Could she have been doing that when I saw her? Maybe, but the timing is tight. Jeanine got cell service sometime that day. I guess Greta could have called her and come right over. More likely, she was here again later. I didn't see her go in the house with my own eyes, though. I didn't see her do anything but poke around in the yard."

"Did she say why she was in the yard?"

"She made some lame excuse about checking for hurricane damage." Faye tried to make sure that her voice communicated how hard she was rolling her eyes at Greta's lameness.

"She's an insurance adjuster. She's allowed to do her job."

"Well, yeah. As long as she isn't overstepping herself. Florida is full-up with crooks trying to make a buck off of old people. I know for a fact that Greta tried to get Emma Everett to sign a power of attorney that would give her control of her insurance reimbursement. Is that illegal?"

"Not unless she was coercive about it. I've known some fishy public adjusters, and Greta Haines may well be one of them, but I've never heard any complaints about her."

Faye snorted. She tried to keep it quiet so he wouldn't hear it on the other end of the call, but she failed.

"It's not necessarily illegal to ask somebody for a power of attorney," the sheriff said. "Maybe Jeanine wants somebody to help her manage her personal business. She's entitled to authorize someone to do that. Adults get to decide how their own affairs are managed. That's the very definition of being an adult. Ain't it? And it's the reason powers of attorney were invented."

Faye snorted at him again.

"However," he went on, "Greta's got a license that requires her to maintain ethical standards. The licensing board might have something to say about it if that power of attorney doesn't meet their rules."

"Yeah, but even if what Greta's doing is legal, it doesn't mean that her motives are on the up-and-up. Maybe she was trying to get her hands on the captain's house, now that Jeanine's going to inherit it. And maybe she's got some kind of back-channel deal with the tree contractor who's going around town with her. Cyndee Stamp's her name."

"I know Cyndee Stamp. She's Greta's cousin."

This was news to Faye.

"Their family relationship raises some more questions," the sheriff said, "because it's not cool for an insurance adjuster to funnel work to a family member, especially if she's using an ethically questionable power of attorney to do it."

Faye rose from the table, twitchy with nervous energy. She might as well use that energy to see if anything else in the house looked fishy.

"I'll do some more checking into the Greta-and-Cyndee situation," the sheriff said, "but it's a far reach to say that Cyndee and Greta murdered the captain, just because they have some fishy business practices. As for the captain's rare books, maybe we should make sure some of them are actually missing before we go too far down that alley, don't you think?"

"Yeah," Faye muttered as she thought dark thoughts about insurance fraud and elder abuse.

"Faye, I get the definite sense that you think I should be handling the captain's death differently, despite the fact that it was very probably accidental." The sheriff's voice was remarkably calm for someone asking "Do you think I'm incompetent?"

Faye tried to answer him, but he kept going. "Do you care to tell me what you think I should do about a drowning case with not the first sign of foul play? That's a pretty weak basis for a presumption of murder."

Faye might have a suspicious nature, but she was honest. "No. I've got nothing but some missing pictures, a missing visitors' log, and some shady characters that were seen around the house. And a dead drone."

"I've got no clue who shot Ossie, and that's for true."

Now even the sheriff was talking like Ossie was a human.

"I'm listening to you, Faye. I am. You're telling me that the shady characters who've been seen at the captain's house had at least a half-baked excuse for being there. And we don't know for sure that he didn't move the pictures and paperwork himself. Tell me you haven't turned that whole house upside down."

"No. I haven't."

"I know you've been hired to help with law enforcement before, so let's talk for a minute, professional to professional. I know what I saw when we assessed the body on-site, and so do you. There was nothing to suggest a struggle, not under the water and not on top of it. Nothing to even suggest that he fell out of the boat and couldn't get back in. The medical examiner said that he most likely drowned, but the evidence isn't conclusive. A heart attack or stroke wouldn't be out of the question, but a violent attack is."

He paused, like a man working hard to lay out a convincing

argument. "You want me to treat this like a murder, but that's hard to do when the body says something different."

Faye closed her eyes and sighed, glad that the captain's last moments didn't involve a beating or a struggle. "Has the autopsy told you anything else yet?"

"No sign of foul play. Some of the lab work is still out. Blood alcohol was undetectable."

Faye studied the beautiful green teacup. "The captain was a complete teetotaler. Literally. He drank almost nothing but tea. And root beer."

"Then that explains the undetectable blood alcohol levels. The toxicology lab's still working, but they haven't turned up any drugs yet, legal or not. No poisons, either."

"So there's no sign of a murder."

"Affirmative. And don't forget this. A clean toxicology report doesn't just reduce the possibility of murder. It reduces the likelihood that he committed suicide."

"Suicide? Oh, that's not possible. I never saw him without a smile."

"Do you know how often I hear the family members of suicide victims telling me how happy they were before they offed themselves? By the way, suicide by drowning isn't too common, but would you care to guess what demographic group is the most likely to die that way?"

"The captain's?"

"Yep. Older, Caucasian, and male. It hurts to get old alone, and the numbers say that it's harder for men. We can't rule out the possibility that an older man without much close family might not tell anybody that he's too depressed to go on."

Faye walked through the captain's cherished library, brushing her hand over the gilt lettering on old leather books. "He was in the right demographic for a cardiac event, too."

"Affirmative. It wouldn't have had to kill him, just incapacitate him so that he couldn't save himself from drowning. Autopsies aren't foolproof in these cases, but the medical examiner did find water in his lungs. Everything about the condition of the body screams 'accidental drowning.' And there's nothing about his house to suggest otherwise, but it does seem weird that those pictures and that sign-in sheet are missing."

Somehow, despite the sheriff's towering pile of evidence that was supposed to make her feel better, Faye still wasn't completely sure that her friend wasn't murdered. As long as that possibility existed, she wasn't sure that she would ever rest well again.

"I hear you, and I understand what you're saying," she said. "Tell me why I can't let this go."

"The truth is, Faye, I don't disagree with you. There's no arguing that all the evidence points to a tragic accident. Still, there are a few tiny, cold, uncomfortable things that don't really count much as evidence, but they bother me. You pointed out one of them yourself. Nobody ever knew of Captain Eubank going diving. He never said he didn't, but he never said he did. And we all know how much he loved to talk about his hobbies. Is that even circumstantial evidence? Yeah, I guess, but it ain't strong."

Faye looked around at the shelves of books. A tranquilizer dart sized for a rhinoceros couldn't have shut the man up if somebody asked him a question about Micco County history. And she was supposed to believe that he was a secret scuba diver?

"Here's something weakly, barely circumstantial that I bet you don't know," the sheriff went on. "Considering our location here on the Gulf, it's no surprise that we deal with more than our share of drowned scuba divers. Usually, the victim is found without his mask, because it's just a reflex to rip it off when you're terrified. And there's usually a weight belt right there around the victim's waist that they didn't or couldn't get off while they were trying to get to the surface. It's a sad thing to say, but scuba divers usually die from panic. The literature backs me up on that."

His words called up the searing image of a human being trapped underwater, struggling with panic and despair. Faye had been holding onto hope that the captain hadn't known what was happening. She'd prayed that he'd died quickly, without panic and pain. She was afraid that the sheriff was about to obliterate that hope.

"The captain didn't fit the usual profile, and that's bothering me. He'd shucked his weight belt, so he wasn't in a total panic. Most likely, he made a mistake or his equipment malfunctioned, and he saw that he was running out of air. He dropped the belt, just like he was supposed to, and he tried to make it to the surface, just like anybody would do. The autopsy suggests that he took water into his lungs at some point, but that could easily happen in those last moments when he's trying to get to open air. Probably, this was all a tragic accident, but I'm an investigator and that means I'm suspicious at heart. I understand why you don't want to let this drop."

This attitude surprised her. She said, "I appreciate that, Sheriff."

"Bottom line, Faye? Captain Eubank just didn't make it, and that breaks my heart. Nothing will bring him back, but the world will feel like a better place if I can find out what happened to him."

"Then I don't suppose you mind if I look around his house a little more before I go?"

"You're doing exactly what a good friend would do, but you need to get out."

Faye thought this was a remarkable change of attitude. "I'm sorry. What?"

"You said that there were some photos missing? And a sign-in sheet?"

"Yes."

"Well, then, now I have a possible theft to investigate. Have you touched a lot of stuff?"

Faye looked regretfully at the teacup. And the spines of the captain's books. And the worktable and chair. And the doorknob. And the desk's drawer pull.

"Um…yeah? I did touch a few things. But I already told you that the place has got to be full of my fingerprints."

"Yeah, but I don't want you to smudge somebody else's. Leave everything as it is and stop touching stuff. I'll get Baker and her assistant back out there to look for physical evidence later today, but I want to talk to you myself right now. At the very least, you can show me all the places where you've been leaving a trail of fingerprints."

Chapter Thirty-One

Faye didn't know how to atone for the fact that she'd left finger-prints all through the captain's kitchen and library. Oh, heck, she'd probably also left a broad trail of hairs, clothing fibers, and footprints, not to mention skin particles that were just loaded with her DNA. But then so had Greta, and they'd both had Jeanine's permission to be in the house.

At first, she thought her best plan was to go wait for the sheriff in her car, so that she wouldn't do any more damage. Then she thought about how she'd go about opening the door without adding another set of her own fingerprints to the mess that was already there. And if she used the hem of her shirt to cover her fingertips when she turned the knob, would she be wiping off the prints of a thief? Or a murderer?

Of course, if she just stayed where she was, sitting on an antique wooden chair in the captain's beautiful library, she'd continue to drop bits of her DNA on his gleaming oak floor in the form of hair and bits of skin. So what was she supposed to do? She decided that the library was already heavily contaminated with her DNA, but if she avoided touching anything, she could keep her fingerprints and skin oils to herself. She shoved her hands in her pockets.

It took about five minutes of reading the spines of the shelved books for Faye to decide that she might go stark raving mad before the sheriff arrived. Fortunately, her ringing phone saved her from both boredom and madness.

The call came from someone she didn't know, but the number was local. She answered it, and a hoarse, angry voice began speaking as soon as she said hello.

"There ain't no call to be interfering in anybody's business. Their livelihood! What'd you say to Emma Everett and Jeanine Eubank, anyway? What right d'you have to tell them my paperwork ain't up to snuff?"

Confused, Faye took a moment to respond. She'd definitely interfered in Greta Haines's business, but this was not Greta's cultured, upper-crust voice nor was it Greta's meticulous grammar.

Faye's mother had taught her to use particularly meticulous grammar when she was angry and thus in danger of cursing, so she said, "To whom am I speaking?"

"This is Cyndee Stamp, and you oughta know it. I run an honest business, and there ain't a thing wrong with me paying a visit to two nice ladies and asking if they need me to do some tree work for 'em. Where do you get off, telling Emma Everett and Jeanine Eubank that I might maybe be a crook? I ain't never been so embarrassed as I was this morning, making follow-up calls just like always, and getting an earful of spite from Ms. Everett."

Faye could just imagine what kind of spite Emma would put in the ear of somebody trying to cheat her. "You're right. There's nothing wrong with making a business call, doing some work, and getting paid for the work you did. I do that kind of thing every day of the week. I don't, however, ask old ladies to sign over their insurance checks. I especially don't slip them the paperwork to sign over those checks without explaining the consequences of their signature."

"Um...what? I hate paperwork and neither of them ladies ever got any from me, not yet. I give my clients a written estimate when they ask for it, not before. I do my work. I give 'em a bill, and they pay it. Ain't none of my business what goes on between them and their insurance companies."

Faye thought that she might just believe Cyndee. Then again, she had been stupidly trusting before.

"Does your cousin Greta Haines ever contract her clients' work to you?"

"Um, yeah. She brings me business, she pays me for the work, and she takes a cut. When did that get to be illegal?"

"Maybe it's not illegal. But you might want to talk to Greta about where she gets the money she uses to pay you. I'm pretty sure her business practices are unethical—so unethical that they could cost Greta her license—and they may well be illegal. If I didn't want to lose my own business, I'd check into how she's running hers."

There was a wordless sound on the other end of the line, as if Cyndee didn't know whether to thank her or curse her. Instead, she simply said, "I'll do that," and ended the call.

Fifteen minutes later, Faye was very glad to see the sheriff pull into the captain's driveway. Her wait wasn't quite over, however, because he took the time to walk around the house before coming in.

This gave Faye a chance to think that he was right to be thorough, but she doubted that he was going to find anything because she knew for a fact that Greta had a key. He wouldn't find any signs of a break-in if she was the one poking around in the captain's stuff.

Then she saw the sheriff walking around toward the side door, putting on a pair of crime scene gloves. A moment later, he stuck his head in the door and said, "Come out here. I found something. Somebody's broken into this house."

———

The evidence of breaking and entering was not subtle. Someone had broken a windowpane in the captain's master bath. Faye had missed it when she went looking for the photos, but Lieutenant Baker had looked in there during her walk-through. This meant that somebody had broken the window since the afternoon of the day that Amande discovered the captain's body.

The vandal had chosen a window on the opposite side of the house from the driveway. It overlooked one of the captain's monumental azalea beds and it was shaded by large trees that kept it from being visible from the street, the back yard, or the neighbor's property. It was well-hidden from anybody who wasn't poking around in the bushes or standing in the captain's bathroom.

Summer breezes played with the lace curtains the captain's aunt had hung in that window long ago, when the house was hers. Their hems brushed against broken glass strewn across the windowsill.

Faye was so glad that it hadn't rained. Jeanine had said that she didn't want anything out of the house, but she might feel differently if Faye brought her these antique curtains and offered to hang them for her. Jeanine had lost so much to the wind and rain, and she'd lost so much to death. She might enjoy having something so lovely at her windows.

"But Greta knew where the key was," she said, not willing to give up her pet theory that the unpleasant woman had been the one who stole Joe's photos and the sign-in sheet. "Why would she break the window?"

"Well, maybe somebody else did it, somebody besides Greta."

"She might have already broken in before Jeanine told her where to find the key. Maybe on the day I saw her in the yard."

The sheriff gave a brisk nod. "You're right. It could have been her. We can't afford to eliminate anybody at this point."

"Or it could have been her cousin Cyndee Stamp, the tree contractor. I just got a threatening phone call from her."

The sheriff's voice was concerned. "What kind of threats?"

Faye thought back through the conversation and corrected herself. "Maybe 'threatening' is too strong a word, but she definitely wanted to tell me how I should behave. And I don't think she knows about Greta's little powers of attorney."

"Maybe Cyndee is the one who's been in the house. Come look at this."

He walked to the base of a large tree that overhung the corner of the house.

"See the damage to the gutters?" He pointed up. "And the siding is scraped really bad. It's even splintered here and here." He pointed to two battered boards that were impossible for anybody standing in the back yard to miss. "It looks like that big limb broke off. You can still smell the sap."

He wasn't wrong. The turpentine-y smell of pine burnt her nostrils.

"The storm brought down a lot of branches all over Micco and Wakulla Counties. You've seen that, Faye. The captain was lucky that this one wasn't bigger and that it didn't hit the house squarely."

"I see it and I smell it, but I can tell you that the house wasn't like this both times I was here before. Everything I could see was immaculate when I saw Cyndee and Greta—shingles, siding, window, everything."

"You're sure?"

"I'm sure. The captain had already made everything shipshape before he died. The house and yard were neat and beautiful on his last day."

Sheriff Rainey didn't question her memory. He didn't try to get her to doubt herself. He took her statement at face value, because why shouldn't he? This made Faye feel respected and heard. It made her respect him as a law enforcement officer.

"You're right about how the captain kept his house and yard," he said. "Setting aside the tree and the damage to the siding and gutters, the broken window is the critical clue. It has to be evidence of a break-in."

"Exactly. Or sabotage. Maybe I'm too suspicious, but I have to wonder whether Greta and Cyndee damaged the house, and maybe even broke the window. That way, they could ensure that there would be an insurance claim she could file for Jeanine."

"Thus giving them a chance to skim some or all of the money for themselves?"

Faye laughed and said, "Yeah. That's what I was thinking. Like I said, I'm suspicious."

"So run me through the timeline," he said. "When have you been at this house this week?"

"I was here the day before we found the captain's body, which I think was the day he died."

He pulled his phone out of his pocket and started taking notes.

"And when did you see Ms. Haines in the captain's yard?"

"One day later. The afternoon of the day we found him. I had stopped by the dive shop down the street, and I saw her SUV in the driveway."

"Did she go in the house that day? And did she have the key yet?"

"I don't know the answer to either of those questions."

"Then pardon me while I call Jeanine Eubank and see if she remembers when she told Greta Haines where to find the captain's house key."

Chapter Thirty-Two

While the sheriff was on the phone with Jeanine, Faye went out to her car. The photo the captain had given her was still there, lying flat on the back seat. She laid it carefully on the hood of her car and took a photo of it with her phone, then took it with her when she rejoined the sheriff.

When she went back in the house, the sheriff was already off the phone. He shook his head and said, "Jeanine Eubank doesn't remember when she told Greta how to get in the house."

Faye said, "That's too bad. Greta and Cyndee confuse me. I find it completely believable that they sabotaged this house to try to get Jeanine's insurance money, making it look like a branch had come down and damaged it. But is that related to the captain's death?"

"Considering that we're still not sure the captain's death was anything but an accident, I can't say. I do know that I've dealt with murders that were committed for a lot less money than the value of this house."

"The missing photos and visitors' log don't seem to fit in with any insurance scam," Faye said. "The photos were aerial shots of the Gulf, which is where the captain died, but they were taken days before he left us. Here, take a look."

She handed him the original print that the captain had given her.

"This is the only photo Joe gave the captain that's still available to us," she said. "Joe's helping clean up a house where there's no cell service yet, but I just texted him to say he needs to make you copies of the rest of them. He'll get the text when he's done for the day. It'll take a little while, because the files are on his computer's hard drive at our house, but we can get them to you tonight."

The sheriff nodded his thanks.

"I keep thinking about that missing visitors' log," she said. "The thief didn't want anybody to have access to that. This could support my theory that somebody had been visiting the library regularly to identify valuable books worth stealing. But I also remember something the captain said on that last day."

"And what was that?"

"He said that people were in and out of the library all the time, asking about the *Philomela*. If any one of the treasure hunters looking for that ship believed that they were about to find her, would they want to shut up the man who helped them with the search?"

"It would show a terrible lack of gratitude, but yeah. Criminals do think that way."

———

Sheriff Rainey was having fun as he watched Faye Longchamp-Mantooth walk around the captain's library, trying hard not to touch things. Maybe he should just hand her a pair of gloves, since it was so hard for her to keep her hands to herself.

She was a tactile person, which probably went along with her work as an archaeologist. When she dug up something interesting like a spear point, she probably wanted to hold it. Maybe she hefted it on her palm to assess how heavy it was for its size. She probably rubbed a thumb over its flat surface to see how the chipped surface had worn over time, then ran the same thumb along its edge to see how well it had retained its sharpness.

She might even lick artifacts at times. He'd heard that this was one way to tell a bone from a rock that just looked like one, but maybe that was a technique from days gone by. Good-quality lights and magnifiers were easy to come by in the twenty-first century, but an archaeologist's tongue might have been the only tool available back in the day.

Dr. Longchamp-Mantooth struck him as a woman who would do whatever it took to get the work done. If she'd been working in the days when Howard Carter was finding King Tut for Lord Carnarvon, she totally would have licked the artifacts when the situation called for it.

She was busy telling him how that single-mindedness could be useful to him.

"It would be easier if the captain had bought a freakin' computer and hired a kid to input the contents of his card catalog, but he didn't. I could do that for you, and then we could use the electronic catalog to see if any of the captain's books were missing. Even better, you could hire my kid and just pay me to supervise her a little. It would be cheaper, and it honestly wouldn't take her all that long. This isn't work that your deputies are trained to do."

She was very persuasive. He had caught himself trying to nod yes to Faye's suggestion (or was it a demand?) but he had so far avoided hiring her firm by accident.

"Not to insult you, ma'am, but I would still want a deputy in the room while you're doing this stuff. You make a good point, and I might well hire you and your daughter to inventory this library eventually, but right now I can't spare that deputy."

"You mean to keep an eye on us."

"Whatever you want to call it."

They were still standing there, silent and more than a bit adversarial, when his phone rang in his pocket and changed everything. Lieutenant Baker's voice was even and calm, but Sheriff Rainey could hear the echo of something dark and disruptive in its cadences.

"We've found Captain Eubank's boat. And it was dragging Nate Peterson. The officer on the scene says his arm was hooked around one of the ladder's rungs. He was trying to get out of the water but he just couldn't manage it."

Rainey's reflexive response was to go into overdrive, running to his car and asking questions like "Where's the boat right this minute?" so that he could get there as quickly as possible. Based on the tone of Baker's voice and the way she'd referred to Peterson, almost like cargo, he presumed that the man was dead, but he forced himself to stand right where he was and gather the information he needed.

"What's Peterson's condition? Is he dead? You make it sound like he's dead."

"No, he's not dead, but he's damn close to it."

Chapter Thirty-Three

"So you're saying that Nate is unconscious, seriously ill, and in an ambulance?" Faye asked. "And that he was found with the captain's boat?"

The sheriff had dropped his poker face. Faye could see that he was confused, he was upset, and he was scared. It was disconcerting to watch the man in charge of protecting her community struggle as he decided his next move.

She spoke gently, looking for information but also hoping he realized that she was on his side. "Do you think this means that Nate was involved with the captain's death in some way?"

"Don't know," the sheriff said. "The captain's boat apparently drifted in close to shore and got hung up in the tidal swamps west of Manny's place, between the marina and your friend Emma's house. All that vegetation was doing a pretty good job of hiding it, or we'd have found it before now. Maybe it's been there all this time. Maybe not. Hard to say."

Faye pictured the geography of the area. "So that's on the same side of the creek as the marina. And it's on the same side of the marina as the spot where Ossie got shot down."

"I don't know if it means anything. It's a fifty-fifty shot on both counts. The captain's boat has gotta be somewhere, either east or west of the creek and either east or west of the marina. But yeah. That's where it is."

"How far from the marina?"

"Don't know for sure. That swampy area to the west is pretty thick, but it doesn't go on forever. The boat's location had to be pretty secluded or somebody would have seen it, so I dunno. A mile, maybe? Much farther than that and you get back into a populated area."

"Who found it?"

"One of Manny's customers saw it on the way out to take her kids fishing. It must have been pretty obvious that things weren't right when she saw an empty boat with an unconscious man floating behind it. That poor woman deserves a medal for hauling a hundred-and-eighty-pound man—plus the weight of his diving gear—into her boat. Do you know how hard it is to get a grip on a body in a wetsuit? It's heavy, slippery, dead weight. I hope her kids were big enough to help."

Faye remembered Captain Eubank floating dead in the water, and she shivered.

"Manny says that he didn't see Nate leave the marina today, even though he usually stops to say hello on his way out," said the sheriff.

"Just like the captain used to do."

"Sort of. Except the captain presumably just walked from his car to his boat and took off, like he always did. There's nothing unusual about that, except he skipped talking to Manny. Nate, though… I've got to do some thinking about how Nate got himself in this situation. He didn't leave the marina on his boat. A neighbor checked his house, and it's sitting right there in the driveway on its trailer."

"Maybe he went out on the captain's boat, which means that he knew where it was."

"Could be. I guess it's possible that he went out with somebody else and they left him out there. Then maybe he came across the captain's boat while he was trying not to drown. But that would mean that the person he went out with is a freakin' psychopath."

"Because nobody reported Nate missing?" asked Faye.

"Exactly."

This, too, echoed the captain's death.

Another awful possibility occurred to her. "Or maybe he went out there with somebody who's also incapacitated or dead, and maybe they were on that person's boat. This would mean that there could still be another boat out there that we need to find. And another body, dead or alive."

"I don't know what you mean by 'we.' You don't work for me, and I haven't hired your firm to help me out, either. In case you haven't noticed, people in boats are turning up dead and nearly dead. I do not want your help, because your children seem to like their mother just fine. I want you alive for their sake."

"My children and I live on an island with their father. We're in boats all the time. I won't feel like my family is safe until I know why people are floating around in the Gulf dead, or close to it. If you would let me help you find out what's going on, maybe we could get to the truth quicker."

The sheriff didn't ask her to play crime fighter. He went straight to practicalities. "I'm heading to the hospital. If Nate regains consciousness—when he regains consciousness—I need to talk to him immediately. While I'm doing that, there's something I'll ask you to do. But don't take this as a sign I'm going to make you some kind of honorary deputy or something."

"Anything," Faye said.

"Go home now and email me files of the photos that you think were stolen from the captain's house. I want to get a look at them as soon as possible."

Faye looked at her watch. The afternoon was gone, so Joe was probably already waiting for her at the marina. It was a good thing that Amande had brought her own boat so they wouldn't have to wait for her. She said goodbye and got behind the wheel.

Her car rolled toward Manny's Marina as easily as if it had memorized the way. As she traveled the captain's street, she saw an object levitating high in the air. It moved up, down, forward, and back, and none of those motions were anything like the flight of a natural creature.

Faye looked around to see who was flying a drone. There, a city block ahead of her, stood a man she recognized as Ray Peterson. Nate's dad was standing in the parking lot of the small commercial building that housed his newspaper. He was intent on the controls in his hand, watching the flying device drop slowly toward the ground.

———

Ray studied the face of his cell phone, strapped to his new drone's controller. More accurately, the drone belonged to the newspaper, not him. This meant that its purchase price was tax-deductible.

His new drone had given him a glimpse of Crawfordville from the air, showing him its street grid and surrounding countryside. The highway cutting diagonally through the town's heart had been obvious, and so had the swampy area northwest and west of town.

He'd seen the sheriff's car parked outside the captain's house, beside the car that belonged to Faye Longchamp-Mantooth, the archaeologist wife of Nate's friend Joe. He wondered what they could be doing there together. Checking out the captain's collection of curiosities, maybe, as if they could be useful in figuring out why the captain was dead? Ray didn't see much likelihood of them solving the crime while standing in a library.

Down the street, he had watched Thad climb into his father's old truck. He'd gotten on Highway 319 and headed south. Was he heading to Manny's Marina, one of his usual drinking spots? Or was he heading to Panacea, where he kept his daddy's old boat, a Willard Marine 30 Trawler that was older than Thad but was too much of a tank to ever die. It was hard to say.

Ray had spent a couple of seconds watching a redheaded woman walking down the sidewalk in front of Thad's place. He'd had no reason to track her movements. In fact, she'd only caught his eye because of the lovely color of her hair. Ray had other things to do, so he appreciated the hair for a moment and then moved the drone east.

On the far eastern side of town, he finally saw what he was looking for, two people who were up to no good. One of them was on a roof, diligently prying up shingles that had made it through the hurricane just fine. The other was in a tree, breaking off limbs and letting them fall to the ground.

Ray thought it was about time for his newspaper to do an exposé on insurance fraud.

———

Faye watched Ray guide the drone with precision to a landing spot near his feet. She wondered if he realized that it really wasn't okay to be flying it over people's private property. If not, his neighbors would be telling him soon.

Just as she was wondering what he was doing here when his

son was terribly injured, she saw him take his cell phone out of the drone's controller, look at its face, and put his hand to his heart. Ray Peterson backed away from the grounded drone, leaving it sitting on the asphalt-and-gravel parking lot. He touched the screen a single time and slapped the phone to his ear.

For a moment, he just listened, hunching slowly forward as if hearing news that hit him like a spear to his chest. Then he was running to his sleek red sports car, phone to his ear, and throwing himself behind the steering wheel. As Faye neared the spot where he had stood flying his drone, Ray Peterson's Maserati was already in drive. She stopped her car dead in the road to let him out of the parking lot, so that he could be on his way to his son's side.

Too torn up to question why traffic was parting to make space for him, Ray floored the Maserati's accelerator, charging onto the street. The powerful car's tires spun, scratching up gravel as he made tracks to wherever Nate was.

———

As if Faye's phone were psychically linked to her daughter's, several beeps heralded the appearance of a series of texts on her phone screen just as she was arriving at the marina. Faye could tell that Amande had typed them over a period of time while one or both of them was out of range, and now they were coming through in a single information dump. Their casual spelling and lack of punctuation made it clear that Amande, whose grammar was perfect when she wanted it to be, knew how to disable autocorrect.

finished my rounds early so gonna
check on emma and head home

emmas doing fine and she wants to
know if ur drinking enough h2o

you woulda thought michael hadnt seen
emma in a century so I said yeah when
she invited him for a sleepover

michael thinks emma is a goddess probly cause
she feeds him jelly and white bread on command

Sorry if he comes home hyper and w/
sugar coming out his ears

so. exhausted. SERIOUSLY.

gonna go home and eat some leftovers and crash

take your time coming home cuz you
and dad got nobody to feed & clean up
after but yourselves & youre welcome

Joe was waiting for Faye at the marina, just as she'd expected. He was sitting with Manny on his usual bench outside the bar, surrounded by the kind of junk food he ate when he was stressed—corn chips, beef jerky, and cheese sticks. Joe believed that most problems could be solved by salt and grease, but it was a sign of Manny's stress level that he, too, was chowing down on junk when his snacking style usually ran more toward fruit and nuts. Faye wasn't sure she liked being close enough to Manny to know this.

Manny left Joe chewing on cheese sticks and intercepted Faye before she could get to her husband. Speaking too quietly for Joe to hear, he asked, "You heard about Nate?"

Faye nodded.

"Joe's taking it hard. Keeps saying that Nate risked his life to keep him from being shot when he was too stupid to keep himself safe. You know—on the day Ossie got shot down. He wants to know why this had to happen to Nate when he wasn't around to help him. I got no answer for him." Manny patted Faye awkwardly on the arm. "You okay?"

"I'm fine," Faye said. "I just want to understand what's happening. It's like I was living in a safe, secure bubble until the hurricane came through and then boom. Terrible things started happening to people."

"Nate wasn't unconscious the whole time. After he got here, I mean. I was trying to make him comfortable while we waited for the paramedics to get here, and there were moments when he was awake."

"Lucid?"

"I wouldn't say he was lucid. It wasn't like you could ask him a question and get an answer. I know I must have said, 'What happened to you, Nate?' about a dozen times and didn't get an answer once. I thought maybe he'd stayed down too long and run out of gas to breathe, but I checked his gauge. It showed plenty of pressure. All of his gear looked perfectly fine."

"Did he say how long he was out there?"

Manny shook his head. "But he was conscious, 'cause he kept telling me how bad he hurt. Tried to get me to go in the bar and pour him some liquor to take away the pain. Straight brandy's what he wanted. I woulda totally poured him a shot of brandy, if I woulda thought it would make him rest easier until the ambulance came, but I didn't dare. I figured it might kill him. That didn't stop him from asking, though."

"Could you see any injuries?"

"You mean like the bloody foam that was coming out of his

mouth? Yeah, he's injured. My best guess is a collapsed lung or an air embolism. He came up too fast from wherever he was diving. When that happens…well…I guess it's like your lungs burst. Or they leak air or whatever mix you're breathing into your blood vessels. None of those are good things."

Faye's hand went to her own chest. For an instant, she felt like she was the one who was underwater and couldn't breathe.

"I'm not a doctor," Manny said, "but I think that's what happened to Nate. It's what I told the sheriff, anyway."

Faye felt like she was reliving something terrible, a nightmare that had only just happened. "He was in scuba gear? Is Nate a diver? Or is this like the captain, where somebody just shows up hurt or dead in scuba gear that nobody's ever seen him wear?"

"Nate lives to dive. He dives every chance he gets."

"Do we know that for a fact?"

"Oh, yeah. I sell him gear, and I hear him telling tales about the cool things he's seen down there. This ain't at all like the captain, where he looked uncomfortable in his gear, even when he was dead. But it's still weird."

"Because Nate's got enough diving experience to avoid getting an air embolism?"

"Exactly. If Nate came up that fast, it means that something went really wrong."

Where was Nate diving when things went so wrong? Faye thought of the captain's belief that the *Philomela* was nearby, maybe even at The Cold Spot. Was Nate looking for it? Had this terrible thing happened to him just off the coast of her island?

No, that couldn't be right. The water at The Cold Spot was too shallow to cause Nate's terrible injuries. If surfacing quickly after diving in six feet of water could kill a person, Faye would have died snorkeling before she hit her teens.

And yet Nate lay at death's door. Faye could feel a nameless danger all around them, one that had consumed the captain and was trying to take Nate. She couldn't name it, but she couldn't avoid speaking of it, either.

"Maybe he stayed down there too long, waiting until it was too late to come up safely." Faye studied Manny's face to see whether an experienced diver agreed or whether he thought she'd lost her mind. "Maybe there was something on the surface that scared him even more than an air embolism or the bends."

Manny nodded. "That's what I was thinking, only you put it into words better than I could've. Why don't you two go home and check on Amande? I'll call you if I hear something, but I worry about her out there all alone. Especially when there's so much happening that I don't understand."

Faye went weak in the knees at the thought of Amande, alone and vulnerable in a place that was supposed to be perfectly safe.

She started to walk toward Joe, ready to get in a boat and hurry home, then she paused and drew her phone out of her pocket. She pulled up an image of the photo that the captain had given her, handed it to Manny, and asked, "See anything weird about this picture?"

He took the phone from her hand and expanded the photo to get a better look. "Nope. Making it bigger don't help."

"Recognize any of the boats?" she asked.

He shook his head. "Can't say for sure, since more boats come through this marina than you'd believe. Too much glare off the water to see any details, and there ain't nothing nearby to give them any scale. I'm gonna say no."

She squinted at the phone's face. "The one with the yellow bimini catches my eye. It's not in all the photos. It wasn't even in the photo printed in the paper, but I keep looking at it. I've never seen a bimini quite that color."

"That's a really light yellow, and my customers are practical. They don't go for nothing that shows dirt so easy. Unless it's white, so they can spray the heck out of it with bleach. Without bleach, the mildew gets away from you. Can you imagine something that color covered in mold and mildew? Even a chrome yellow would hide mildew better than that creamy pale yellow. Yeah, I think I'd have noticed if I'd seen that boat. But why are you asking about that one boat? There's others in the frame, too."

Faye took the photo back. "I'm curious about all of them. I'm also curious about the photos themselves. Prints of some of them got stolen from the captain's house. The ones in Ossie's memory got blasted out of the sky. The ones in Joe's phone got lost or stolen. I just got to wondering about the boat with the yellow bimini because it's in some of the photos, and it *is* such an unusual color."

"I'll keep an eye out for it," Manny said. "Oh, in case you haven't noticed, Nate's boat is gray with black trim. And a black bimini. So this boat ain't his, if you're wondering."

Faye walked quietly over to Joe and sat down beside him on the bench. It was hard for her to even think about Nate's condition, because accepting it meant that she couldn't push her own fears away. She was afraid to get in her own boat and go to her own island, because she was scared of something unnameable in the water. Or on it. Or deep underneath it.

There was something wrong about the water lapping at the shores of her island. It had killed the captain and now it had tried to kill Nate. And Amande was out there in the middle of it.

Faye was afraid to stay where she was, on a deck overlooking that same water. She was afraid to drive to Emma's house and wrap her arms around her son, because doing this would leave her daughter alone on Joyeuse Island, surrounded by water. She was afraid to move from the spot where she was standing and she was afraid to stand still. With loved ones strung out across the county, where was she supposed to be and what was she supposed to do?

Joe wrapped an arm around her shoulders, and said what she knew to be true. "I'm going to call Sheriff Mike to go get Emma and Michael. And then we need to get in the boat. Amande's not safe out there all alone."

Yes. Joe was right. It was obvious where they needed to go and why. Michael was safe with Emma—probably, oh God, he was only probably safe, but he'd be safer when he was with a retired but armed officer of the law—but Amande was alone. She needed them.

They got in the boat and opened up the throttle, leaving Manny standing alone on the dock as he watched them go.

Chapter Thirty-Four

Joe cut the motor. As soon as its racket died down, Faye pulled her phone out of her pocket. She'd had time to think of some things that the sheriff should know, so she called him.

"How's Nate?"

The sheriff's "Well…" was hesitant, like a time-waster that would delay the inevitable truth. "They've got him on oxygen and an IV of something or other, and they're transporting him to someplace that has a hyperbaric chamber. It's urgent that they get started with that, as I'm sure you know, particularly since we don't know how long it's been since he got sick."

"What do his doctors say?"

His voice was soft. "They just don't know, but it's serious and it could get worse. The embolism could cause a stroke. His organs could be permanently damaged. It's gonna be a while before we see how things play out for him."

Faye thought of Nate, standing on a dock and peeling off his clothes because he couldn't wait to get his boat out on the water. Youth and love for life had flowed through him. "Did he regain consciousness?"

"He was in and out the whole time I was with him. He tried

so hard to tell me something, but he just couldn't get it out. My contractors are gonna test his equipment, but they told me when they picked it up that they didn't see anything obviously wrong with it. The pressure gauge was low, but the tank wasn't empty. We're guessing that the embolism happened because he'd been diving deep and came up too fast, but we don't know why he took that risk."

Faye tried to imagine having something important to say but no way to say it. It seemed like the definition of hell. "I know people dive alone, but it seems incredibly dangerous. Yet we've got two people within a week who either had terrible accidents while diving alone or else they were abandoned in the water by someone who's not talking."

The sheriff said, "If anybody was with the captain or Nate, I'll get them in for questioning and they'll talk."

Faye said, "I've been thinking so hard, trying to come up with something helpful. I didn't come up with much, but I did want to tell you that I saw Nate late yesterday afternoon. It might not have been long before things got bad for him."

If she was right about that, then Nate had floated in the Gulf, injured, all night and all day. Her breath left her at the thought.

Faye forced herself to focus. "I saw Nate with two other men. One of them is a young man named Cody. He works for Manny, and that's all I know about him."

"I know Cody. I see him around the marina, coming to work and going home in a john boat. Keeps a way bigger and nicer boat up the creek from the marina at his house. Not much more than a kid, just a few years older than your daughter. It seems to me like I've seen him eyeing Amande, in fact."

"So I hear."

"Cody works hard. Plays hard. Clean record, as far as I know. That's about all I can say."

"The other man I saw with Nate is named Thad. You know—the one who owns Thad's Surf and Dive Shop. It's right down the street from the captain's house and the newspaper office. I'm not sure whether that's important, but it seems like it could be."

"I know who Thad is. He's never been in any trouble, either. Did you see the three men together at Thad's store?"

"No. They were in Nate's boat. I saw them heading out on the water yesterday. They were in high spirits. There's no law against having a good time with your friends, but I sure hope they had a designated boat pilot, because Thad and Cody were already drinking before the boat left the dock. As far as I could tell, though, Nate was sober, which is good because he was piloting the boat."

"I'm going to need to talk to Cody and Thad, and soon. If tonight's like most nights, they'll be drinking at the marina after sundown."

The three men in Nate's boat had all exuded the kind of arrogant carefree self-regard that tended to make Faye irrationally angry, so she tried to stuff that anger. It wasn't helpful. She also tried to stuff her concern that these dudes arrogantly thought that they were good enough for her daughter. And worse, she needed to stuff her concern that they might try to do something about it. It was important to set aside her irrational thoughts, because she had some rational ones that the sheriff needed to hear.

"I think it's possible that those guys are looking for a sunken ship. I told you about it—the *Philomela*. And maybe they've found her, but I doubt it. I took a good look at the spot that the captain thought might be the site of the shipwreck, and I saw nothing."

"Without checking with me?"

"I was in water where I swim once a week, at least. Right off my island. Do I need to ask you before I do that? How about when I take a walk on my own land?"

"I kinda wish you would, but I guess that's too much to hope for. The problem is that between the captain, Nate, and Ossie, we've got bad things happening on land and sea, and they're happening in places that have always been perfectly safe."

The sheriff wasn't telling Faye anything new. She wanted a safe haven for her family, and she didn't know how to find it.

"Anyway, I didn't see any sign of the *Philomela*," she said, "but that doesn't mean that Nate's buddies aren't out there looking for her. And maybe Greta. Judging by the size of her boat, Greta could have already found the *Philomela*, hauled all her sunken treasure ashore, and turned it into cash. Not that I think it's a sure thing that the *Philomela* was even carrying treasure. Even if none of them are anywhere close to finding her, you're the face of law enforcement who's closest to their amateur treasure-hunting escapades."

"Well, that sounds just awesome."

"No joke. And it means that you need to be aware of what's going on. If they've found the thing and word gets out, there will be professional treasure hunters coming in here who know what they're doing. Worse, there will be amateurs who don't. People diving on that boat could get killed. One of them probably already has and another's at death's door."

"Big money attracts big crime."

"Exactly," Faye said. "I think that Thad and Cody know something. Maybe Nate's condition will shake them up. They just might talk to you now and I think you should force their hands. If people are out there diving on an old, dangerous, and possibly valuable shipwreck, you need to know about it. Lives are at stake."

———

Ray got to the emergency room in time to see his son before the ambulance took him for barometric treatment. There wasn't much time, only time enough to sit in the chair at Nate's bedside, holding his son's hand.

Nate was silent, fighting for breath, until the nurse tending him stepped out into the hall. Then his eyes opened and met his father's.

His lips formed a word, then another, but Ray heard nothing but a gasp and a sigh. Still holding his father's gaze, Nate raised a finger, so slightly, and crooked it.

Perhaps no one but his father could have understood this gesture, but Ray did. He dragged his chair even closer to the hospital bed and leaned forward. With his ear brushing Nate's lips, he could hear words instead of gasps and sighs.

In order to hear Nate, he was forced to lean forward hard. Before long, his sixty-year-old back was spasming good and hard, but he ignored it. His boy was talking, so Ray kept listening until Nate had said all he had to say.

Chapter Thirty-Five

The house was quiet when Faye and Joe entered, stopping in the kitchen on their way to Joe's office. The sheriff needed the digital files on his computer, and Joe's antiquated system for dealing with photos wasn't going to make it easy to get them to him. For one thing, the files were way too big to email at a usable resolution, not unless they planned to be chained to the computer all night and all the next day. Printing out a big stack of photos at high resolution would take an inordinate amount of time, too, and then they'd still have to take the physical images back to shore. Faye wondered if they should just put Joe's desktop computer on the boat and ferry it to shore.

They sounded very married, even to Faye's ears, as they stood in the kitchen making sandwiches, bickering the whole time.

Faye led with, "It's a good thing one of us lives in this century. I have a cloud storage subscription. We can upload the files to my account, send an invitation to the sheriff so he can see them, then crack open a couple of beers, because that's it. The whole thing's done. You should listen to me when I tell you about this kind of stuff."

And Joe was having none of it. "That seemed like a whole lot of trouble when I just wanted to take a few pictures. Who knew that the newspaper would want them?"

"And law enforcement?"

"Well, yeah. You're not planning to tell me that you knew the sheriff was going to need my pictures. Because you didn't."

Faye was busy telling Joe exactly how easy it would be to zap the photos where they needed to go when she remembered how slow their internet connection was. As she opened her mouth to say, "Maybe we better take the beers to your office to drink while we wait for your pictures to float slowly up to the cloud," Joe plunked a stack of photos on the counter next to her ham sandwich.

"Maybe I live in the Stone Age, but here's something for you to look at while we're waiting for my computer to talk to the clouds. Or whatever it is that you're planning to do with it."

"What are these? Did you print out all those pictures you took with Ossie? No, that's not possible. You must have taken hundreds of them, but there's only twenty or so in this stack."

"Nope, I didn't print them all. But I did print two copies of the ones I gave the captain, one for him and one for me. I was giving him my very best shots out of all the pictures I took, so I thought 'Why not make some prints for myself?'" He waved them at her. "These are them."

"So this stack of pictures in my hands is exactly like the ones you gave the captain? The ones I saw in his library? Well, except for the photo that was in the paper, because he'd already given it away."

"Yep. And unless the captain scrambled them—which I doubt, because you know how neat he was—they're even in the same order."

She rifled through the stack of photos, looking at the pleasure boats with their colorful biminis and trying to find the scene she remembered from Nate's article. None of these photos were quite right. One of them was close, but it showed the boat with the yellow bimini and Faye was dead certain that she hadn't seen it in the paper. Its path snaked in and out of the scene in stop-motion as she flipped quickly through the prints.

"The photos are important somehow," she mumbled, mostly to herself but she knew Joe would hear. "They keep getting stolen. First somebody took them from the captain's house. Then they took the ones stored in Ossie's memory. And then your phone disappeared, which I guess had some of your drone pictures on it."

"Yeah. I put 'em on there so I could show 'em to people. But you know, Faye, Ossie didn't just get stolen."

He was right. Somebody had blasted Ossie apart.

Faye felt herself giving in to panic. Someone had gone to extraordinary lengths to eradicate Joe's photographs, destroy the device that had taken them, and steal a device where they'd been stored. Was the person who had done those things satisfied now, confident that a critical secret was protected? This would be an unwise position for that person to take, since the pictures in her hand were proof that the thief had failed.

The photos felt radioactive. The captain, one of the few people to see them all, was dead. Nate Peterson had seen at least one of them, and he was fighting for his life. There was another target, an obvious one, and he was standing beside her. Was Joe's life in danger?

She couldn't stop shuffling through the photos. If she could just figure out what made them dangerous, maybe she could protect Joe.

"Faye." Joe was saying her name, and it probably wasn't the first time. She was too freaked out at the thought of somebody stalking her husband to think clearly.

"Faye, don't forget. I've got more pictures on my office computer."

"Why don't you go on and wake up the computer? Make sure you remember what folder you stored the photos in. Stuff like that. There's something I want to check out."

Faye had sent Joe on his way so she could do her favorite thing, which was to obsess on the internet. She was having a little trouble concentrating, though, because Joe had decided he needed another sandwich before he vacated the kitchen and gave her room to think.

Trying to block the sound of Joe's knife bumping around in a mayonnaise jar, she focused on a single question: If the *Philomela* was the key to everything, and she thought it was, what had it been carrying that was worth murdering someone over?

She knew that blockade runners mostly hauled cash crops like cotton and tobacco out of the Confederacy, dodging the Union ships that blockaded southern ports. Their destinations included ports in the Caribbean, on Bermuda, and beyond. Cally's oral history said that the *Philomela* had been headed for Havana after it left Joyeuse Island, and it was definitely on the list of known ports for blockade runners.

If the *Philomela* had gone down right after it left Cally, it would have been loaded with trade goods grown by people living in the Confederacy, things like cotton, tobacco, rice, and indigo. It didn't seem to Faye that this kind of cargo would be worth much after a hundred and fifty years underwater, if it had survived at all.

But what if the *Philomela* had made it to Havana? What if its captain had sold the trade goods and loaded the ship with desperately needed food, but also with the kind of luxury items that would yield the most profit possible from a crowded cargo hold?

What would those luxury items be? Faye thought that they might include silk, paintings, jewels, silver, gold, books, wine, or liquor. Maybe all of the above. Would they have survived in a condition that would still interest treasure hunters? Jewels certainly could have survived, which was why they constituted the classic image of treasure from a sunken ship. Liquor and wine, too, might have had a shot, as long as they were stored in something sealed well enough to keep out saltwater for a long, long time.

Silk, paintings, and books? Surely they would have rotted beyond repair.

In a war zone, guns were moneymakers for those willing to risk their lives smuggling them in. Since there was a war on and the Confederacy did not begin the war with significant weapons manufacturing capabilities, the *Philomela* was almost certainly carrying weapons as it ran past the Union gunboats into blockaded Southern ports. Guns would be a lot more likely to survive a long stint underwater than perishable goods. There were collectors who would pay a pretty price for Civil War weaponry, even after being submerged for all this time.

The ship would also have been carrying money, of course, so that the captain could purchase another load of cash crops and do the whole thing again. If any paper money had survived that long underwater—English, Confederate, Union, or the currency of some other nation—it might be worth something on the collector's market, but gold was the currency that sang a siren song for people who dreamed of sunken treasure. Faye knew that any treasure hunters diving on an old shipwreck would be hoping for gold ingots, but they wouldn't turn their noses up at guns, liquor, table silver, or jewelry.

If Captain Eubank had been killed by someone trying to protect the location of the *Philomela*, would the killer have been brazen enough to offer goods traceable to the ship for public sale? Maybe. Greed made people stupid. And also, recreational divers who stumbled on a wreck would not be experienced in fencing their goods. The internet might seem to them to be an anonymous way to go about it.

Faye went to the obvious place first. She checked eBay for listings of old gold coins or ingots, but nothing from the right time period had been listed during the past week. She had the same result on a search of antique jewelry sites. Nobody had tried recently to unload saltwater-corroded, Civil War–era guns, either. To really be sure they weren't out there, she'd need to search every pawn shop and the home of every black-market-shopping collector in the world, but this was a useful first-blush result.

Moving away from eBay, Faye did a general web search for some specific nineteenth-century luxury items that could have survived a century and a half of being wet. Here, she struck pay dirt.

A man in south Georgia had been posting on social media about his recent purchase of a stash of brandy and rum that was more than a hundred and fifty years old.

Manny had said that Nate was talking about brandy. Maybe he didn't want brandy to drink. Maybe he was trying to tell Manny why someone had tried to kill him.

The local paper of the man who bought the old rum and brandy had done the only logical thing and sent a reporter right over. With the lightning speed of modern media, the article was already online.

Faye shook her head at the foolishness of it all. The looters might have been smart enough not to list their loot on eBay, but they had sold it to somebody too stupid to keep his dubious shopping habits to himself. Did it truly not occur to him that people selling really old stuff on the quiet might be crooks?

And what about the newspaper? Did the reporter think this purchase of ridiculously old liquor was legitimate? If he'd asked the man where the rum and brandy had come from, he hadn't reported it in the article. To be fair, though, he'd written the piece in such a way that readers might read between the lines. He didn't seem to like the man he was interviewing, which was also something that the average reader could certainly read between the lines.

Faye was pretty sure that the reporter thought rich people should buy cheap liquor that did its job of getting them drunk, then spend a little bit of the savings on something important like feeding people or buying them medicine. Faye thought she and that reporter could be good friends.

The thought of drinking mid-nineteenth-century rum made Faye's breath catch in her throat. It brought home the reality of the trade in enslaved human beings. Africans were brought to the West Indies, where they were forced to grow sugar cane that became molasses. Molasses was sold to New England rum makers. Rum was shipped to Africa and traded for people who were sold to the West Indies, and truthfully to all of the New World, and this started it all over again. This shameful triangle went on for centuries, and now a too-wealthy-for-his-own-good man in Georgia had paid a probably unholy sum for rum distilled from human misery.

Actually the sum paid for that rum wasn't just probably unholy. Its unholiness was certain. If he hadn't paid a ridiculous amount for the rum and then bragged to someone about it, the newspaper wouldn't have sent someone to report on his conspicuous consumption.

The liquor-buyer had prattled on about how lucky it was that the labels were still somewhat legible. The newspaper had printed a photo of some of the old bottles, and it was obvious to Faye that the labels weren't damaged by mere age. They had been soaked in water, and she'd bet it was seawater.

Those bottles of rum and brandy were a morning's drive from Crawfordville. Faye was as certain as she could be that they came from the shipwreck that the captain had been chasing.

The liquor-buyer had said, "I opened a bottle of the brandy and I take a sip of it every night at bedtime. My stash of liquid gold is big enough to last me for years at that rate."

The reporter had asked what would happen when he ran out.

"I'll buy more, no matter the price. I've never slept better, and that's worth something."

The reporter, who Faye figured would never in his life be able to afford such an extravagant sleep aid, was allowed to take his own sip of the old brandy. How else could he could write the most complete story possible?

His article concluded with a statement that suggested he was not as grateful as the liquor-buyer might have liked. "It tasted good, but drinking a hundred-dollar bill should taste good."

Faye imagined bottle after bottle, cases and cases of them, all filled with the alcoholic equivalent of hundred-dollar bills. Now she knew for sure that the *Philomela* had gone down carrying cargo valuable enough to inspire a thief. Or a murderer.

Joe must have gotten carried away with his sandwich-making, because he slid a sandwich, tall with roast beef, lettuce, tomatoes, and pickles, in front of her. He set an open beer beside it and said, "When you finish whatever it is you're doing, bring this with you. We can chow down while the computer's clouding." He picked up the stack of photos and headed for his office.

Faye blew him a kiss and shot off a text to the sheriff with a link to the article, suggesting that he get this man on the phone and find out everything he could about who sold him that old brandy. As she hit "Send," she heard Joe calling her.

"Faye. Come quick."

Because denial is a powerful survival mechanism, she had almost convinced herself that there was no reason to be scared by the time she reached Joe. He stood in his office door and a breeze wafted through it. The balmy air smelled like pine trees and the sea because the room's single window had been broken. The glass had been two hundred years old, so its loss was a kick in the gut for Faye. Shattered shards of it covered the floor completely, reaching into all four of the room's corners.

Joe's computer was gone, as Faye had feared or guessed or expected. The only thought left in Faye's head came out of her mouth.

"Where are the children?"

Chapter Thirty-Six

Faye loved her house, but she knew it was too big. It was too big to furnish, too big to clean, too big to heat and cool and insure. It was way too big when it came to paying property taxes. On this night, the distance from the old house's aboveground basement to Amande's upstairs bedroom was just too damned far.

After the first moment of panic, she had realized that Michael was safe. She knew this because Amande had texted that she'd left him with Emma. Amande had also said that she was tired and was coming home early. Thus, their daughter had to be somewhere in this big house, alone. She had to be.

Both Faye and Joe were calling out for Amande as they scuttled up the narrow sneak stair that had carried her enslaved ancestors up from the basement, past the main floor with its towering ceilings, and up to the bedrooms where they had waited on their captors, night and day. The sneak stair opened into their bedroom with its finely detailed murals, painted by those same enslaved ancestors.

Their work boots clattered on the heart pine floor as she and Joe ran for their bedroom door, which led out onto the landing at the head of the massive circular staircase rising through the center of the old house. The staircase had collapsed during a hurricane that had almost consumed the whole house, and the landing had gone down with it. Faye and Joe had spent a long, long time rebuilding it, all by historically accurate methods and completely by hand.

Faye knew every brick and crevice of the old house, because she'd patched, polished, and painted every inch of it. She knew every board under her feet as she ran to find Amande.

When she thought of the thief (or was it thieves?) shattering the rippled glass of windows her ancestors had hung in the 1800s, she felt personally violated, but this was a feeling she could survive. When she thought that the thief (or thieves?) might then have hurt Amande, her heart twisted in her chest and threatened to stop beating.

Nothing in Faye's life mattered but the people she loved. Everything else was expendable.

Every original bedroom in the house opened onto the reconstructed landing, including Amande's. Their daughter's room was the place where Faye had slept while she dreamed of a family, the family that would someday come to live with her in this house that was way too big for one lonely woman.

When the door to Amande's room burst open, Faye's heart stopped as she waited for a single split-second to see who had opened it. Was Amande safe, or would the person on the other side be the same one who had broken a window and stolen Joe's computer?

When she saw the beautiful curves of her daughter's face, framed with unruly curls the color of the burnished pine floors under her feet, Faye was so overcome with relief that her legs failed her. She plopped onto the beautiful floor under her feet and let the tears come.

"What's wrong?" Amande asked.

For one of the few times in their married life, Joe did all the talking. He led with, "Are you okay? Somebody broke in the house. Did you hear them? Or see them? Amande, are you okay?"

Amande dropped the box in her hands, a long and slender white gift box with golden lettering. "Oh, my God. No! I didn't hear anything. I've been home at least an hour. Do you think it happened before that?"

Faye thought back through the trek from the basement to this spot. She doubted Amande could have heard anything happening down there, not even if the burglars had smashed the window with a baseball bat and then flung the bat through the window against the office's heavy oak door. The thick, tabby cement walls of the basement were so sturdily built that they could have contained the sound of a bomb blast.

Faye was still weeping, and for no good reason since her daughter stood there in perfect health, but she was able to gasp out, "It could have happened any time since we left the house this morning."

Joe looked a lot calmer than Faye, although there was something a trifle unhinged about the way he grabbed Amande, hugged her, held her out to look at her, hugged her again, and kept chanting, "You're okay. You look okay. Do you think you're okay? Do you feel okay?"

Faye, though she might look stupid as she sprawled helplessly on the floor, still clung hard to reality. She sorted through the facts as she knew them. First, they had been robbed. Second, they didn't know why. And third, they didn't know when.

"Y'all," she said, trying to be heard over Joe, "somebody could still be on this island. Several somebodies, actually. We've got to go. I just wish we'd been able to get those picture files to the sheriff, because I'm guessing they're the reason Joe's computer got stolen. They must be pretty dang important, but they're gone now."

"Not all of them," Joe said, turning his focus from Amande to Faye.

"Of course they're gone. Since you wouldn't sign up for the cloud storage I told you about, they're not floating in the ether. Even the prints you gave the captain got stolen, all except one, and I already gave it to the sheriff. Your computer's gone. Your phone's gone. Ossie's gone, and her memory chip went with her. We haven't bought the backup hard drive you wanted yet. Are you saying that you saved the files somewhere else?"

He was still holding the duplicates he'd made of the prints he'd given the captain, so he waved them in her face. "We don't have computer files, but we have hard copies."

"That short stack of photos isn't much help. I just can't believe that, out of all the photos you took, these are all we've got left. They stole hundreds of images. We have maybe twenty, and only because you stuck them in a kitchen drawer instead of taking them to your office."

Something about the existence of those photos in the kitchen, the room where Faye's family gathered around the table to eat and talk and laugh, put a hot iron lump in her stomach. She didn't know what made them dangerous, but they obviously were. How many times had somebody stolen or destroyed those same images?

Underscoring their untouchable nature was a simple, incontrovertible fact: the captain was the last person who had seen them, and he was dead. No, that wasn't exactly true. Faye had looked at the photos on that last day with the captain, so the two of them together might have been the last to see these shots. This was not a comforting thought.

And then there was Nate. There were any number of reasons

he might have found himself grievously injured and afloat in the Gulf, but he too had sent Ossie into the sky. He was directly linked to at least one of the drone's photos, the one he'd published with his front-page story. Now he was gravely injured. Ossie's photos were somehow poisonous.

And those photos weren't yet out of their lives. She and Joe were holding twenty prints, but the sheriff would be holding them just as soon as she could unload them on him.

She wanted them out of her house.

Chapter Thirty-Seven

Sitting sprawled on the floor at Amande and Joe's feet, Faye couldn't come up with an answer to the question of why anybody had been in her house in the first place. How did the thief know that stealing Joe's computer would solve a lot of problems for anyone who wanted those photos out of circulation?

"Joe, who knew the details about where you kept your photos? Both the physical ones and the electronic files?"

Joe's hearing was better than perfect, so the fact that he didn't seem to hear her was evidence that he, too, was at the end of his rope.

Faye's position on Joe's file storage habits was changing rapidly. If he'd been as adept at file handling as the average middle schooler, it would have been a lot harder for their adversary to put the photographic genie back in the bottle. Maybe it could have been done by kidnapping Joe, torturing him for his passwords, and then killing him. Faye was deeply grateful that this hadn't proven necessary.

And maybe this was an important clue. The person trying to squash Joe's photographs out of existence clearly knew that it was possible to do so.

She thought through the major players in the events of the last few days. The captain was no better at managing his electronic life than Joe was.

Thad didn't know Joe, and he had no reason to know anything about Joe's file storage habits. Faye didn't know much about him, other than that he worked down the street from the captain in a store he'd inherited from his father. He came to Manny's Marina from time to time to hang out with his buddies, but Faye didn't ever remember seeing him with a boat of his own. Surely a dive shop owner would have a boat. The odds were good that he kept it at a marina nearer his home in Crawfordville, maybe in Panacea. He apparently admired Amande, not that Faye could see how this was related to any criminal activity.

Cody didn't know anything about Joe or his file storage idiosyncrasies, either, as far as Faye knew. All she knew about Cody was that he worked for Manny in the dive shop and he lived in a rented fishing cabin up the same creek where Manny's boat slips were. He rented space from Manny for the boat repair business that paid his bills, and that business had enabled him to trade up to a boat that was way more posh than the rest of his life. He, too, was one of her daughter's admirers.

Greta Haines, as far as Faye was concerned, was a crook. Like the others, she had an enviable boat. She used Manny's boat ramp to get it into the water. Faye wasn't sure whether Cyndee Stamp was a crook or whether she had a boat of her own, but she hung out with a crook and had access to a crook's boat, so she stayed on Faye's suspect list.

Samantha Kennedy remained on the periphery of it all. Faye knew of no contact between Samantha and any of the suspects, but Faye didn't like the way she was hanging around Jeanine. She could potentially be romantically linked to any of the three young men, which put the disturbing thought in Faye's head that she might be jealous of Amande, but she knew almost nothing about Samantha outside of her professional life. She did know that the woman was far more interested in old books and drawings than she was in up-to-the-minute photos taken by drone.

Manny sat at the center of all these things, at the marina where the captain and Nate had presumably left shore and gone to disaster, but Faye knew of no reason why Manny would know anything about how Joe stored his files. Nate, however, would. She could just imagine the conversations that had passed between Joe and his friend Nate before that front-page article.

Nate would have been saying, "What do you mean you can't send it to me from your phone? I have a deadline."

Joe would have been saying, "What's your hurry? I can print it out and bring it to you next time I'm in town."

It would have been stupidly easy for Nate to ask as many questions as it took to nail down the locations of everything that needed destroying.

"Joe."

He was still busy asking Amande whether she was okay, so she tried again.

"Joe, did you and Nate talk about how you stored your photos? And where?"

"Sure thing. He was real interested in how Ossie's pictures got stored, because he was wanting to get a drone like her for his newspaper work. He was asking me about it on the very day she went down. Right when it was happening, actually."

Well, there it was. Evidence that Joe's friend may have been behind this effort to lock down a bunch of aerial photos that showed…something. Did any of these people—or all of them—think that The Cold Spot marked the location of the *Philomela*? Because Faye was sure that it did not.

Did someone think that safeguarding the location of the

Philomela was worth the risk of shooting Ossie down? Or of breaking into their home?

Her heart went cold. Was the explanation for the captain's death as simple and ugly as that? Was he dead so that his killer could keep hiding the location of a sunken treasure?

The irony of this burned Faye's heart, because she had been to The Cold Spot and she knew that there was no treasure there. The captain had died for nothing. Nate was suffering for nothing.

Who did the killing and the maiming? Thad? Cody? Were they working together? Was Nate in on it until they turned on him?

Maybe Greta and Cyndee? They seemed greedy enough, but they didn't fit into her theory that the guilty party had unique knowledge of where Joe kept his photos.

Samantha? Faye knew the woman's library skills were formidable. If anybody could find that shipwreck's location without ever dipping a foot in the water, it would be Samantha. That knowledge alone would be enough for a treasure-hunting diver to cut her in on the haul.

Though she'd been working hard to like Manny better, for Amande's sake, Faye couldn't deny that he was uniquely positioned to make sure that the captain and Nate got out on the Gulf unseen. Like all of her other suspects, he was in charge of his own schedule. It would have been so easy for him to arrange to be on the captain's boat with him when he died. He could have killed him…somehow. Faye wasn't quite clear on how the captain had died, and she didn't think the sheriff was yet, either.

Manny could have dragged the captain's boat onto the mud flats west of his marina and walked back to the marina through the swamp. So could any of the others.

Joe could be in danger from the person who hurt Nate, who

was probably the same person who shot down Ossie while Nate was busy distracting Joe. Nate and this person could have been partners in crime until the partner decided to cut Nate out. If the criminals were turning on each other now, anything could happen.

Faye stared at the apparently dangerous photos in her hand. "Where is the shot that Nate printed? It stands to reason that the most important one is the one that the most people saw, but it's not here. These are all just a shade different from each other, and none of them is the one from the newspaper."

"Yes, it is." Joe took the deck and paged through it quickly, selecting a photo and holding it out to her. "This is the one."

She looked at it, puzzled. The boat with the yellow bimini was positioned near the southernmost edge of the shot, but it emphatically hadn't been visible in the newspaper. She was sure of it. She would have remembered the sunny color.

There was another reason she was sure that she'd never seen this photo. There was another anomaly in the water. Once she'd finally given it a good hard look, she couldn't unsee it. A deep-blue shadow was located just south of the yellow-topped boat. Its contours were far more subtle than the clear-edged dark spot that she and the captain had seen on another photo, the one that had revealed the location of the subterranean spring. It was an indistinct shadow, just an oblong area that was very slightly darker than the surrounding water. An amateur like the captain might not have realized what he was seeing, but Faye couldn't take her eyes off it.

This thing couldn't possibly be natural. Its edges were too smooth. The two corners to the north were too close to ninety degrees, which was a sharp contrast to the way the other end of it faded away, as if it had broken off or been buried in sand. This long, dark…something…lay on the seaward side of the little boat with the yellow bimini. It lurked like a submerged whale, dwarfing the small craft.

This was a photo that Faye could believe that someone might want to hide, for she felt sure that she was looking at a long-lost shipwreck. Perhaps it was the *Philomela*, found again after a hundred and fifty years underwater. Perhaps it was something newer, a sunken cargo ship that was potentially as valuable but far less romantic. Or perhaps it was something even older, a tall-masted sailing ship that had been protected by sand until the hurricane scoured it away.

It was time to go. Faye and Joe had business with the sheriff, and they needed to get their daughter out of harm's way immediately. It was way too dangerous to stay on Joyeuse Island.

Unfortunately, Faye was having trouble getting up off the floor. Maybe it was because she was emotionally flattened or maybe it was because she'd been pushing herself beyond her physical limits since the hurricane blew up her life. She wasn't sure. As she put a hand on the floor, hoping she could push herself to her feet, it brushed the box that Amande had dropped.

The box fell open beneath her hand. Faye leaned over to look at it and saw a bracelet, obviously made of real gold and so heavy that it must have cost many hundreds of dollars. More likely, it had cost thousands.

The embossed cardboard gift box had come from a jewelry store that would never stoop so low as to carry something cheap. A card lay next to the box, but it said only "Cody," so it told her exactly nothing about a man who was apparently very serious about her daughter. Or, at the very least, he was a man who was financially serious about her daughter.

In reconstructing that moment later, Faye was always pretty sure that she'd done nothing wrong, at least not in the moment. She had done nothing but pick up the box, look at the bracelet and the card, then look up at her daughter's face. These are things that any person might do. They weren't the actions of a manipulative and controlling mother. Faye knew this to be true.

To be fair to Amande, though, perhaps Faye paid the price that night for the things she'd already said. She paid, in that awful moment on the floor, for weeks of questions about Manny, for months of single-minded focus on Amande's college plans, and for her unending schizophrenic need for her daughter to live a full and happy life while simultaneously never leaving her mother's side.

With all of that conflict as prologue, perhaps her simple glance up at Amande's face actually was sufficient cause for the eruption that followed.

Amande towered over Faye, even when they were both standing. At that moment, from Faye's perspective on the floor, Amande looked like a righteously indignant giant. She leaned down, snatched the bracelet in its box out of Faye's hand, and said, "That was a gift to me. I can keep it. I can wear it. I can give it back. And I can take my boat far, far, far out in the Gulf of Mexico and throw it overboard. This bracelet is not your concern."

And then she used those long legs to step over Faye and sweep down the spiral staircase. Turn by turn, she moved away from her mother, even though Faye had never said a word to make her go.

She scrambled to her feet, leaned over the bannister, and called out, "Amande, I love you. I'm sorry. Please don't go."

There was no answer. All she heard was the bang as her daughter slammed her way through the door to the sneak stair that would take her to the basement and out of the house. For all Faye knew, she intended to leave forever. Faye hurried through her own bedroom to the top of the sneak stair and ran headlong down the winding and uneven stair treads without ever considering the risk of a broken ankle or a broken neck.

Joe's voice echoed down the stairwell. "Amande? Honey, what's going on?"

Amande turned to answer him and Faye felt a glimmer of hope that she was coming back. But her next words stirred up the fear again.

"I've got to go, Dad."

"Honey, where are you going? It's late and the thief could be anywhere on this island. Your mom and I are just about to get on a boat and take you with us to stay with Magda and Sheriff Mike."

"Manny's apartment's tiny, but there's a lot of buildings at the marina and he owns them all. I know he'll find me someplace to sleep. The booths in the bar have nice comfy benches. Maybe I'll just curl up on one of those after the drunks go home. It'll be better than being here. You two can stop worrying about me. It makes you unhappy, and it's making me miserable."

Faye was still saying "Don't go," when the door to the outside world closed behind the daughter who was walking away from her.

Chapter Thirty-Eight

*I'm Manny and I'd love to take your message, but the fish are bitin'
and I've gotta help my customers catch their fair share. Leave a message
on this phone, and I'll get right back to ya. Unless one of you
fine people wants to hold down the fort so's I can go fishin'. Naw. I
didn't think so. Leave a message...*

Faye cut off Manny's voicemail message by thumbing her
phone off, wishing that she were holding an old-fashioned dial
phone so that she could slam down the receiver properly. Of
course, an old-fashioned dial phone wouldn't have been much
good to her as she hustled down an island path to the dock
where her boat waited. The sound of Amande's boat motor
revved loud, then quickly began to fade as she moved away fast.

"Amande will be okay." Joe sounded more hopeful than certain. "Yeah, she's got a couple minutes' head start on us, but
look. We can see her running lights from here."

This was true.

"Faye, she's as good in that boat as you are in yours and she's
an adult. We're gonna have to trust her to take care of herself for
a few minutes. There's no way we can catch up to her before she
gets to the marina, but she's safer there than she is here and it

ain't possible that she could get lost. She says she's going to sleep there tonight, and I believe her. I honestly think that Manny wants the best for her. He wants it almost as much as we do."

All this was probably true, but Faye still wanted to chew iron nails and spit out the heads.

The sun was going down fast as they reached the dock, so she moved to stand under the security lamp that illuminated it. She wanted one more chance to thumb through Joe's dangerous pictures while he got the boat untied and the motor started.

It was hard to focus on the images. Faye kept glancing around at the shadows where the person who stole Joe's computer might still hide. They needed to get out of there. They needed to catch up with Amande. They needed to protect her, and they needed to protect themselves.

Somehow, she pushed her fears aside and looked at the photos, really looked at them. It was fitting that, while standing in a spot of light in the gathering darkness, a sunny spot of yellow was the thing that spoke the truth.

Faye pulled her phone out of her pocket and searched for the web edition of the Micco County newspaper. There, on the front page of a paper just a few days old, was the answer.

"I know why the captain's pictures were stolen and I know why your computer's gone."

"How'd this picture tell you that?"

She held out her phone in one hand and a photo in the other.

"Look. Somebody at the newspaper cropped the original photo before printing it. Maybe it was Nate who cropped it. Not sure. Coulda been his dad. Like I showed you, the uncropped photo shows the location of a shipwreck that may be the *Philomela*, south of The Cold Spot. It's obvious that it was cropped off to protect the location of the wreck, but the photo was cropped harder than necessary if the person's goal was just to hide the wreck. I think it was done so that the yellow bimini wouldn't be in the frame, either. What do you want to bet that the person who did the cropping knows why the captain took his boat out, probably hoping to find this very ship, and never came home? Maybe that person was with him."

"Ain't taking that bet. You're pretty much always right."

Joe was a smart man.

"Before the captain died," Faye said, "your pictures needed to disappear because they could give away the location of a shipwreck that was going to make its finders a whole lot of money. That much is clear. I think the boat was cropped off, too, in case somebody found out that the wreck was being looted. This photo is evidence that could point to whoever was doing the looting."

Joe took the photo from her hand and held it closer to his eyes, looking for a killer.

"After the captain died, pictures of the wreck and the boat really needed to disappear. Maybe he drowned by accident or maybe he was drowned on purpose. Either way, nobody reported his death. This photo ties a specific boat to the shipwreck that the captain was obsessing over. If he died while he was diving on that wreck, then anybody who was diving with him is in danger of a murder charge. What if the sheriff saw this picture and went looking for somebody whose boat has a yellow bimini? We know they're not real common, so whoever owns this boat would be in for some uncomfortable legal scrutiny."

She held out the phone. The yellow blob was just north of the shadow that she believed was the *Philomela*. "Somebody in that boat might have been diving on the *Philomela* at the very time you took the picture. Days later, the captain mentioned the *Philomela* to me and died within a few hours. I think that the killer found that shipwreck by doing research with the captain's collection."

"The captain's sign-in sheets would answer that question."

"Yeah," Faye said. "The captain figured all of this out. Everybody knows that he talked too much, so the treasure hunter offered to take the captain to look at the wreck and then made sure he drowned."

"It wouldn't have been all that hard," Joe said. "We know he wasn't a diver."

"No kidding," Faye said.

"Look how close the wreck and the yellow boat are to shore. You've been saying that The Cold Spot is too shallow for the captain to drown there. Well, the *Philomela*'s in water that's deeper than that, so it ain't too shallow for drowning, but it also ain't all that deep. If it was, we wouldn't be able to see her. Do you really think the captain drowned there? Is that water deep enough that Nate could get hurt by coming up too fast?"

"I think the killer took them diving someplace deeper and farther from shore," Faye said. "The captain wouldn't know the difference. And maybe Nate was told that they were going somewhere else to see something new and wonderful at the bottom of the Gulf. If they were partners, why would he question it?"

"Nate's a reporter," Joe said. "Maybe he got too close to the truth."

Faye waved the picture at Joe. "Somebody really needed this photo to stop existing. And I guess they needed the people who saw the uncropped photo to stop existing."

Oh, Joe. Will they be after you now?

"Because somebody else might try to go out there and take stuff before they can finish stealing it?"

"Well, yeah," Faye said. "But also, the State of Florida's going to want a big cut, at the very least, and settling that dispute would tie up their right to dive on the wreck for a long time. It took Mel Fisher years to get rights to the treasure he found on the *Nuestra Señora de Atocha*. Why wait that long if you can avoid it? And why take the risk that somebody else will go out there and take the treasure you've worked so hard to find?"

"Who found the wreck?" Joe asked. "Because that's probably who killed the captain. Do you think it was Nate? Or Thad or Cody?"

"An academic has been sniffing around his library. Samantha Kennedy is her name. You remember her. We interviewed her. Well, she knows her stuff. If you told me she'd found a shipwreck using library methods, without ever getting her toes damp, I'd believe you."

Joe knew they hadn't hired her, so he knew that Faye had her doubts about Samantha Kennedy.

Faye was still rattling through suspects. "The captain's visitors could just have easily been the insurance adjuster and tree surgeon that I told you about, Greta Haines and Cyndee Stamp, coming to coerce him into signing away his right to his own money. They could've been softening him up by pretending to be interested in his library. Or maybe they actually were interested. Greta could be using that big boat to loot the *Philomela* every minute of the day that she's not cheating old people. But my money's on either Thad or Cody. And maybe Nate, too, but he couldn't have been working alone."

Faye heard herself say "Cody" and "Thad" and "Nate," and imagined her daughter being wooed by the man responsible for the captain's death. She needed to do something. She and Joe needed to get off the island, and they needed to let the sheriff know what was going on.

"We have to go. Let me try talking to Amande before you crank up the motor too loud for me to hear."

Faye dialed Amande's number, but her daughter was evidently still angry. The call went straight to voicemail, so Faye left a message:

Somebody dangerous is out there, and I'm not sure any of us are safe. Joe and I are coming to you as fast as we can. I'm calling the sheriff. When you get to the marina, find a crowd. So go in the restaurant, I guess. Yeah. Go sit in the restaurant, and wait for the sheriff there.

Then she dialed the sheriff and got no answer. She left a message, but what she needed was the reassuring voice of someone promising to take care of everything.

———

Amande's running lights were still visible on the horizon. Every now and then, they winked out of sight when her boat slid down into a wave's trough.

And every time, they reappeared. Faye could only pray that this kept happening.

———

Faye knew that Joe hated shouting over the sound of a boat motor, but he was doing it. "The person—people?—diving on the shipwreck. They found it 'cause the captain shared his books and maps with them. Right? Couldn't they have just shared the treasure, instead of killing him?"

He shook his head like a man who didn't have it in him to be a criminal. He couldn't even imagine it.

Faye had a bit more of a dastardly streak. She could totally imagine being a criminal now and then. She just didn't have it in her to follow through on her larcenous ideas.

Faye used her dastardly streak to explain things to Joe. "Try to imagine the captain staying quiet about a shipwreck. I can't. He had to be shut up."

As Faye thought it through, she doubted that the captain had even recognized the real *Philomela* in Joe's photo. The dark blotch at The Cold Spot was far more obvious. It would have been so easy for an evil person to offer to take him out there. Even when he said he didn't dive, he'd happily suit up if he was with someone who promised to keep him safe. The captain had trusted everybody.

But the murderer had sabotaged his gear and taken him someplace else, someplace way deeper than The Cold Spot. Or maybe sabotage hadn't even been necessary. It would probably be easy to take a trusting person with no scuba experience diving, then keep him down there until it was too late. The captain didn't know his equipment, and he would have believed whatever his fellow shipwreck researcher told him.

It was a pretty perfect crime to Faye's way of thinking. No marks on the body. No crime scene evidence. No visible equipment tampering.

She couldn't shout all of this over the roaring motor, so she just yelled, "Somehow, somebody killed him. Probably tampered with his equipment."

Joe asked, "Do you think that's what happened to Nate?" and Faye could see how much he was hurting for his friend.

Faye stopped trying to talk over the wind and the motor. She slashed her hand across her throat, signaling for Joe to cut the motor.

"Yeah, that may well be what happened to Nate. Getting double-crossed by a friend when you're deep underwater is one way for an experienced diver to die."

"Was he in on it? Was he okay with stealing from the wreck?

And…Faye, this is awful…was he okay with killing the captain? That doesn't seem like the Nate I know."

Faye sat quiet with her feet braced against the deck as one wave after another rocked the boat's hull. She was growing convinced that Nate was complicit in Ossie's destruction, and she had no reason to think he wasn't capable of worse, but there wasn't any driving need to rub Joe's face in his injured buddy's possible guilt.

"Coulda been his friends Thad and Cody. Coulda been Greta or Cyndee or Samantha. Thad has a dive shop and Cody helps Manny run one, but that doesn't mean they're the ones diving on that ship. And it doesn't mean that they're responsible for Nate's condition. Let's hope Nate pulls through. If not, maybe Thad and Cody will be able to clear up those questions."

———

Thad has a dive shop and Cody helps Manny run one.

Faye's own words echoed in her head. It was dark, and she could hear nothing but the boat's racing motor, so no sensory input was coming in to drive that sentence from her brain.

How would you try to kill an accomplished diver?

Faye wasn't sure, but it seemed to her that someone who worked in a dive shop would have a pretty good idea. She had been in two dive shops within the last few days. What had she seen in each of them? Racks of gear and a tank-filling station with multiple cylinders of pressurized gas.

She remembered what the captain's gear had looked like—mask, tank, flippers, wetsuit—and nothing had been out of the ordinary. Not visibly, at least.

Not visibly.

Like a bolt, she realized that the most important thing that a diver took underwater wasn't visible. It was the invisible gas in the tank that provided a diver with lifesaving oxygen.

Faye wasn't a diver, but she'd spent enough time at a marina to have picked up the lingo. Divers didn't say that they had air in their tanks. They called it "gas," and one reason for that was the varied gas mixtures that they used. This was why dive shops didn't just have oxygen tanks onsite. They had oxygen, nitrogen, and helium, so that they could fill divers' tanks with gas mixes suitable for the diving they planned to do.

Faye knew that most recreational divers used compressed air, filtered and dehumidified, but divers who wanted to go deeper or stay down longer needed different mixes. "Enriched air," which allowed diving at greater depths with reduced decompression times, was composed of nitrogen and oxygen, and the percentage of each component could vary according to the situation. Other mixes included helium at various concentrations to increase depth limits or dive times even more.

All these mixtures were safe when used as intended, but what if the person doing the mixing wanted to kill you? Too much nitrogen would induce nitrogen narcosis, a state of inebriation known as the "rapture of the deep." Tank volumes weren't infinite, so extra nitrogen meant there was less room for oxygen. Adding more helium than safety allowed reduced oxygen in the mix even more.

Too little oxygen would kill you, but it wouldn't happen immediately. As you drifted off into a nitrogen narcotic rapture, you would slowly suffocate. And your pressure gauge would show that you had gas the whole time.

Because you did. You just didn't have oxygen.

Faye wasn't sure whether investigating a diving death included testing the mix of gases in the dead person's tank. A quick web search on her phone wasn't much help, but she did see that the equipment testing was often done by outside contractors. It had only been two days since the captain had been found, and that wasn't a lot of time for the tank to go to the contractor and get tested. This delay could be giving the murderer time to empty the *Philomela*, kill the witnesses, and prepare to disappear.

And would the excess helium even be measurable? Faye remembered enough chemistry to know that helium molecules were tiny. If anything was going to leak during Nate's long day floating in the Gulf, the helium would go first.

Cody and Thad both had access to the equipment needed to pull off this kind of murder. And they had the necessary knowledge. Which one did it? Or was it both of them?

Worse, they'd both shown an interest in her daughter that Faye would call harassment, since Amande wasn't welcoming it and they weren't giving up. Faye had a queasy feeling that a man who had done murder to amass enough money to disappear wouldn't hesitate at grabbing a woman to take with him.

The sheriff hadn't called back, so she texted him.

Make sure that your investigators check
the gas in those two scuba tanks. Oxygen?
Nitrogen? Helium? Right mix? Wrong mix?

We need to know.

Chapter Thirty-Nine

Amande was running her boat at top speed so she didn't hear her phone ring, but she felt it buzz in her jeans pocket. She slid it out, checked the screen, and saw that it said "Mom."

She declined the call, and she also declined to listen to the message. What she had to say to Faye was better said by text, when she wouldn't have to hear the hurt in her mother's voice.

She took some time to think about what to say to Faye. When she was ready, she steered the boat with her elbows long enough to shoot off a string of return texts.

Then she set her phone to silent, resolved to ignore any vibrations in her pocket that might come from a mother intent on convincing her to pick up the phone.

———

Faye tried to be patient as she waited for Amande or the sheriff to call her back, but she honestly didn't have it in her to wait very long. She had one eye on the phone in her hand as Joe headed for the marina, throttle open.

"Did you call the sheriff about the break-in at our house? Or Lieutenant Baker? Or 911?" Joe hollered over the wind and the motor.

"Went straight to the sheriff. If I called Baker or a dispatcher, they'd just send out a deputy for a small-time burglary. We need more than that."

"He didn't pick up?"

"Nope, but I texted and said it was urgent."

"The man's probably taking a bath. It's that time of the night. Give him a few minutes."

"I'm just gonna keep texting. When he gets out of the tub, he'll have a million texts and they'll all be from me."

Bracing herself against the boat's motion, Faye used her phone to snap a picture of the print showing the possible shipwreck and the telltale yellow bimini. It took her a few tries to get the flash right and to take a shot that wasn't too blurry, but she managed. She sent it to the sheriff with a text saying,

Somebody at the newspaper cropped this print
because it shows that the Philomela was wrecked
someplace south of here. (I think. Look at the
shadow near the boat with the yellow bimini.)

Maybe Nate did the cropping.

Or maybe he's in the hospital because the
person who did it wants to shut him up.

Maybe somebody at the newspaper is in on it.

But who? Surely not his dad.

Then she just kept texting, because it seemed important to have all her suspicions in writing, even if they were floating around as cell phone signals, waiting for somebody to read them.

> Also, somebody broke into our house
> and stole Joe's computer.

> Still have a handful of prints but they're
> all we've got left of his drone shots.
> Will send photos of those too.

Once she'd communicated the critical information, she indulged in some speculation-by-text while she kept hoping that either he or Amande would text back.

> Doubt Nate had time to steal the com-
> puter and then float around in the Gulf
> until he nearly died. Not all in 1 day.

> Wish I knew Nate's timeline better. Was he
> part of a group that had been looting the
> Philomena before he got hurt? Or was some-
> one else working alone to loot the ship
> and kill people who knew too much?

> Did somebody try to kill Nate so they
> didn't have to split the money? No clue.

> Same questions apply to the captain. I truly
> believe he was a diving newbie. Did some-
> body sabotage his gas and let him drown?

> Or maybe Nate's partner (partners?) killed
> the captain and Nate wasn't having it.
> Maybe they tried to shut him up by sabotag-
> ing his tank but he was a better diver than
> the captain and he managed to survive.

As the last text left her phone, flying on invisible electro-magnetic waves toward the sheriff, wherever he was, Faye felt a series of vibrations. They signaled that a string of texts had traveled on their own electromagnetic waves to her. She prayed that they were from Amande.

And they were. Unfortunately, they did not say anything resembling, "I got your message and I am going someplace safe to wait for you." They said,

> im okay

> i just don't want to talk right now

> dont know when im coming home
> but it wont be tonight

> if something's wrong ill text

> otherwise presume im fine

> i do love you both

———

Faye tried not to think about the daughter who wasn't speaking to her. She figured that helping the sheriff lock up any criminals running around Micco County would be a concrete way to keep Amande safe.

Shouting over the boat motor's whine, she said, "We've gotta get these photos to Sheriff Rainey," she said. "If Ossie was flying low enough, you might have even gotten the yellow-topped boat's registration number. The sheriff has people who may be able to blow these pictures up enough to see that."

This, of course, was probably the reason somebody had blasted Ossie into tiny mechanical bits.

Joe grabbed her wrist and made her look him in the face. Seeing his lips move didn't make it easier to understand him over the motor's racket. He said something starting with "You," repeated it a few times, then gave up and cut the motor again.

"You can't be telling the whole county that you know something about that boat. What if you're right? What if somebody really is trying to lock down my pictures because they're hiding something?"

Joe was right, so there was nothing to do but tell him so. "You make a good point."

He wasn't finished making his point, so he didn't let go of her wrist. "You already talked to Manny about that yellow-topped boat, didn't you? What if he's in on it?"

Faye had been suspicious of Manny for quite some time, so she was shocked to realize that she so firmly believed in his innocence that he hadn't been a serious suspect in any of the scenarios she'd been considering. This could have been a deadly mistake, since Manny, too, had access to his own tank-filling station. He could have used it to kill somebody just as easily as Cody.

"Manny? Do you really think he's dangerous?" Faye felt like she had too many clues and they didn't quite line up. "The facts we know point to the owner of a boat that we're pretty sure isn't Manny's, unless he's hiding a yellow bimini somewhere. I don't even think he has a personal boat. If he ever has time to go out for fun—and it doesn't seem like he does—he probably takes one of the boats he rents to tourists. The yellow bimini doesn't match Nate's boat or Greta's, either. I don't know what Thad's boat looks like, or Cody's. I don't even know if Cyndee or Samantha have boats, but I'm thinking no. Regardless, I really doubt that any of them gets away from land, stops to change biminis, and then does it again before coming home."

"That don't make a bit of sense."

"Exactly. Yes, Manny could still be involved, and Amande's going to get to him before we do. We've just got to hope that he's not a killer and that she stays safe until we can catch up with her.

Chapter Forty

Faye looked up from her phone, scanning the watery horizon. The running lights on Amande's boat were dim in the distance, but they were there. She knew where her daughter was going. She was going to Manny.

For reasons Faye didn't understand, she was relatively okay with that. In her heart, she believed that Manny would protect her daughter.

But Thad? Cody? Some other nameless person who liked to dive and liked money enough to kill for it? Any of them could be waiting at the marina for a young woman who was naive enough to think she was ready to take on the world.

But she wasn't. Nobody was ever ready to take on the world. All anyone could ever do was make a leap of faith and hope that somebody was there to help when the world let them fall.

———

Sheriff Rainey's phone was waiting for him on the bathroom counter while he showered, so he had heard the flurry of texts come through. Micco County wasn't a big place and it didn't have an awful lot of crime, but he did actually have more open cases than the captain's death investigation. Nevertheless, he knew in his heart that Dr. Faye Longchamp-Mantooth was sending the flurry of texts that was generating constant beeps while he washed the shampoo out of his hair. This theory was based on the fact that very few people had her utter focus, so they weren't capable of a string of texts the size of an old-school encyclopedia.

He tried to dry himself off while he read texts alerting him to possible problems with scuba tanks, as well as a shipwreck "south of here" and a mysterious yellow bimini.

———

Because Sheriff Rainey's life wasn't complicated enough, he got an urgent call before he finished drying himself. Lieutenant Baker was still working the missing persons case like a person who didn't need sleep. Or even a shower.

"We got him," she said. "The ringleader of the looters, I mean. And get this. It's the husband of the missing woman."

"I never liked him."

"Yeah." This single syllable communicated the depths of Baker's contempt for the man.

"What about the neighbor?"

"Still no alibi for the first three days after the storm. Still acting suspicious as hell, but he's walking free because I've got nothing to tie him to the looting. Or to the missing woman and kid. Yet."

———

Faye's text to Sheriff Rainey, telling him to talk to a man in south Georgia about some ridiculously old brandy and rum, was interesting. So were her thoughts about the captain's death, especially the part where she thought someone at the newspaper was "in on it," but he wasn't sure what the best thing was for him to do right that minute. And he did think it was important to do something right that minute because the breathless tone of Faye's texts was setting off his trouble radar.

He tried to call her, but got a text back saying,

> On the boat going fast. Too loud
> to talk. Texting is better.

So she was on a boat, but it was a coin flip as to whether she were coming to shore or going home. He texted her back to say,

> Slow down and tell me what's going on.

Her return text didn't help much.

> If the rich rum-buying guy or the newspaper
> folks point you in the direction of Manny, LET
> ME KNOW. My daughter's running straight
> into his arms right now. We're trying to get
> there. Please meet us at the marina.

So that answered his question of what to do next. He needed to get the straight scoop from Faye, and Manny's Marina was as good a place as any to get it. Because he was not stupid, he called Baker, told her he was heading to the marina, and asked for backup. Then he got on the road, listening all the while to Lieutenant Baker, who was not happy at being ordered to waste her time calling Faye's rum-buying guy. The fact that she was supposed to do that while driving to the marina to be his backup was the last straw.

He listened to her objections, which were detailed and well thought out, but they changed nothing. Nobody ever said that working in law enforcement was all fun and games.

———

Amande's boat was tied in its usual spot. Faye felt a momentary relief. They knew where she was, at least. Well, this was true unless she'd gotten in her car and driven away to parts unknown. Or been stolen away by a murderer.

She and Joe hurried up the dock toward the bar and grill, the beating heart of Manny's Marina. Peering through its windows, she could see people inside. They were mere shadows on the window blinds, but they were alive and moving. They gestured with their forks as they laughed. They jostled their way between crowded tables as they made their way to the bar or to the bathroom.

None of those shadows were her daughter. Faye would have known Amande by her graceful, forthright style of movement.

She didn't see Manny, either, but he was probably on the far side of the room, working the bar. Savvy owners knew nobody else could bartend as well as they did. Employees might slip drinks to their friends. They might overpour and destroy the profit margin. They might underpour and leave the clientele peeved. Manny had a mind for business and he was smooth. The bar and grill had been popular under all its owners, but Faye had never seen it this full.

Joe opened the door for her, and she stepped inside. The place was dimly lit for socializing, but it was still brighter than the outdoors. Her eyes took a moment to adjust. She spent that moment looking for Amande.

When her dazzled pupils had tightened enough for her to see, Faye saw Manny right where she'd thought he would be, elbows on the bar and surveying the room to be sure his customers were happy. Thad and Samantha were sitting at the bar across from him, having an intense conversation, all emphatic nods and eye contact.

Greta was sitting almost elbow-to-elbow with Thad. Cyndee was perched on the stool beside her with her long limbs arranged uncomfortably in the tight space. Both women had their eyes on their drinks, but Faye could see them stealing glances at the handsome Thad and Manny.

Nate's dad Ray sat on Cyndee's other side, tapping on his tablet computer and drinking. His presence rang warning bells in Faye's head. Why was he here, instead of at the hospital with his seriously injured son? And why was everybody she could reasonably suspect of murdering her friend in this room, except for Cody? Was the marina some kind of common denominator?

Of course it was. Thad, Greta, and Manny were all boaters. Ray probably was, too, and Faye knew for a fact that he was a regular in the bar and grill. Cyndee seemed to go where Greta went. Samantha seemed a bit out of place, but she and Thad were sharing some powerful chemistry. Maybe they were simply on a date.

There might have been many nights when all these people were here. The only missing strands of the net that Faye was trying to untangle were Cody and Amande.

Then she raked her eyes around the room and learned that she was wrong. Cody was indeed right there in the room with her, completing her roster of suspects. He was standing on the far side of the room, between the bar and the rear exit. And he was deep in conversation with Amande.

Faye would have run to her daughter, but she was hampered by an obstacle course of crowded tables full of people enjoying Manny's catfish, not to mention drinkers getting drunker. She slalomed between the tables, swerving from left to right when she really wanted to plow straight through.

As she stumbled past Manny, she heard him asking Thad if he'd seen a boat with a yellow bimini, and she died a little inside. She was sure that the person who owned that boat was killing people, maybe just to shut them up about it.

She lurched toward Manny, trying to shut *him* up. This was her fault. She had done this. She had asked Manny about a yellow bimini. Now he was innocently trying to get her question answered for her. And the fact that he was asking it told her something. It meant that he wasn't the guilty person trying to make that yellow piece of canvas go away.

"I'm sure I've seen one," Thad said. "They come in all colors, but my customers like colors dark enough to hide mildew. Burgundy. They like burgundy. And navy blue."

Manny repeated the question to Greta and Cyndee. Both women raised their eyes from their drinks and shook their heads no.

Greta said, "I've seen some cool custom ones in the colors of football teams. You know—orange-and-blue for the Gators, garnet-and-gold for the Seminoles, aqua-and-orange for the Dolphins. But I can't think of anybody who has a yellow one, not off the top of my head."

Cyndee said, "Me, neither. Though, you know what? Yellow would look pretty awesome with a black boat. Especially if you put some fine little yellow pinstripes on the black. Why'd you wanna know?"

Before Faye could get close enough to tell Manny to shut his loose lips, she heard one of her favorite voices speaking in its familiar low alto.

"Hey, let me ask you something. Do you know anybody who has a yellow bimini on their boat?"

Oh, Amande. No. Don't be asking dangerous questions.

She hadn't reached her daughter yet, but she was close. Cody was closer, leaning in with his ear to Amande's lips. His hand gripped her side possessively, palm to her waist and fingers splayed from the base of her bra to the curve of her hip. Someday, someone was going to touch Amande that way and she would like it. This was not that day.

Amande was letting him touch her, despite the fact that Faye could see her vibrating with revulsion. Or maybe it was fear. And maybe Cody was enjoying that fear.

What was he saying? Faye needed to hear him answer the question, and then she needed to slap him senseless. Better senseless than unconscious, though, because that's what Cody would be if Joe got to him first.

Cody's tone was quiet, romantic even, but Faye's ears were tuned to it. He said, "No, I don't know anybody with a yellow bimini. Never seen one, actually. I don't think they even make 'em that color."

The answers banged around in Faye's head. Greta had said, "I can't think of anybody who has a yellow one, not off the top of my head," and Cyndee had said, "Me, neither." Thad had said, "I'm sure I have," before he said he couldn't think of any specific boats. Way back when she'd mentioned it to Manny, he'd said, "Can't say for sure, since you wouldn't believe how many boats come through this marina, but I'm gonna say no."

Cody, and only Cody, was denying that there even was such a thing, which beggared belief. Maybe most people didn't choose that color, but manufacturers surely made it. Cody did boat repair, so he must get catalogs that showed all the colors of paint and canvas that he could use to customize a watercraft. Also, he pumped Manny's fuel, which meant that he probably saw more boats in a day than anybody in the room. As far as Faye was concerned, he protested too much.

Cody's fingers pressed hard into the soft flesh of Amande's side and the young woman flinched.

"Why do you care about boats or biminis or anything yellow? Why are you asking me this question, little girl?"

Faye needed to press her fingers into the soft flesh of his throat. She lunged in his direction and struck her shinbone hard on an empty stool.

Faye yelped as she felt the nerves in her shin scream. The oak stool crashed onto the wood floor with a terrible clatter.

"Faye? Is there a problem?" The question came from behind her.

It was the sheriff speaking. As he pushed his way into the bar and grill, he let the screen door slam behind him, and its wood-on-wood bang echoed the sound of the stool hitting the floor.

Faye saw the panic on Cody's face and she knew it could be deadly. He stood straighter and pulled his jaw down toward his collarbone. It was a reflexive defensive motion designed to protect his throat, but it made him look like a cornered cobra spreading its hood. Amande let out a small squeak as he dug his fingers even further into her side, and the sound enraged him.

"Shut up."

She twisted toward him and opened her mouth to speak.

"I said shut up." Smooth and fast, the hand that wasn't grasping Amande dipped into his pocket and came out with a dive knife.

He flipped it open, pressed it to her throat, and said, "I'm out of here. I didn't want to go until I got that ship picked clean, but I've hauled up enough stuff to support me for a real long time.

'Specially if I go to some cheap-ass country where my dollars go a real long way. Maybe I'll take this pretty girl with me. Seems like she thinks she's too good to go anyplace with me when I'm being nice."

Chapter Forty-One

Cody wrapped his arm tighter around Amande's midsection, still holding a six-inch blade to her throat. The young woman's eyes darted from Manny's face to Joe's, but they settled on Faye's. There was terror in Amande's eyes, but trust, too. Faye, who was fighting against the shock wrapping its cold blanket around her shoulders, knew that she would rather die than betray that trust.

If something happens to Amande...

She forced herself to fully acknowledge her fear.

If he kills Amande and leaves me alive, I'll go to my grave remembering that look on her face.

Faye wasn't going to let that happen. If this man took her daughter's life, he was going to have to take Faye's, too.

She took stock of the situation. The sheriff was behind her and he was certainly armed, but it would be almost impossible for him to shoot Cody without taking the risk that his knife would sink into her daughter's throat. Besides, between the sheriff's gun and Cody sat a room full of people who had been innocently enjoying their drinks just five seconds before. Shooting Cody was too risky.

Cody yelled, "Everybody stay right where you are."

Faye watched the terrified eaters and drinkers weighing their next moves. Should they drop to the floor and hide under their tables? Should they run for the door? They didn't know and so, for the moment, they were frozen in place.

Since Cody was armed with a knife, not a gun, running for the hills was a high probability proposition for everybody in the room who wasn't Amande. Still, everyone knew that all bets were off if the sheriff opened fire. And they knew that sudden moves on their part could startle the man holding a knife to the delicate skin just below Amande's mandible.

For now, they were motionless, but it wouldn't take much to send them stampeding to safety. A few of them had toddlers and babies in their laps. Those people slowly, very slowly, folded forward, wrapping their arms and torsos around tender little bodies.

———

Amande was having trouble finding a place to focus her eyes. Cody had jerked her to him so roughly that her head had whiplashed hard, and she was dizzy. The sharp knife edge against her throat awakened something primal in her that wanted to scream, vomit, cry, collapse. The knife's edge made her see dark spots floating through the darkened room, and it kept her from believing that a uniformed man wearing a badge could do anything to help her. The floating dark spots meant that she couldn't see him, not really, not with a dark room between them and a dark night behind him.

The room was silent except for the hushed breath of dozens of people. No clothing rustled. No shoes scuffed.

Cody's voice was deafening in her ear. "Nobody needs to get hurt, not even this little bitch."

He took a step backward. The only way to keep the sharp edge from slicing her skin was to take a step with him, so Amande did.

She could feel the people who loved her more than she could see them. There was the shadow of her dad, standing near the door where the sheriff was. He was dim and far from her, but she held her gaze until the very sight of him pushed the dark spots out of her field of vision. Knowing he was there made her feel stronger than she really was. Amande knew that her dad was good all the way through. He believed the best of people until he just couldn't. It took a lot to push a man like that to vengeance, but she knew in her bones that if Cody hurt her, her father would track him like an animal until he had nowhere left to hide.

She felt Cody dragging her toward the bar's rear exit. Everything in her said that she shouldn't pass through that door. She shouldn't let him take her into the dark.

As they shuffled backward together, Manny came into view to her right, just inside her peripheral vision. She had known him all her life, but she'd never seen tears on his face before now. He stood at the open cash register, with shining glasses and liquor bottles arrayed behind him, just as she'd seen him stand since she was a little girl. Manny knew how to make people happy. Long ago, he had explained to her that what he did was very important. He helped people enjoy the great blue sea without a care, and he greeted them with a cold drink and a smile when they came home to a reality that often wasn't very pleasant. If Cody took her out into the dark and she didn't come back, she would be sad to leave Manny.

Amande's grandmother had loved Manny in the special way that old women love charming young men who bring them daisies and bourbon. She had paid him the compliment of trusting him with her granddaughter. Amande missed her grandmother and she wondered what it meant to die. If Cody pressed harder on the knife handle, hard enough to slice her jugular vein, would she see her grandmother again? What about her mother, Justine, who had run away from baby Amande? Justine had kept running until cancer stopped her dead. If the knife did its job, would Amande finally meet the mother who gave birth to her?

She would rather stay with the mother she had, the one who cared about her so much that Amande sometimes chafed under her love, the one who was standing so nearby but not quite near enough to touch.

Amande's eyes found Faye's and she comforted herself with what she saw there. If she had to die, it would be in the company of someone who saw her and knew her and loved her anyway.

———

Manny, standing at the bar, was the only person in the room who could see Cody's back, so he was the only person who saw the bulge under his jacket. The bulge was the shape and size of a handgun, some kind of semiautomatic unless Manny missed his guess.

This bulge complicated Manny's life considerably. His first priority was Amande, and it would always be Amande. He simply loved her, as much as if she were his own baby girl. More than that, he admired her. Nobody east of the Rockies would have expected that the abandoned child of two heroin addicts, raised by an old woman with no education and no money, could have grown into the vibrant, loving, dynamic person standing just out of his reach. Setting aside his own feelings, he owed it to Amande's grandmother to save her precious baby.

But Manny had a second priority. He stood in a room full of

people who trusted him to entertain them and, at a bare minimum, to keep them safe. If Cody reached around behind him and pulled that gun out of his waistband, Manny's guests would be at risk, all of them, and he wouldn't stand for that. He began plotting a way to get between Cody and Amande.

And between Cody and his gun.

———

Sheriff Rainey knew he was personally responsible for this hellish situation. All he'd done was walk through the door, but criminals knew that he was the law walking around on two legs. And they hated him for it.

When he'd made his entrance and unwittingly put all these people in danger, he hadn't had a clue who killed the captain, nor did he understand what had happened to Nate Peterson. Faye Longchamp-Mantooth seemed to have some idea of what had been done to the captain and Nate, but he didn't, not really. Cody's current behavior made it obvious that he was guilty of something terrible, and it was most likely the murder and attempted murder.

Yes, he'd had his suspects and Cody was one of them, but he'd had no evidence pointing directly to him. Heck, poor Nate could have killed the captain, for all he'd been able to determine. Nate's current condition, quite serious according to his doctors, didn't mean that he hadn't committed murder while he was still hale and hearty.

The sheriff reflected that he'd solved this crime simply by wearing his badge into a bar. This didn't make him feel very good about himself as a top-flight investigator.

———

Cody was now within reach of the door that would take him out into the night, and Faye's daughter with him. He hovered near it uncertainly, and Faye saw his problem. With his left arm around Amande's body and his right hand holding a knife to her neck, he didn't have any hands left to operate the door. He covered his hesitation with aggression, speaking to the crowd with a sneer.

"Here's what's gonna happen. I'm going out this door and I'm getting in my boat and I'm taking her with me. You people are going to let me go and you won't come after me if you want her to stay alive. Maybe I'll take her with me where I'm going. Or maybe, when I'm far enough away, I'll give her a life jacket and leave her floating in the water to wait for you. You're gonna wait four hours—no, five—before you come looking for her. If you don't, the body you find floating in the water won't be alive."

Faye tried not to think of her daughter afloat as a living needle in a big, watery haystack. She tried not to think of sharks and hypothermia. She tried not to think.

Cody lowered his lips to Amande's ear. "Need you to do something for me, honey. Reach over there and turn the door-knob for me, then open the door real slow. I'm a little twitchy, so be real careful not to upset me. Okay?"

Amande didn't nod, because the knife's big blade was in the way, so she whispered a barely audible, "Okay."

Faye saw her reach for the doorknob, but her arm wasn't long enough. Seeing this, Cody edged closer and the back of her hand brushed the knob, but her arm wouldn't rotate enough for her to grasp it. She and Cody commenced an awkward dance as he tried to maneuver her into position without turning his back on anybody. This effort was not entirely successful.

When he turned and Faye saw him in profile, she saw a bulge above his rear waistband that put the taste of ashes in her mouth. Manny stood to her left and she could see that he had a clear view of the man's back, too. He knew what Amande was up against.

Cody shifted his grip on Amande so that she could reach the doorknob. As he did this, his jacket shifted enough to reveal what was under the bulge. The handgun was small, matte-black, and terrifying. Faye let her gaze shift Manny's way. Their eyes locked and it was obvious that he saw what she saw.

Without speaking a word, they understood each other. Something needed to be done before Amande passed through that doorway.

———

Amande had twisted herself into a position that let her reach the doorknob while still being physically restrained by a knife at her throat. Her hand lingered on its worn metal, unwilling to open the door and let the night in.

Cody used the fingers gripping her torso to pinch Amande's side, hard. His breath was hot on her cheek as he said, "Any day now, bitch," but the maneuver to let her reach the knob had put a few inches of spaces between them. If she was going to make a move, now was the time.

She looked for her mother. Faye was there, just an arm's-length from Manny but farther from Amande. She was too far to reach, too far to touch, but Amande could look in her eyes. She saw comfort there.

Faye held her gaze and her face told Amande everything. No, not that. She didn't want to see that.

Amande didn't want to see self-sacrifice on her mother's eyes. She saw it in the set of her jaw and in her ready-for-anything stance. Amande didn't want Faye to give herself up for her. How could she signal the word "No" without shaking her head or moving the neck where a blade rested?

She couldn't. She could only watch as her mother waited for her chance.

Cody nudged Amande to open the door and she had to move herself another inch away from him to get enough leverage to twist the knob. Her eyes were still on Faye as a bit more space opened up between her and Cody. It was even possible that the blade was one hair's-breadth farther from her neck. Now was the time.

At that instant, Faye's eyes dropped to the floor at her feet and rose again, telling Amande what she had to do. Amande was terrified, but if there was anything in the world that she trusted, it was her parents. Craning her neck back as far from the blade as she could manage, she did what her mother asked. She let her knees buckle, trying to slip between Cody's arms and trying to let herself drop. He had the reflexes of a very young man, or she would have made it. As it was, he caught her under an armpit before her knees hit the floor.

———

Faye saw Manny's eyes on the gun. They told her how he planned to make his move, and she let him do it. He went high. He went for the gun, knowing that this would leave him wide-open to the knife.

Faye went low, knocking Amande loose from Cody's grip. They dropped to the floor, and Faye made herself as big as possible, sprawling over her much-larger daughter's crumpled body. Then she waited for the slash of a blade or the stunning impact of a bullet.

———

Amande lay flat on the floor. Her flyweight mother was on top of her, using her tiny body as a human shield. Once the room stopped spinning, Amande planned to shake Faye off and pin her to the floor. After all, Amande was the one stupid enough to spend time with Cody-the-murderer. She should be the one exposed to blades and bullets. Unfortunately, her head had hit the floor pretty hard, so she was having trouble operating her arms and legs.

A pair of deck shoes blurred past her face and she wanted to be ill. Now Manny was risking everything for her, too, and that just wasn't how things were supposed to be.

———

Manny saw Faye wrap both arms around Amande and drop her to the floor, away from the knife. It was time to gain control of the gun.

He grabbed a roll of quarters out of the cash register, holding them in his right hand where they would add heft to his punches. Then he broke a bourbon bottle on the side of the bar, crafting himself a wickedly sharp weapon for his left hand. He lunged at Cody with both the fist and the bottle swinging.

He resisted the overwhelming impulse to give the knife a wide radius. He had calculated his odds of snatching the handgun out of Cody's pants, and they were best if he faced the knife and went straight for his target. If he lost a little blood in the process, so be it.

Manny saw the knife carve a slash into his arm more than he felt it. He would feel it later, if there was a later.

———

Ray Peterson threw a bar napkin on top of his tablet computer and dropped an expensive fountain pen on top of it.

He rose.

———

If he'd been navigating through an open space, Joe knew that he could have reached Amande and Faye in just a few long steps. In this crowded bar? It would take him a long time to get there. Too long.

He had just one option. He needed to go up and over.

Joe put his size fourteen foot on the seat of an empty chair and used it to leap onto the nearest table. Hopscotching from table to table, he launched himself from the last one, confident that his flying body would strike Cody dead-center.

There was a single problem as he took flight. Somebody was in his way.

———

Lieutenant Baker's first indication of trouble came when she opened the door to the bar and grill and walked into a scenario that made no sense at all.

She saw Cody standing over Faye Longchamp-Mantooth and her daughter. She saw Manny and his homemade weapons. She saw Joe's face, nine feet above the floor, as he ran across a room full of tabletops. She saw Nate Peterson's father put a gun to Cody's chest.

And she saw how wrong she'd been.

———

The sound of a gunshot at close range deafened Faye, and presumably Amande, so they were both spared the sounds of Cody's suffering, which didn't last long. Shot through the heart, he died quickly.

They did, however, hear the words spoken as Ray Peterson yanked a snubnose .38 out of his pocket and pressed its muzzle against Cody's chest.

"What kind of monster leaves his friend for the fishes to eat?"

Cody's pleas for mercy were pathetic and Ray brushed them all away. He just said, "This is for Nate. You can tell Satan hello for me," as he pulled the trigger.

And then all sound was blotted out for Faye by that single gunshot, even the screams of a roomful of people.

Chapter Forty-Two

"You're the one who cracked the case," the sheriff said to Faye, as they sat in his office and tried to disentangle what had happened to them. "You deserve to see this." He slid a tablet computer and a cocktail napkin across his desk toward her.

The napkin was covered with the elegant, stylized script of a rich man writing with an expensive fountain pen. In large letters and numbers, he had written down the passwords to open the tablet and to access his note-taking software. Faye used them, and she found the notes Ray had taken for two explosive articles he was writing for his newspaper.

One set of notes was a meticulous compilation of the sins of Greta Haines. Ray had before-and-after photos of multiple properties that she'd sabotaged to drum up business. Faye recognized the captain's house and yard among photos he'd taken both by drone and with a handheld camera. Ray had testimony from people pressured to sign powers of attorney. And he had witnesses prepared to testify that Greta had worked the same scams during the last hurricane. She was going down, and she would likely take Cyndee with her.

The other notes were for an article to be co-written with Nate. They included a transcription of Nate's testimony, taken at his sickbed:

After Joe sent me his photo, I showed it to Cody and Thad. Since it showed the *Philomela*, we decided I should crop it, so nobody else would know where it was. Cody's yellow bimini was so obvious. It said, "Hey, look at me!" and we didn't want anybody to know we'd been down to the wreck.

That was the only time we dived on the wreck together, and we just took one bottle of brandy as a souvenir. We weren't ever going back, as far as Thad and I knew, because we liked the idea of protecting it from people who would destroy it for money. At least, that's how Thad and I felt.

Cody talked me into finding out where Joe stored the photos, saying that they were dangerous. They could show treasure hunters where the ship was. I thought that was a little extreme, but it was fun feeling like a secret agent. I helped him figure out how to destroy Joe's pictures. I cropped the cover photo. I helped steal that one bottle of brandy. I own those mistakes, but that's all I did. I didn't know Cody killed the captain until I realized he was trying to kill me.

I didn't know that Cody was hiding in the swamp when he shot Ossie. He heard the sheriff and Joe make plans to fly Ossie with Lieutenant Baker, so he hid and waited to shoot her down. I accidentally made things easier for him by taking her up before the lieutenant got there and by doing such a crappy job of flying her.

It didn't occur to me that the shooter was Cody until I was in the middle of telling him everything Joe said about where he stored the photos. I realized that something wasn't right and I called him on it, but he seemed sorry. Said he'd gotten too caught up in the shipwreck. Acted like he wanted to make things up with me by going out for a dive someplace new, deeper than we usually went. (I really should have suspected something when he didn't invite Thad.)

My guess is that he sabotaged my gas. Too much helium and nitrogen. Not enough oxygen. I know the symptoms of nitrogen narcolepsy, and I have a pretty good idea what it's like to die from lack of oxygen. That's what it was like.

I realized what was happening and kicked hard for the surface. When I got there, Cody and his boat were gone.

I had a long time to think about things when I was floating out in the Gulf. It's clear to me that the captain died the same way that Cody wanted me to die. There was no way that the captain was going to stay quiet about Cody using his library to find the Philomena. Cody had never imagined that people existed who couldn't be bribed to shut up, so he had to do something. But he knew the captain well enough to know that if he promised to take him diving and keep him safe, the captain would believe him. How anybody could kill a man like the captain is beyond me.

Somebody has to stop Cody before the same thing happens to Thad. And who knows who else?

It took Faye a moment to come up with the words for what she was feeling. When she did, she said, "I know exactly why Ray shot the man who did this to his son. What's going to happen to Ray?"

"He killed Cody in front of a crowd. It wasn't self-defense. He showed up with a gun and he left us this note, so there was at least some degree of premeditation, although he can certainly afford a lawyer who'll say it was temporary insanity. And maybe it was. So I don't know. I do know that it's going to be hard to find a jury in Micco County who will want to see Ray suffer for what he did."

Faye knew that she didn't.

———

Faye Longchamp-Mantooth had hardly shown herself out of the sheriff's office when Lieutenant Baker showed up on his doorstep.

"I was wrong," she said. "If it weren't for Dr. Longchamp-Mantooth, Cody might have gotten away and taken that young woman with him."

"I suspect Cody would have found Amande to be more than his match. She'd have probably brought him to us, hog-tied and with a signed confession pinned to his shirt."

Baker wasn't in the mood to joke.

"I should have respected your judgment."

"You were right about the missing woman," he said. "The neighbor came forward as a witness as soon as word got out that we'd arrested the husband for looting. That neighbor's gonna be a local hero when word gets out, because he put a battered wife and her kid in his car, drove twenty-four hours, dropped her off at her sister's, slept for twelve hours, turned around, and drove home. And never breathed a word to anybody about where she was until the man who hurt her was safely in jail."

"So I heard. I understand that the neighbor's wife's got a future as a local hero, too," Baker said. "She had the good sense to get video of the missing woman telling why she'd run away, complete with closeups of her cuts and bruises. And cigarette burns. Even if we hadn't nailed him on the looting, we'd have him on the domestic violence."

"You're kind of a hero, too, Lieutenant. You put her sorry husband in jail."

This made Lieutenant Baker laugh out loud. "Up next to Dr. Longchamp-Mantooth and Manny laying down their lives? Or the next-door neighbor who probably saved her life? No way. I'm just a cop who was right about one case and wrong about the other."

"Same here, Lieutenant. But sometimes you're not right at all, and this time we know that neither of the bad guys is going to be hurting anybody any time soon. Cody won't hurt anybody ever again. You were right to chase your case and I was right to chase mine. I think we should enjoy the moment, don't you?"

—

Several long days sitting in the hospital at Nate's bedside had convinced Amande that she knew all there was to know about him. Faye was amused, but she did enjoy listening to her daughter explain things from Nate's point of view. Maybe he was as innocent as he claimed.

Faye had a suspicious soul, but she was inclined to believe him. And she was inclined to believe his father's obvious remorse. Ray blamed himself for not finding out the truth in time to prevent the attempt on Nate's life. He was having trouble finding a way to take responsibility for the captain's death, but he was on a roll, guilt-wise. Give him time, and he'd find a way.

Faye sat at the bar at Manny's Marina, eating breakfast with her daughter as Amande prepared for her daily "Let's go cheer Nate up!" trip to the hospital. Manny had done an admirable job of frying their eggs with just his left hand. He would be working in a sling until the deep cut that Cody had carved into the muscles of his right upper arm had healed. Somehow, Manny managed to give that arm sling a hip pirate charm. He gave his spatula a deft bounce, and a patty of hash browns flew into the air, flipped, and landed right beside Amande's fried eggs.

"Hey, Manny. Got any hundred-and-fifty-year-old brandy on one of those shelves behind you?" Amande dug her fork into her hash browns and waited for his answer.

"Naw, but I've got some that's pretty good. Smooth, and it don't cost a hundred bucks a sip. But you're not twenty-one yet, are you, little girl?"

"Nope, but you made me a promise you'll have to keep when I get there."

Faye held her breath. She knew that Amande had been hanging onto this promise for years.

"I promised a long time ago that I'd tell you everything I know about your birth father when you're twenty-one, and I will. I'm warning you that he's a nasty piece of work. But, you know, when you blast into his life, you'll either cure him of that or you'll make him pay for every terrible thing he ever did."

"Maybe I'll do both."

Faye saw Sheriff Rainey walk up behind them. She could see that he was listening to Amande's challenge to Manny and to her birth father and, she supposed, to life itself, but he was pretending like he wasn't. He settled himself on the stool next to Amande, caught Faye's eye, and said hello. Other than that, he didn't speak, but Faye could see him listening to Amande's rapid-fire chatter. If the young woman noticed, she didn't seem to care.

"Nate's not your average snotty, rich guy," she said, shaking her egg-coated fork in Faye's face to emphasize her point. "Well, he was, but he's learned a lot, what with being double-crossed by a man he thought was his friend. And spending a lot of time in a hospital bed."

Faye would have added, "Not to mention floating alone in the Gulf of Mexico for hours and hours, in pain and on the brink of death," but she hadn't yet recovered from Cody's threat to do the same thing to Amande. Also, she didn't want to glorify Nate too much. Amande was capable of doing that all by herself.

Amande had warmed to Nate after she'd extracted his side of the story, slowly but persistently. She had sat with him in silence as his lungs began to heal, and maybe she'd spent that time remembering those moments when she'd believed that Cody would be tossing her overboard, too, to float alone and perhaps to die.

She'd drawn the story out of him slowly, like a spinner coaxing a thread from a ball of raw wool. It would be the sheriff's job to make sure Nate was telling the truth when he claimed to be innocent of anything but stealing a single bottle of brandy off the wreck of the *Philomela*, but even suspicious Faye found his story convincing. Amande's suspicions had faded away once she decided that Nate wasn't such a rich daddy's boy after all.

Faye had decided to believe Nate. For one thing, his story hung together logically. And for another, one thing about his story tracked with what she knew to be true. The captain would have certainly asked too many questions for Cody to be comfortable leaving him alive. Also arguing in Nate's favor was the fact that Cody had tried very hard to kill him.

"Nate says Cody got the mixture of gases right for killing the captain," Amande said. "Obviously. Because he died. But Nate is young, and he knows diving, and he knows his body. After Cody left him to die, he woke up just long enough to realize that he had to get to the surface, even if he burst his lungs open doing it."

Faye shivered at the thought of what Nate had gone through. The moment underwater when he realized that he might not have enough air to get to the surface haunted her. So did the moment when he looked around from the spot where he floated, gravely injured, and saw nothing but open water in all directions.

"Cody's boat was the one with the yellow bimini," the sheriff said. "Correct?"

"Not anymore, but yep. It used to have one. Nate says Cody must have been out there every free minute after they found the wreck, even at night, looking for things he could sell. It's dark enough down in the wreck that you're gonna need lights, day or night. Might as well dive at night, too. That tracks with Manny's time sheet records. Cody didn't put in many hours on those days. It was easy for him to come and go without being seen. It's not easy to walk through that swamp, but you can get from the marina to Cody's house that way. No problem. And it wasn't any problem for him to walk home after he killed the captain and grounded his boat in the swamp."

Faye had spent time on that creek. This story was plausible.

Manny, who wasn't above eavesdropping, refilled Amande's coffee. "Don't forget. Killing Nate meant that Cody didn't have to split the money he got from selling the liquor. If you want my opinion—"

Faye hadn't asked for it, but Manny had skyrocketed in her estimation since he had laid his life on the line for Amande.

"—I think Thad was next. He's real lucky that we all stopped Cody when we did. And also"—he topped off Faye's coffee cup—"I believe Nate when he says he didn't know what Cody was up to. When you scratch off a layer of the rich-boy attitude, he's a stand-up guy."

Amande beamed and Faye resolved to be okay with Nate dating her daughter. Not that she had any say in the matter.

Faye glanced at the sheriff. "Did he find anything else on the *Philomela* besides the old rum and brandy?"

"Not that we know of. What would you wish for?"

318 Mary Anna Evans

"There's a book that may be on the boat, autographed. Even considering that it's been soaked in saltwater and nibbled by fish, I'd give a lot to have that book."

The sheriff looked at Faye oddly, but she didn't explain. Faye was telling the truth that she'd love to have Cally's book, but a romantic part of her liked to think of it at the bottom of the sea, forever.

"If Cody had gotten away with all that old brandy and rum, he would have done very well for himself."

What did the sheriff mean by "very well"? How much had Cody really made on that rum? Faye tried to do the math on crates of old liquor, but she didn't have enough information. Still, she didn't think that they held the kind of immeasurable wealth you'd expect from a ship loaded with gold and jewels. Had they held enough liquid gold to justify murder?

Faye decided that she didn't have the information to answer that question, either, because she couldn't fathom doing the kind of premeditated killing that Cody had. Brutal honesty required her to admit that she would do some shady things to save Joe's life or the lives of her children, but coldblooded murder for a few thousand dollars or even a few hundred thousand dollars? Millions?

No. She couldn't imagine it.

"Did I tell you that I've hired Samantha Kennedy to help us run the captain's library?" Faye asked the sheriff. "Since Jeanine gave it to us on the condition that we keep it available to the public, we've got to take care of it. We need somebody who knows how. The money left in the captain's grant will help us get started, but it'll take all my grant-writing skill to get it renewed. Emma and Ray have donated enough money to make those grants go further, and donations of all sizes are coming in from all the captain's friends. Samantha is more than capable of helping me administer the library and its funding."

"I thought you didn't trust her," Amande said, her mouth full of cherry pie.

"I wasn't sure, until fingerprint data showed that Cody was the one who broke a window to get into the captain's library and steal the photos and sign-in sheet. Samantha sheds tears every time she thinks about how badly she was tempted to break into that library. She came close, but she never did it. And she absolutely did step up and help the sheriff and lieutenant administer first aid to all of us that night, even Cody. She might not be cut out to be a field archaeologist, but she was paying attention to the first aid training at field school. Magda gave me a chance when I was struggling. I think Samantha has earned her chance."

Joe arrived, Michael in tow, and dropped onto the stool next to Faye. The sheriff nodded at Faye and said, "I'll leave you people some privacy," as he left.

"Are you people finished worrying over the killings and all that?" Joe asked. "Because if you're not, I'll go find someplace else to eat. We all just lived through a bad time. Seems to me like there's no point in dwelling on it."

"Sure thing, Dad. We can talk about something else." Amande studied the swirls of cream on the surface of her coffee. "In fact, I have news."

Faye wondered how Amande had squeezed any extra thoughts into a mind that was so full of Nate Peterson.

"Spit it out," Joe said. "I knew you had a secret."

Faye had not known, but Joe was so tuned in to the people around him that he could sometimes pass as telepathic.

"I'm starting school full-time in the spring. It's too late to register for the fall semester, and I've still got stuff to do, like help with the hurricane cleanup. You know that's gonna take months and months. Emma wants to pay me to do her insurance paperwork, which I told her was stupid, but she said she'd put the money straight in my college account if I said no. I'm gonna help Miss Jeanine, too, but I'll eat dirt before I let her pay me. Not after she gave us the captain's whole library. We owe her forever for that. Good thing we've got a big house with a lot of empty rooms to hold all those books."

"School?" Faye asked, failing to match her husband's air of nonchalance. "Brick-and-mortar school?" She desperately wanted Amande to go away to college, and yet she didn't want her to go away.

"Thank you for not saying 'real school.' My online classes are quite real, thank you very much. But yes, a brick-and-mortar school."

Afraid that Amande was going to add, "And it's half a continent away in Nevada," Faye held her breath and waited for the other shoe to drop.

"I've been talking to Magda."

This wasn't good. Magda had probably told her to apply to colleges in Australia.

"I told her that the family business needed an underwater archaeologist real bad. Here we sit right on the coast, and we're losing business left and right to companies that have divers."

"I could learn—" Faye began, but Joe and Amande's snorts drowned her out.

"Repeat after me, Mom. 'I don't have to be the one who does everything.'"

Faye tried, but she couldn't make her lips form the words.

"Nobody swims at the surface better than you do, but you're terrified of deep water." Amande's voice was gentle but it told the unvarnished truth. "It's so, so, so obvious. I've never known you to fail at anything so, yeah, you could learn. But why should you be miserable when I would love being down there? I'm driving to Tallahassee tomorrow, and Magda's going to show me around her university. Introduce me to the right professors. Stuff like that. She says that there's a field school in Australia next summer that would be just perfect for me!"

Faye had some choice words for Magda and her Australia obsession, but she knew her friend and mentor was right. Amande needed to carve out her own professional niche that was separate from her parents'. Magda would be a superb role model for Faye's daughter, just as she had been for Faye.

"Magda also says that she wants to talk to you about teaching some classes at the university. I think you should do it. It wouldn't kill you and Dad to live in Tallahassee during the week while you taught. You could go home to Joyeuse Island on the weekends. We're coming up on the day when Michael needs to go to kindergarten, and you're going to have to figure out how to get him there. It'd be a heckuva lot easier to do that in Tallahassee."

Now Faye's daughter was trying to help Magda run her life. Charming. But Amande and Magda weren't wrong.

Amande was still rattling on. "You'd be surprised at how much college credit I've piled up from all those online courses. I can start right in on my archaeology courses and I'll be diving by summer."

In Australia.

Faye's daughter was going to the other side of the planet. In the special way of mothers, Faye could glory in the knowledge that her daughter was going to see the world while she grieved her impending absence deeply.

"You'll get your dive instructor's license eventually?" Faye asked, although it was a given that her ambitious daughter planned to amass all the credentials there were.

"Sure thing," Amande said before she poured a tremendous slug of caffeine and cream down her throat.

"When you do, will you teach me to dive, sweetheart?"

Faye might be terrified of The Cold Spot, but she'd do whatever it took to be shoulder to shoulder with her daughter.

"Absolutely, but get ready to kick hard if you're planning to keep up with me."

NOTES FOR THE INCURABLY CURIOUS

I frequently hear from readers asking whether certain plot elements in Faye's adventures are real. I feel a responsibility to history and to the real people who lived it, so I do my best to get the facts right and to make sure that my fictional events are at least plausible. In the case of books set near Faye's home on Joyeuse Island, I also think it's important to keep the fictional history of the area consistent. Thus, the fictional Joyeuse Island has been established through four books—*Artifacts, Findings, Isolation,* and *Wrecked*—as being near the fictional Micco County and the factual Wakulla County. Or, as I like to think of it, Micco County exists adjacent to Wakulla County, but in some other dimension that is not ours. Joyeuse Island and Micco County also exist in a slightly different timeline, as the nameless hurricane portrayed in *Wrecked* is smaller and less devastating than 2018's Hurricane Michael, which inspired it.

The *Philomela* is, alas, imaginary. I modeled it on the *Syren,* an iron-hulled, sidewheel steamship with two steam engines that made a record-setting thirty-three runs through Union blockades during the Civil War, which is particularly noteworthy for a ship that sailed for less than two years before she was captured in Charleston Harbor.

Sopchoppy, Panacea, and Crawfordville are real towns in Wakulla County, but don't go looking for Thad's store, Ray's newspaper, or the captain's house, because I made them up. The spring boils in local creeks are real, though, and Spring Creek, where Faye and Joe kayak, is famous for its multiple submarine springs, which have a combined discharged estimated in 2000 by the Florida Department of Environmental Protection to be 1.25 billion gallons a day. Several of them have smooth areas of upwelling water at the spring boil like the one I describe at The Cold Spot.

There are a number of offshore submarine springs like The Cold Spot off the Florida coastline, including the Crescent Beach Spring off the Flagler County coast, which is reputed to have served as a freshwater source for long-ago mariners, and the Mud Hole off Lee County's coast, which is famous for discharging warm, murky water beloved by fish and by people who like to fish. The spectacular archaeological work that I describe at Wakulla Springs and in the Aucilla River is real, and Faye's hope that the submarine spring at The Cold Spot could prove as fruitful is, I think, justified. I like the idea that Amande could come home from her underwater archaeology studies and help her mother discover something very old and very special.

ACKNOWLEDGMENTS

I'd like to thank all the people who helped make *Wrecked* happen. Erin Garmon, Tony Ain, Michael Garmon, Rachel Broughten, and Amanda Evans read it in manuscript, and their comments were incredibly helpful. The late Robert Connolly's suggestions and guidance regarding archaeological details have added realism to the entire series, and his suggestions as I planned *Wrecked* were, as always, an inspiration. I will miss him a great deal. I am grateful to Nadia Lombardero and Art Watson for their scuba diving and boating expertise. They get the credit where I got things right, and I get the blame where I did not.

As always, I am grateful for the people who help me get my work ready to go out into the world, the people who send it out into the world, and the people who help readers find it. Many thanks go to my agent, Anne Hawkins, and to the wonderful people at Sourcebooks and Poisoned Pen Press who do such a good job for us, their writers. Because I can trust that my editor, Barbara Peters, will help me make my work shine, I can stretch myself creatively and try new things, and that's a wonderful place for a writer to be. I'm also grateful to the

University of Oklahoma for providing the opportunity for me to teach a new generation of authors while continuing to write books of my own.

And, of course, I am always (always!) grateful for you, my readers.

ABOUT THE AUTHOR

Photo by
Nadia Lombardero

Mary Anna Evans is the author of the Faye Longchamp Archaeological Mysteries, which have received recognition, including the Benjamin Franklin Award, the Oklahoma Book Award, the Mississippi Author Award, and three Florida Book Awards bronze medals.

Mary Anna is the winner of the 2018 Sisters in Crime Academic Research Grant and is an assistant professor at the University of Oklahoma, where she teaches fiction and nonfiction writing. She speaks widely on fiction writing and on the work of Agatha Christie.

Check out her website, maryannaevans.com, where you can subscribe to her e-newsletter; her Facebook author page at facebook.com/maryannaevansauthor; and her Twitter account at @maryannaevans.